Comfortable DISTANCE

D0752643

Kenna White

Bella
BOOKS
2009

Bella Books, Inc.
P.O. Box 10543
Tallahassee, FL 32302

Printed in the United States of America on acid-free paper
First Edition

Editor: Marissa Cohen
Cover Designer: Linda Callaghan

ISBN 10: 1-59493-152-6
ISBN 13:978-1-59493-152-9

Dedication

In loving memory of my sweet daughter, Annie.

To Sharon, for understanding and caring. We all should be blessed with such a friend to help lead us through the darkness of life's tragedies and back into the light. Thank you from the bottom of my heart.

Acknowledgments

A big thank you to the skippers of Puget Sound who generously offered their sailing knowledge to this landlubber. After a few months on a houseboat, I began to understand the love affair with nautical life and why men go down to the sea in ships.

Also, a thank you to my bro for being my rock. Love ya.

Chapter 1

Dana's desk was strewn with sketches. Some were finished cartoons, ready to be scanned into the computer and sent to the publisher. Some were only rough ideas not yet fully developed. She applied a few last strokes and held the sketch up for a final check. She had drawn a dog, a female black Scottie named Ringlet to be exact, tethered to a leash. Her coat was clean and brushed to a shiny gloss. Dana had learned how to suggest such things in a simple pen and ink drawing. The dog had a bow pinned to the top of her head and she had a proud though annoyed expression on her face. The dog's human, a thin figure of a woman, was dressed in shorts, tank top and running shoes. She had a shy smile as she trotted into the park, holding the dog's leash. The bubble over the dog's head read: *I hate it when she's trolling for lesbians and I'm the chum.*

Dana added a line here and a stroke there, examining

1

every detail. She was a creative perfectionist in her work. She had a classic education in fine arts with a master's degree from the University of Washington. She spent a summer in Europe studying the masters and was accomplished in watercolors and pastels. She had a flair for brightly colored pen and ink images, and the wall above her desk held several of her works. She could work pretty much anywhere with some of her best sketches coming on the spur of the moment in the most bizarre places. The tools of her trade were a black calligraphy pen and a tray of watercolors. From these humble beginnings Dana drew one of the best-loved, amusing characters in the gay literary world.

Dana Robbins, aka Robinette, was the artist behind Ringlet, a well-published syndicated cartoon. Ringlet was a perky little mutt with a curious personality and a propensity to find trouble where trouble didn't exist. Dana had discovered her cartoon talent quite by accident. She had added a few cartoon sketches to a report for a continuing education class on social art. The professor didn't care for her point of view in the report but gave her glowing marks on the character she drew. Like many of those things touched by fate, a classmate knew someone who knew someone and six months later Ringlet was born.

"This one is ready. What do you think, Ringlet?" Dana said, tilting her head as she gave it a final inspection. Dana signed Robinette to the corner of the sketch and set it aside to dry.

She had been at her desk since six a.m. Much to her surprise, it was now after eleven. She stood up and stretched, her slender white tummy exposed between her shirt and jeans. Dana was thirty-two years old with strawberry blond hair. It was long and lusciously wavy but usually held back in a ponytail to keep it out of her work. During the summer she had freckles across her nose when she stood in the sun too long. She was normally cheerful and friendly with an artistic flare. Until three weeks ago, she also had a girlfriend, one who didn't understand or accept Dana's decision to move out. Nor did she accept Dana's explanation as to why she needed some time alone to think. For months Dana felt something eroding their relationship, but Shannon didn't

2

agree. Whether it was a serious problem or a minor difficulty, Dana knew she needed a few months away from whatever stress was eating at her. When she heard Morgan Faylor's turquoise houseboat was for rent, she knew it was just what the doctor ordered.

Dana made a cup of coffee, curled into the wicker rocking chair on the houseboat deck and watched the boats entering the harbor. It was the second weekend in July and in Olympia, Washington that meant Lakefair, a week-long festival in the downtown streets and the boardwalk along the harbor. A nearly nonstop parade of boats had been passing by her deck for days. Everything from luxurious cabin cruisers to single-mast sailboats slipped into the marina and took up temporary residence, adding to the party atmosphere. It was a beautiful day and if Dana was lucky she could spend a few hours with her sketch pad on her lap, finding inspiration for a cartoon or two.

Just as she had put pen to paper, a spider dropped down from the ceiling.

"I wish you'd do that somewhere else," she said. The complex spider's web was already draped across the corner. Frowning at the spider, she moved her chair to the other side of the deck. How spiders found their way onto a houseboat was a mystery but they frequently did. She tried to remind herself spiders brought luck, as Morgan had told her the day Dana moved onto the houseboat.

It was more of a house than a boat. It had a living room, a fully equipped galley, a bathroom with a wooden Japanese soaking tub, and a loft bedroom with bedside windows that looked out over the harbor. What it didn't have was a motor. Propulsion was at the mercy of a hired towboat, but Dana didn't mind. She wasn't going anywhere. She just needed a place to live. The idea of living in a marina near downtown Olympia seemed like a good idea, or perhaps just an interesting one. Life on a houseboat was certainly different. Dana had never spent the night on a boat before three weeks ago. In fact, other than a ferry, she had never been on a boat at all before she loaded up her car with clothes and art supplies and moved onto the turquoise blue houseboat.

Dana was deep into her drawing when she heard giggling from a boat two slips away. Curious, Dana glanced in that direction. The two women on the rear deck of the day cruiser didn't notice her. They were too busy kissing and fondling each other to notice anything. Dana was about to go inside and leave them to their fun when one of the women, a young brunette with a butch haircut, pulled the other's shirt off, revealing two of the largest breasts Dana had ever seen. The first woman immediately began sucking one of the dark brown nipples, bringing a loud moan from the owner. Dana slid down in her chair, hoping to remain invisible and not embarrass the lovers.

The brunette fumbled the woman's shorts and underpants off and tossed them aside.

"Oh, baby," the woman groaned, grabbing the chrome railing around the bench. "Give it to me."

Dana slid further down in her chair, trying to decide how she could get inside without them noticing her. She couldn't help but be a little envious. It had been a long time since she had spontaneous heart-pounding sex like that.

"Yes! Yes!" the woman shrieked, writhing to her partner's touch.

Dana smiled to herself as she crawled across the floor and through the open door, allowing the women their privacy. As soon as she was inside, the telephone rang. She quickly shut the door and ran to answer it.

"Hello," she whispered.

"Hello? Is someone there?"

"Hello," she said, realizing no one could hear.

"Hi, Dana girl. Did I interrupt anything?"

"Hi, Ruth Ann. No, I was just watching the boats coming in." She wasn't going to admit she had been watching two women having mind-blowing sex.

"Yeah. Aren't they something? Did you see the big one with the helicopter pad on the top?" No one in the world had an accent like Ruth Ann Smith's. It was the product of a childhood

4

in Alabama, teen years in New Hampshire and adulthood in Washington.

"No. I must have missed that one. Was there a helicopter on it?"

"No. They had patio tables on the top with umbrellas that looked like grass skirts. I'd say they planned on having one hell of a party tonight." Ruth Ann had a hearty laugh.

"Do they all do that? Have parties, I mean."

"You bet. That's what makes Lakefair special. More beer, barbecue and boobs than you can shake a stick at."

"I've noticed some of that already," Dana said, watching a boat chug past with a pair of bathing beauties sunbathing on the deck. Their bathing suits were little more than floss and postage stamps.

"I thought I'd let you know we've moved up the time. Come on over about six. Connie said seven is too late for us old folks. When we were your age, we could eat late and it wouldn't bother us. But at sixty-five, if we don't eat dinner until eight o'clock, we'll be up all night."

"Okay. What else can I bring?"

"Nothing. Just a bottle of cheapo vino. Or whatever else you want to drink."

"Are you sure? I'd be glad to make a salad or dessert."

"Nope. Connie has it all under control. We do this every year and she has a pretty good handle on the food."

"How about you, Ruth Ann? Do you help in the kitchen?"

"No, I stay out of the way. That's my duty and I do a bang-up job of it. I make ice and fill glasses. I think she's going to let me open the chip bags this year though."

"If you need help, send up a flare."

Dana looked out at the far end of the marina closest to downtown. She couldn't see it for the row of tall cabin cruisers but over there somewhere was Ruth Ann and Connie's boat, the *Kewpie Doll*. They had been partners for thirty-four years. Ruth Ann insisted it was thirty-five, but who was counting. They had been living on their 1958 forty-six-foot cabin cruiser for three

5

years. It used to be a weekend destination but the fascination grew into a lifestyle, and unable to resist, they'd finally moved onto it fulltime. Like many of the permanent residents across the marina, they loved the adventure of living on a boat within walking distance of downtown shops and cafes. They could pretend to live a seafaring life without ever untying the dock lines.

Ruth Ann and Connie had mothered Dana ever since she'd moved onto the houseboat three weeks ago. This call was Ruth Ann's daily check-in. Normally, she'd call with a transparent excuse that somehow ended in a maternal lecture on how Dana shouldn't hesitate to call if she needed anything, anything at all, no matter how minor, no matter what time. Then she would make sure Dana had their telephone number, both of their cell numbers, and the security code to the gate to their dock, just in case it wasn't the same security code as her gate, although it was and had been for months. Ever since they invited Dana to come to their Lakefair boat party Ruth Ann had a perfectly legitimate excuse to call and she did, every day, sometimes twice a day.

"I thought I'd give you a heads-up on who'll be at the party tonight. First there's Bev. She'll be the one wearing a cowboy hat. She always does. She's from Houston and you know what they say. You can take the lesbo out of Texas but you can't take the hat off her head. Bev's a looker, too. Damn nice rack." Dana could hear someone in the background censure Ruth Ann's comment.

"Was that Connie?" Dana teased.

"Yes. You'd think she never saw a nice pair before." Ruth Ann laughed. "Anyway, Bev's a massage therapist. Real sweetheart. Her girlfriend couldn't come. She had some family reunion thing in Portland this weekend."

"And Bev wasn't invited to go along?" Dana said curiously.

"Oh, yeah. She was but Bev said they aren't at that point in their relationship where she wants to meet the whole family just yet. Between you and me, I don't think they will ever be at that point. I don't particularly care for her girlfriend. But that's none of my business." Ruth Ann's voice trailed off as if throttling her. "Then there's Kathy. Who knows what she'll be wearing. Something funky, I'm sure. And her hair may be some strange color, like purple or orange. But she's a sweetie, too. She's getting over her last relationship. That makes two this year. Poor Kathy! She really liked this one. Kathy works for a car dealership up in Tacoma. You'll like her. She's fun to be around. And then there's Christy." Ruth Ann stopped and laughed. "Christy is a character. You can't miss her. She's got square shoulders like a football player. In another life she probably was one. Christy works with Connie at the Transit Center. She drives the Shelton bus. She's also the Casanova in the bunch. I'm sure she'll give you the once-over. Just smile and ignore her. She's not dating anyone right now, but we'd know it if she was. She'd be bragging on how big the girl's bazooms were or how often they did it. Marty is another one of the group. She was coming but she called this morning to say she had a wicked migraine and not to expect her. She gets those barfing kind of headaches. She's our hairdresser. She's an Amazon beauty. It's a shame you won't get to meet her. Actually, she'd probably remind you of Shannon. So maybe it's just as well she won't be here. And then there's Dr. Jamie Hughes."

"A doctor?" Dana said curiously.

"Doctor as in professor doctor out at the university. She said she'd be here but who knows? If she gets busy in her lab, she may forget to come altogether. She knows scientific stuff no one else ever heard of."

"How did she get into your group?"

"She scuba dives in Budd Bay. Her research boat used to be moored next to ours. We knew her before she moved her boat out to West Side Marina. They don't have the access to downtown like we do so they can't charge as much slip rental, so it's cheaper and Jamie said it was closer to where she needed to be. She lives right across the harbor on the west side of the Budd Bay. The tan apartments with balconies, I think. Jamie is older. Not as old as Connie and me, lord knows, but older that the rest of you girls. You can't miss her. She's the tall, quiet one with glasses. She always looks like she's contemplating some great hypothesis. Sometimes

I wonder why she puts up with us. Other than her, you'll be the only one at the party who went to college. We certainly aren't on Jamie's level, education wise."

"That shouldn't make any difference. Friends are friends, regardless how much education you have."

"Yeah, but I feel like an idiot when I'm around her."

"She's that overbearing?" Dana said.

"No, not at all. But when you're around someone that smart, it's hard not to feel a little dumb. She's a sweetheart. A little quiet and analytical sometimes but nice."

"She must date someone from the university then," Dana said.

"Not her. Dr. Jamie Hughes is having a romantic relationship with each and every slimy creature in Puget Sound. She's on a first-name basis with them all." Ruth Ann laughed. "Don't worry about meeting the girls. They're going to love you."

Dana hadn't planned on worrying about it. Meeting Ruth Ann and Connie's friends wasn't a life altering event. Dana only agreed to go because Ruth Ann kept needling her about getting out and meeting people. It was easier to give in and go than listen to her daily list of reasons why she should. And Ruth Ann and Connie were nice people. Dana had met them through Shannon's work. An evening on their boat with a few of their friends might be just what she needed to find a little balance in her life.

"Dress casual," Ruth Ann added. "I'm wearing shorts and a T-shirt. So is Connie. Jamie is the only holdout. She'll probably wear professor clothes or something. Now, you've got the gate code?"

"Yes."

"See you at six."

"Bye-bye," Dana said and hung up, glancing out the window. The women on the nearby boat had finished and left. Dana had just settled back into her chair with her pen in hand when the houseboat telephone rang again. She reached for the cordless, expecting it to be Ruth Ann with a last-minute question or instruction, but it was Shannon. Dana sat holding the handset, staring at Shannon's name flashing on the screen. Finally, it stopped ringing. The light flashed, indicating she had left a message. Dana was sure it was only the first of many now that she had her telephone number. She went back to work without checking it. At least she tried. Whatever inspiration she had been working from was gone. Shannon's call had drained her concentration. She went inside to shower and change for the party.

Chapter 2

Dana locked the door and headed down the dock. She was late. The party had started thirty minutes ago and she was still fighting the urge to stay home. A last-minute idea for a cartoon panel kept her hunched over her sketch pad well past six and she was surprised Ruth Ann hadn't called yet. Maybe she wouldn't be missed. After a few hellos, Dana hoped she could blend into the background and slip away.

It was only a few hundred yards to their side of the marina and the *Kewpie Doll* moored in slip twenty-three. On foot it took ten minutes and two blocks to circle the boardwalk. During Lakefair, every inch of dock space was filled with boats from as far away as the San Juan Islands and beyond. When the marina filled to capacity, boats were simply anchored in the harbor, their occupants happy to row or motor ashore in dinghies or inflatable rafts the locals called rubber ducks.

Dana keyed in the security code and opened the gate. The dock was abuzz with boaters enjoying the carnival atmosphere. She was greeted by several partygoers as she made her way down the dock to Ruth Ann's boat. The *Kewpie Doll* was pointed into the dock, her back decks facing the harbor. Like Dana's houseboat, Ruth Ann and Connie had an outside slip with an unobstructed view of Budd Bay and all its activities.

"Hello," she called, tapping on the side of the hull near the access gate.

"Hey, there you are," Ruth Ann said, grinning at her. She unlatched the gate and waved Dana aboard. "I wondered what happened to you. I was afraid you fell overboard." She wrapped Dana in a warm hug. Ruth Ann was a stout woman with short gray hair that curled naturally to look like a Brillo pad. She had a middle-aged waddle under her chin that jiggled when she talked. She was wearing jean shorts and a 2004 Seattle gay pride T-shirt.

"I'm sorry. I got busy with Ringlet and time got away from me."

"You aren't supposed to work during Lakefair," she scolded. "It's party time."

"Is that Dana?" Connie said, hurrying out to give a hug of her own. Connie was also a bit overweight but was a happy woman. Her eyes gleamed and her body language told Dana she was genuinely glad to see her. Connie was a driver for the city bus company and had learned that a smile got her more cooperation than a scowl. Her hair was a peculiar shade of brown, something between auburn and persimmon. At least it was this month. "Come in and get acquainted, honey. I have to go stir or we'll be eating burnt hamburger. Make yourself at home. *The Kewpie Doll* is at your disposal. Get her some wine, Raggie." Ruth Ann's dearest and closest friends called her Raggie. Dana hadn't heard exactly why but she still called her by her rightful name. The name Raggie sounded crass to her.

"Everyone's on the upper deck watching the babes on the boats coming in. Let's get you something to drink and you can join them." Ruth Ann winked.

"I hope these are a decent year," Dana said, handing her two bottles of wine.

"How would we know?" she chuckled.

Ruth Ann handed Dana a glass of wine and showed her the basic layout of the boat. It had two bathrooms, two bedrooms, a galley, a small living room, an inside and an outside dining area, and two decks, one of each level. Both decks had patio tables and chairs. The ones on the top deck had umbrellas.

"Raggie, I need a hand in here, sweetheart," Connie called.

"Make yourself at home. The girls are up there," Ruth Ann said, pointing to the ladder. "Be right back."

"Can I help?" Dana said, looking toward the galley.

"Nope. She probably only wants me to get something down from the cabinet. I'm not allowed to cook," she said and went inside.

Dana stood at the railing, watching a seagull bob in the wake of a passing motorboat. This was one of those postcard images. The water shimmered with the reflection of the evening sun. Mountains scalloped along the horizon. Tiny sailboats in the distance danced across the mouth of the harbor like white-winged moths. Dana couldn't help but smile and drink in the beauty. How lucky was she to live in such a gorgeous place? She had just taken a sip of wine when she remembered what Shannon called a scene like this.

"Fucking nature. Ain't it great?" she would say sarcastically.

Dana choked on her wine. It was amazing how the word *fuck* fit perfectly into almost all of Shannon's conversations. When Dana displayed even a hint of displeasure at such language, she would use it all the more. Dana grabbed the railing to steady herself as she coughed.

"Are you all right?" a voice said from the deck above.

Dana looked up to see a woman leaning her elbows on the railing. The glint of sun reflected in the woman's glasses, temporarily blinding Dana's view.

"Are you choking?"

"No, it just went down my Tuesday pipe." Dana tried repeatedly to clear her throat.

"What is a Tuesday pipe?" the woman asked, pushing her glasses against the bridge of her nose.

"I meant I swallowed wrong." Dana's voice cracked. She coughed and cleared her throat again.

"Sounds bad."

"Dana, are you okay?" Ruth Ann called. "Do you need the Heimlich maneuver?"

Dana shook her head, afraid to answer in case she hadn't finished coughing.

"Is someone dying?" Another woman stuck her head over the railing and peered down at Dana.

"I'm fine." Dana had one more feeble cough before her voice cleared. "I just swallowed wrong."

"It went down her Tuesday pipe," the woman in glasses explained.

"Damn the Tuesday pipe," Ruth Ann said. "Be careful, sweetheart. I don't want to have to call the paramedics on you so early in the evening." She smiled before going back to the galley.

"Maybe you should stick with water," the woman with the glasses said. "The booze must be too strong for you."

"I'm not drunk. I just choked."

"But you don't seem to know what day it is."

"Of course I do. It's Saturday. Tuesday pipe is only an expression."

"If you say so." She raised her eyebrows in disbelief.

"Dana, did I hear you choked?" Connie came rushing up to Dana, drying her hands on a towel. She slipped a hand around Dana's waist and gave her a worried look.

"I'm fine, Connie. It just went down wrong."

"What are you drinking?" She took Dana's glass and sniffed it. "Oh, honey, don't drink that stuff. That's Raggie's idea of high society." She took the glass to the galley, pulling Dana along by the hand. "Let's get you some good red wine. You can't beat a

13

nice glass of red wine." She poured a glass and waited for Dana to take a sip. "Isn't that better?"

"Yes, it's very nice."

"Are you feeding her that swill?" Ruth Ann said, carrying a tray of dirty glasses into the galley.

"It isn't swill. It's Cabernet Sauvignon from California." Connie made a stab at a French accent.

"Glorified grape juice." Ruth Ann sniffed the open bottle and raised it to her lips.

"Don't you dare drink out of that bottle," Connie warned, smacking her arm.

"Did I say I was going to drink out of the bottle?" She winked at Dana and set the bottle down.

"Well, you better not." Connie shot her a stern look. Ruth Ann gave her a stern look right back then kissed her. Connie giggled.

"Have you met everyone?" Ruth Ann motioned Dana to follow her up the ladder.

"Not yet."

Ruth Ann climbed the ladder like she could do it in her sleep, carrying two bottles of wine in one arm and an ice bucket in the other. Dana took one step at a time so as not to spill her wine. She wasn't an old sea salt yet.

"Is that the good stuff, Raggie?" A woman in a well-bent straw cowboy hat, halter top and tight jeans met Ruth Ann at the top of the ladder and wrestled the wine bottles from her grip. Judging by the hat, Dana figured this was Bev, the cowgirl from Houston.

"Damn right." Another woman in jean shorts and a tie-dye T-shirt raised her empty glass.

"That's the wine you brought, Kathy." Ruth Ann set the ice bucket on the small table.

"Hell, I don't want that crap I brought. I want something good. What did you bring, Bev?" she asked the woman in the cowboy hat.

"I brought the best wine in a cardboard box money can buy.

They were on sale at Safeway. Ten bucks a box."

"That stuff is dated by the week, not the year," Ruth Ann chuckled.

"We can't call you cheap, can we Bev?" Kathy teased, refilling her glass.

"Hell, no." Bev tipped her hat.

"Gals, this is Dana Robbins. She's the new kid on the block. She's the one I was telling you about."

"Hi, Dana," Bev and Kathy said at the same moment.

"Hello," Dana said, shaking hands.

"I'm going to see about the grub. You all play nice." Ruth Ann descended the ladder.

"Hi, Dana. I'm Christy." A woman in her thirties offered her hand and a pleasant smile. Ruth Ann was right. Christy had square shoulders and was built like a husky athlete.

"Hi, Christy." Dana noticed she had a firm handshake, almost painfully so. She made eye contact with Dana and held it tenaciously.

"You're the one who draws cartoons?"

"Yes." Dana had the strangest feeling Christy was doing something with her finger in the palm of Dana's hand.

"Which one?" she said finally releasing Dana's hand.

"Ringlet."

"Oh, my God," Bev said, overhearing their conversation. "You draw Ringlet? You're Robinette? I love that cartoon. That dog looks just like my mother's schnauzer, except she's gray and Ringlet is a black Scottie. But Zoomer acts just like Ringlet sometimes. Like the time Ringlet fell in the bathtub. She's done that before."

"Your mother's dog's name is Zoomer?" Christy chuckled.

"It's AKC registered. Her name is actually Felice de Zoom Pilar, great-granddaughter of a grand champion. She was going to call her Felice but I told her that name should only be used on poodles. So she picked Zoomer. Maybe you could put Zoomer in your cartoon. She has an attitude."

"I'll remember that."

It didn't take long before Dana felt right at home. She had been taken in by the group. Bev and Kathy seemed fascinated by Ringlet and her antics. Christy, on the other hand, seemed more interested in Dana's blue eyes and pleasing figure. It wasn't until the conversation moved to cars that Christy turned her attention toward Bev and away from Dana's bustline. She also removed her hand from the small of Dana's back. Dana took the opportunity and stepped to the railing, putting a chair between herself and Christy's reach. She hadn't noticed someone sitting in a corner of the deck, her face partially obscured by an umbrella clamped to the armrest.

"I take it you aren't interested in five-speed transmissions," a voice said.

Dana peeked under the umbrella. It was the judgmental woman with the glasses. She had her feet up on the railing and was holding a glass of something amber.

"No. I don't drive manual transmissions. I don't know how to use a clutch."

"But you get better gas mileage with a five-speed." The woman took her feet down and stood up, stretching her back. She was several inches taller than Dana and had a thin frame. Dana wondered if she was one of those tree-hugging eco-maniacs.

"It can't be that much better if I'd spend the difference rolling backward down a hill and crashing into parked cars."

"With driving habits like that, then probably you're better off with an automatic." She turned to Dana and finally made eye contact. "I guess I should introduce myself. I'm Dr. Jamie Hughes. And you're Dana Robbins, right?"

"Yes. How do you do?" They shook hands. Jamie had long fingers that folded around Dana's hand. It was a brief comfortable handshake, unlike Christy's overbearing one.

Dr. Jamie Hughes had brown hair with curls swirling around the edges of her face. Just as Ruth Ann had said, she was older, somewhere in her forties. Her eyes were the most unique shade of brown, almost mahogany. They were also soft, something her wire framed glasses couldn't hide. Eyes and eye color were

16

something Dana noticed about people because she could use it in her cartoons to convey emotion and personality. A raised eyebrow, a slanted lid, a wide glance was sometimes the only way she could show Ringlet's mood. This woman's eyes were expressive and downright stunning. She didn't appear to be wearing any makeup, but her complexion was tanned and even. She wore tan slacks and a navy blue blazer over a white T-shirt. Ruth Ann was right again. Dr. Hughes did wear professor clothes.

"How's your Tuesday pipe?"

"Fine. I changed to red wine." Dana held up her glass.

"Ah. Good. Red is better." The corners of Jamie's mouth curled slightly, revealing a dimple in her right cheek, a dimple that made her look twenty years younger.

"I should be embarrassed over that, shouldn't I? I created quite a scene."

"Blame it on the wine."

"So, you're a college professor? What do you teach?" Dana didn't want to talk about choking anymore. It was embarrassing enough without reliving it over and over again.

"Marine biology and marine ecology."

"Wow. That sounds very…" Dana wanted to say interesting but since she knew absolutely nothing about biology of any kind she couldn't truthfully say marine biology sounded interesting.

"Boring? Tedious?" Jamie said.

"No. Scientific."

"And you draw cartoons."

"That's right. Ringlet."

"Sorry, but I've never seen it."

"It's carried in quite a few GLBT publications." Dana felt the need to validate. She didn't know why, but she did.

"Syndicated?" Jamie asked, surprising Dana with that term.

"Yes."

"Congratulations, but if it doesn't appear in a scientific journal I don't have time to read it."

"Ringlet definitely doesn't appear in scientific journals. My readership isn't quite that scholarly. *I'm* not that scholarly."

17

Dana laughed and sipped her wine.

"Are you telling me I won't see your cartoons in *Microbiological Ecosystems of the Northwest*?" Jamie said with a straight face.

"Um, no. I doubt it."

"There was a cartoon in last month's issue though. It was pretty funny. A pair of anemones were surfing the Web and complaining about the bacterioplankton's magnetic field interrupting the reception."

Jamie seemed to be the only one who understood the joke. She smiled as she remembered it. Dana gave a weak smile.

"I guess you had to see it," Jamie said and took a drink.

"Probably."

"Jamie," Bev called. "What's that?" She was pointing over the side at a translucent glob floating on the surface. It was the size of a dinner plate and looked like snot.

Jamie went to look.

"*Aurelia aurita*. Don't worry, Bev. It won't hurt you. It's dead."

"*Aurelia aurita*?" Kathy said, pronouncing it wrong. "Looks like a jellyfish."

"That's what it is."

"Then why not just say so?" Bev said, tossing an ice cube at it.

"It's a dead jellyfish, Bev," Jamie said and patted her on the back.

"Look, another jellyfish." Bev pointed at one pulsing through the water a few feet from the boat. "Stick your hand in the water, Kathy. Grab it. I want to see your eyes roll back in your head." She giggled.

"Are you nuts?" Kathy said.

"Actually, those aren't harmful to humans," Jamie said, studying the specimen.

"I thought jellyfish were poisonous. Remember that movie *Finding Nemo*? Ellen DeGeneres was a blue fish that got stung by all those jellyfish and was unconscious."

"*Cyanea capillate* are fatal to humans, if enough poison is injected. *Aurelia aurita* are not." Jamie took a drink then refilled her glass at the table.

"Huh?" Bev smirked and batted her eyelashes.

"A Lion Mane jellyfish will kill you. That's a moon jelly. It won't."

"I knew that," Kathy said.

"You did not." Bev scowled at her. "No one knows that shit."

"You'd know it if you were stung by one," Christy said, chugging the last of her beer.

"Have you been stung by one, Jamie?" Bev asked, dropping an olive on the pulsing jellyfish.

"A Lion Mane, no. A moon jelly, yes. Several times." Jamie watched the jellyfish maneuver away from the missile.

"Did it hurt?" Kathy wrinkled her brow at the thought.

"It wasn't something I enjoyed."

"I thought divers wore suits to protect against things like that," Dana said.

"Sometimes, when the water is cold or depending on how deep you're diving."

"Oh, my God," Bev shouted, grabbing Kathy by the arm. "Picture it. Dr. Jamie Hughes scuba diving in nothing but a string bikini and an air tank!"

"What color is your bikini, Jamie?" Kathy giggled. "Transparent white?"

"Itsy bitsy teenie weenie yellow polka dot bikini," Christy teased. "Do you need help getting dressed, doc?"

"Yeah. Those string bikinis are kind of complicated." Bev winked at Jamie. "We'd be glad to offer a helping hand next time you go out."

"I've seen Jamie's swimsuit," Ruth Ann announced as she carried a bowl of chips to the table. "It's a black and white two-piece. Very nice, too." She grinned.

Jamie took a drink, obviously trying to hide her blush.

"Do you fill it out, doc?" Christy gave her a playful poke.

"Of course, she does," Bev said, flipping the side of Jamie's blazer out of the way to expose her white T-shirt. "Even nerdy professors have boobs. Don't you, Jamie?"

Jamie scratched her forehead as if to hide another blush.

"Okay," Jamie said, chuckling along. "Yes, I have boobs. And yes, I wear a two-piece bathing suit but it's not a bikini."

"It isn't much more than one," Ruth Ann shouted from the galley.

Everyone roared with laughter as Jamie blushed again and grinned. Dana thought it was cute that Jamie allowed herself to be the brunt of the jokes. From what she could tell through the T-shirt and blazer, the professor had a perfectly acceptable pair of breasts. Nothing enormous but still nothing to sneeze at.

"Are you going to tell them about that time you were diving in Friday Harbor?" Ruth Ann said.

"No, I am not." Jamie pushed her glasses tighter onto her nose.

"What happened?" Bev said eagerly. "Tell us."

"Yeah, what happened? Your bikini string break?" Christy said.

When Jamie didn't answer, Ruth Ann did.

"Worse than that," she offered.

"Come on, Raggie. Let's hear it."

"Well, you know the old expression about the absentminded professor?" Ruth Ann looked over at Jamie and laughed wickedly. Jamie hung her head and groaned.

"What about it?" Bev encouraged.

"Jamie was doing some highly technical stuff. What was it?"

"It doesn't matter. What happened?" Christy interrupted.

"Oh, please." Jamie went to the railing and scowled out at the harbor.

"It seems Dr. Jamie Hughes came up from her dive, climbed back in the boat, took off her wet suit and voila. She forgot to put on her swimsuit first. She was standing there on the boat, sorting her catch with nothing on but her glasses."

"Naked?" Bev said.

"Yessirreebob."

"What's the big deal with that?" Christy said.

"Her boat was right in the middle of the harbor and a class of junior sailors was zipping back and forth on either side of her. To make matters worse, a harbor tour boat was cruising by."

"Our Jamie? Dr. Cover-it-all-up?" Bev snickered.

"You mooned the tour boat?" Christy laughed wildly.

"She did more than moon them." Ruth Ann gave Jamie's cheek a pat before going back into the galley.

Everyone hooted and teased Jamie until she turned around and held her blazer open in surrender.

"Did you get a sunburn, Jamie?" Christy asked.

"Sunburn, hell. Did you get any offers?" Bev said.

"Were you terribly embarrassed?" Dana asked, knowing if it had been her she would have been.

"I felt pretty stupid, yes." Jamie shook her head and chuckled.

"What were you diving for that made you forget your suit?"

"To tell the truth, I don't remember. It slipped my mind when I realized what I had done."

"What did you do? Dive for cover?" Dana tried to picture it.

"I put my wet suit back on. I had no choice. I got dressed ashore and didn't have anything else to wear. It wasn't that big a deal anyway."

"I bet it was at the time." Dana offered an understanding smile. "And from my vantage point it looks like a perfectly acceptable deal."

"Dana, Jamie, come on. Food's on," Ruth Ann called, waving them to the buffet table. "Come get a plate."

Bev, Kathy and Christy were already swarming around the table.

"After you," Jamie said to Dana.

"So, you're a professor of scuba diving?" That sounded silly and Dana knew it. "I mean you scuba dive as part of your work as a professor?"

"I'm a professor of marine biology at Capital State University during the school year. I do research during the summer. That's when I do most of my diving."

"Research about what?"

"Algae blooms and how toxins affect their amino acids and the food web in Puget Sound."

"I think I understood about half of that." Dana took a paper plate and crushed some tortilla chips on it as a base for a taco salad.

Jamie looked over the choices, tasting a blue tortilla chip.

"What exactly is Ringlet? Some sort of dog, I take it."

"A black Scottie, female, of course."

"Of course. Do you own one of those Scotties?"

"No. I don't have any pets. I live on a houseboat."

"How big is it, this houseboat?"

"Thirty-seven feet long and about twelve feet wide."

"Four hundred forty-four square feet," Jamie said without hesitation.

"Yes, if you say so. And there's a second-story loft. That's the bedroom." Dana continued, piling the layers on her salad.

"How big is the loft?"

"I don't know. Twelve by twelve, I guess." She plopped a spoon of salsa on the top.

"Five hundred eighty-eight square feet."

"Not all of it is livable space."

"Minus the closets and cupboards," Jamie added.

"And the staircase."

"You have a staircase on a houseboat?" Jamie helped herself to a scoop of meat, lettuce, cheese and chips but kept them all separate on her plate. She carefully placed a spoonful of salsa in the middle, not disturbing the individual piles.

"Well, it's a ladder really. I call it a staircase."

"Why not call it a ladder?"

"A ladder is what you use to climb over something. A staircase is what you use to go upstairs. So I call it a staircase." Dana took a fork and mashed the salsa into the pile.

"But you just said it was actually a ladder."

"Are you always such a stickler for details?"

Dana licked the salsa off the back of her fork.

"Not really. You're dripping." Jamie pointed to the glob of salsa hanging off the edge of Dana's plate. Dana caught it with her finger.

"Aren't you going to make a taco salad?" she asked, noticing Jamie's strategically arranged plate of food.

"I did." Jamie took one more chip and ate it. "I prefer to combine the ingredients at the moment of ingestion."

"She means she can't have her food touching on her plate," Bev said, reaching in for a handful of chips. "It's a scientific thing."

"The chips absorb the moisture more rapidly than my rate of consumption," Jamie explained.

"Whatever," Bev scoffed.

"You mean the chips absorb the grease from the meat and get soggy before you get to the bottom of the salad?" Dana said.

"Yes. And the lettuce wilts when exposed to heat."

"The heat being the meat?" Dana said, taking a bite of her salad.

Jamie nodded.

Ruth Ann and Connie waited until everyone had a plate then helped themselves and joined the others on the deck to watch the ongoing Lakefair festivities.

"Does Ringlet like the houseboat?" Ruth Ann asked. "Have you written the houseboat into the cartoon?"

"Not yet. I've put her in a boat, though."

"Don't tell me," Kathy insisted, covering her ears. "I don't want to know. I want it to be a surprise when it comes out."

"What does your girlfriend think of your houseboat?" Christy said, obviously fishing for information.

Dana looked over at Ruth Ann, who had promised not to say anything about her relationship with Shannon. Ruth Ann shook her head adamantly. The one subject Dana didn't want to discuss had popped up. If she admitted to having a girlfriend, she'd have to answer a slew of questions. If she admitted they were separated, that too invited questions she'd rather not answer.

She chose the safe route.

"I don't have one."

Ruth Ann frowned at her.

"Hey, ladies. Dana is free and available." Bev grinned over at her. "Careful, honey. When the word gets out you'll have them beating down your door."

"Are you free for dinner tomorrow night?" Christy asked without missing a beat.

"Thanks, Christy, but I'm not ready for that just yet."

"Sounds like you are getting over someone. Don't worry about it, Dana. We won't pry. We all have a closet full of used relationships," Bev said, giving a reassuring but weathered smile. "Take your time. And you leave her alone, Christy."

"I was just being hospitable." Christy gave Bev a glare.

"Yeah. We know what you were just doing," Kathy said, giving Christy's cheek a pinch.

Homemade ice cream and fresh strawberries followed dinner. So did a fresh round of teasing, this time over Bev's on-again-off again relationship with an Olympia policewoman. She too was a good sport about it, playing the dolt to Kathy and Christy's needling. Dana wandered over to the railing to watch a harbor seal frolic in the wake of a passing boat. She didn't feel like making fun of anyone. That wasn't her idea of entertainment. The temperature had begun to drop. She found her jacket and wrapped it over shoulders.

"Are you cold?" Jamie said, standing a few feet down the railing.

"Chilly. Aren't you?"

"No."

"You were smart. You dressed for the evening. It's amazing how quickly the temperature drops after dinner time."

"Radiational cooling from the water."

"Ah." Dana slipped her arms in the sleeves and pulled the collar up around her chin as a cool breeze blew across the back of her neck.

"Did they embarrass you?" Jamie asked, leaning her elbows on the railing and looking over at Dana.

"About what?"

"Your private life. They don't mean anything by it."

"If you mean my relationships, my girlfriend, no, they didn't embarrass me."

"It's all innocent stuff. Sometimes they forget not everyone knows they are kidding."

"I guess I should be flattered they included me in their fun."

"Yep. That's the way you have to look at it. Don't take anything they say seriously."

"Do you? I'd think you'd be the one who was embarrassed."

"About what? The fact I'm a scientist and view the world through analytical eyes? Not hardly."

"I meant about the bikini and your boobs."

"Oh, that." Jamie grinned at the water. "That's harmless. I usually ignore ninety percent of what they say."

"Only ninety?" Dana mused. "Sounds more like ninety-five percent. Maybe more."

"It's a defensive posture, Miss Robbins. Adapt to the surroundings or succumb to the pressure. Most creatures in nature do that. Is that what you're doing? Adapting to a new environment. Or are you giving in to it?"

"If you mean the houseboat, it isn't that much of a change in environment. It's just a change in location."

"I didn't mean living on the houseboat. I meant living without your girlfriend." Jamie cocked an eyebrow at her. "Are you giving in or adapting?"

"In this case, I'm not sure there is a difference," Dana said, squinting out over the harbor. "What makes you think I'm doing either?"

"Just a hunch." Jamie shrugged. "There are two kinds of creatures in the animal kingdom, Miss Robbins. Predator and prey. Something tells me you're not a predator and that houseboat is nothing more than a temporary habitat in an unstable environment."

Dana looked over at Jamie.

"If I'm not a predator, you think I'm the prey?"

"I think we all are one or the other. Have you ever heard of a cape gander?"

Dana shook her head.

"It's a small worm-like animal that lives in coral reefs off the coast of Australia. To keep from being eaten by bigger fish it often hides under shells discarded by crabs and larger crustaceans. It works part of the time. But just as often it doesn't. The cape gander falls victim to the food chain."

"Are you saying I'm a cape gander?"

"No. I'm saying hiding from a predator may not always be the best decision."

"Oh, really? So you're saying if the cape gander comes out from under the shell and faces the bigger fish, it won't get eaten."

"Not always. But spending its life hiding under someone else's cast-off shell isn't much of an existence."

"Adapt or die?"

"Eat or be eaten. And I don't mean the sexual connotation. Cowardice is not forgiven in the animal kingdom, Miss Robbins. You can hide only so long from the predator. Eventually they win out."

"Your scientific hunch isn't very accurate, Dr. Hughes. I'm sorry but you missed the mark on this one. I am not prey to some predatory creature. And I don't consider living in a houseboat hiding. I'm certainly no cape gander."

"My mistake. I apologize."

Dana pulled the houseboat key from her pocket. It was attached to the gold key ring Shannon had given her on their fourth anniversary. It was engraved with Dana's initials and two interlocking hearts. "This is not the key to someone else's cast-off shell. I chose to live there. I didn't skulk off to hide in it." She held it up, dangling the keys in front of Jamie's face.

"I never said you did. If those keys represent your

independence, then good for you."

"Yes, they do." Dana slapped the key ring down on the railing.

"The keys represent your independence but what does the key ring represent?" Jamie said, looking down at the interlocking hearts.

"As a matter of fact it was a gift from a friend."

"Must be a close friend."

"If it's any of your business, yes, a very close friend." Dana shifted her weight, crossing her arms defensively.

"Predatorily close?" Jamie said, testing Dana's resolve.

"Absolutely not." Dana glared at her presumptive insinuation. "She's not that kind of person."

"What do the two hearts represent?" Jamie touched the engraving, tracing the two hearts with her fingertip. "You and her, pining over one another?" she said melodramatically.

"No, they do not." Dana grabbed for the key ring. She missed, pushing it to the edge of the railing. Jamie quickly reached for it but their hands collided, bumping the keys and knocking them into the water.

"Oh, no," Dana gasped, lunging for it. Jamie grabbed Dana by the waist just as her weight was about to take her over the railing and into the bay as well. The key ring shimmered in the turbid water and sank out of sight.

"Hold on there," Jamie said, pulling her back onto the deck.

"My keys," Dana said frantically, reaching over as far as she could.

"I'm sorry but they're gone." Jamie kept her hands on Dana's waist as she leaned over the railing. "And you're going to fall in if you don't stop that."

"But my keys. Quick! Get a net or something."

"By now your keys are embedded in three feet of mud and silt. It's like quicksand down there. I'm sorry, Miss Robbins."

"Will you stop calling me Miss Robbins? It's Dana. And stop saying you're sorry and *do* something," Dana demanded.

"What would you suggest? Pull the plug and drain Budd

Bay?" Jamie scoffed.

"Yes." Dana peered into the murky water for signs of her key ring. "How deep is it here?" She stepped out of her sandals.

"It's high tide, just starting to go out. It's probably fifty feet, maybe more. It fluctuates but I'd say fifty-three to fifty-five feet this far from the shore. The tidal current can deposit additional sediment, depending on the season and the shipping activity in the basin but I'd say—"

"Oh, shut up and do something," Dana said harshly. "I don't want to hear a scientific explanation. I just want my keys back."

Everyone came to the railing to see what the shouting was all about.

"What keys?" Bev said, joining Dana in staring overboard.

"She knocked my keys in the water," Dana said, pointing to the spot.

"I did not," Jamie said adamantly.

"Yes, you did! I grabbed for them, and you knocked my hand away."

"That isn't what happened."

"Are they your car keys, Dana?" Ruth Ann sounded worried.

"They were, and my houseboat key."

"Don't tell me her keys are down there with my cell phone and the good butter knife," Connie said.

"And that metal thingy that keeps the toilet paper on the holder. Don't forget that," Ruth Ann elbowed Connie as if it was a private joke.

"Oh, God. My mailbox key was on there, too. They said not to lose that because it would cost fifty dollars to replace it."

"I did not make you drop your keys overboard," Jamie said, straightening her glasses.

Dana gave her a smirk.

"Well, I didn't," Jamie stated.

"Instead of arguing why don't you put that scuba diving ability of yours to work and go get them?" Dana pointed emphatically at the water.

"You've go to be kidding." Jamie laughed at the idea, only

making Dana's face more desperate. "I told you the bottom of the bay is a thick muddy ooze and the water is as dark as coffee. I couldn't find an aircraft carrier if it was down there, much less a keychain. And the tide is starting to go out. Who knows where it will end up?" Jamie pointed toward the mouth of the harbor. "I'm sorry but they are gone for good. I'll be happy to pay the fifty dollars to replace your mailbox key, but that doesn't mean I take responsibility for their loss."

"I don't want your money."

"Most people who live around boats have learned to keep valuables in their pocket, not left out on the railing for disaster to strike."

Dana realized not only were her keys gone but the key ring Shannon had given her was gone as well. The expensive gold key ring she had made especially for her now lay at the bottom of the harbor as food for the passing seals. She knew Shannon would ask where it was and why she hadn't taken better care of it.

"She's going to kill me," Dana muttered, giving one last look over the side.

"Who?" Jamie said.

Dana hadn't intended for anyone to hear that.

"No one."

"The other heart?" Jamie suggested.

"Yes." *Damn, this woman is observant*, she thought.

"Pricey gift?"

Dana knew if she said yes she'd sound mercenary. If she admitted the key ring was an anniversary present, there would be more questions about what happened to the relationship, questions she didn't want to answer. Besides, it wasn't any of Jamie's business.

"I happened to like it," she finally admitted.

"Maybe next time you should get one with a float attached to it if you're going to toss it around the deck." There was an I-told-you-so lilt to Jamie's voice and Dana didn't like it.

"How are you going to get in your boat, honey," Ruth Ann asked. "Does your brother have a spare key?"

"No." She hesitated, waiting for another remark from Jamie about preparing for all eventualities and never leaving things to chance.

"Who has the spare key?" Jamie said.

"I meant to have one made. I've only been in the houseboat three weeks."

"No spare?"

"I was going to do it next week." Dana knew that sounded like a flimsy excuse. If someone said that to her, she'd have to laugh and that's just what Jamie did.

"She'll have to break a window," Bev said. "Pick a small one. It'll be cheaper to fix."

"But she has to be able to get through it," Christy said.

"*She* has to get through it, you twit. Not you." Bev gave Christy a smirk. "She could get through a porthole with room to spare."

"It's a shame you have to break a window," Ruth Ann said, rubbing Dana's arm.

Dana checked her watch.

"Maybe I won't have to," she said, digging her cell phone from her pocket.

"Are you calling a locksmith?" Bev asked.

"She'll have trouble finding one to come out tonight because of Lakefair," Ruth Ann said.

"My landlady." Dana pushed in the numbers. "She'll have a key."

The call went straight to voice mail.

"This is Morgan Faylor. Thanks for calling and with a name and number, I'll call you back. Ta-ta!"

"Morgan, this is Dana Robbins. It's eight-forty-five Saturday evening. I'm sorry to bother you but I've locked myself out of the houseboat. Could you please meet me on the dock? I'd really appreciate it. I'll wait for your call. Thanks." She closed the phone and put it back in her pocket. "I better go. Thank you for inviting me, Ruth Ann. It was fun."

Dana said her goodbyes to Ruth Ann, Connie, Bev, Kathy

and Christy, saving Jamie for last. She didn't want to be impolite but it was going to be hard to say it was nice talking with her without choking on the words. "Good night, Dr. Hughes. It was interesting."

"It was nice to meet you, Miss Robbins," Jamie acknowledged, offering a handshake. Dana felt her press something into the palm of her hand.

"What's this?" It was a fifty-dollar bill carefully folded into a neat square.

"I insist."

"I don't want this." Dana tried to push it back into her hand but Jamie slipped them into the pockets.

"It won't cover the keychain but at least you can get a new mailbox key."

"Dr. Hughes, I don't need your money. I'm perfectly capable of paying for my own keys."

"I know you are."

"Take this back, please."

"Good night, Miss Robbins." Jamie climbed down the ladder and disappeared below deck.

"But." Dana was left standing at the railing holding a fifty-dollar bill in her hand. She didn't have time to argue. Morgan could be on her way to the marina at that very moment. She was known for showing up without warning. Dana stepped back into her sandals and headed for the houseboat.

Chapter 3

It was after nine o'clock as Dana rushed around the boardwalk and let herself in the security gate. She trotted down the gangplank in hopes Morgan was already at the houseboat with a spare key. But no one was there. Dana sat down on the storage locker to wait. She had only been there a few minutes when her cell phone rang.

"Hello, Morgan," she said, reading the caller ID.

"Dana, how is life on the houseboat, honey?"

"Did you get my message?"

"No. I saw you called but I haven't listened to the message yet. Oh, wow," she gasped. "Did you see that one?"

"See what?" Dana said.

"The fireworks. Isn't that spectacular? There isn't a better slip in the marina than the one that houseboat is in. Great view. Privacy. Convenient to town. I love it. If I weren't a confirmed princess, I'd live on it myself." Morgan laughed. Whether it was laughing, crying, drinking or having sex, Morgan never did anything halfway. It just wasn't in her nature and she was the first one to admit it. She had life by the gonads and was holding on for all she was worth. An unabashed lesbian, she was outspoken, flamboyant and sincere. Dana's first impression of Morgan Faylor was that she was larger than life and she continued to think so.

"Morgan, I have a little problem."

"What?" Morgan made it sound like no problem was worth the worry.

"I hate to ask but I've lost my houseboat key. It accidentally got dropped overboard. I planned on making spares but dumb me never got around to it. I'm so sorry. I'll be glad to pay for another one and I can come pick it up whenever it's convenient for you." Dana had already decided she would be calling her brother for a place to spend the night.

"I'll be right over." Morgan hung up without waiting for Dana's reply.

"I didn't mean it had to be this very second," Dana muttered, slipping the phone back in her pocket. "But thanks."

Morgan must have driven like a maniac. In six minutes flat her candy apple red Mercedes convertible was pulling into the parking lot above the marina. From the dock Dana could see Morgan's hat bobbing between the sailboat masts. Her posture was perfect. She was dressed in white linen pants and a black v-neck sweater with the sleeves pushed back to the elbow, revealing freckle-covered arms. Her figure was youthfully round and firm and her age was somewhere between fifty and none-of-your-business. She had a girlish wiggle in her walk. Dana could hear Morgan's platform sandals slapping the dock in a quick, determined pace.

"You really didn't have to come right away. I could have waited." Dana opened the gate onto the front deck for her.

"There is no merit in delay," Morgan said, holding up a key suspended from a red and white fishing bobber.

Dana couldn't help but laugh at the inference.

33

"Why didn't I think of that?"

"You have to be a boat person to understand the little nuances of marine life. Or is it marina life?"

"Both I think," Dana said, unlocking the door. "Come in. I'll put the kettle on. You're a tea drinker, right?"

"Tea? I'd love some." Morgan stepped inside and followed Dana to the galley. "This is so cozy. I like what you did with the furniture. Is that a new sofa?"

"Yes. It's a sofa bed."

"That's a good idea." Morgan sat down on it, leaning back and settling in as if she planned on a long visit. She crossed her legs, removed her hat and fluffed her hair. "Now, what's this crap I hear about you and Shannon Verick?"

Dana snapped a look at her. That was exactly the last thing she thought Morgan would ask. Yes, Morgan knew who Shannon was. Dana had mentioned she needed a place to live since she was moving out of her girlfriend's apartment. But that was all she knew. Of course Dana suspected Morgan had the balls to ask almost anything.

"Well?" Morgan leaned her elbow on the back of the sofa and fiddled with a lock of hair at the back of her neck.

"What do you mean?" Dana was trying to formulate an answer.

"I received a telephone call from Ms. Verick last week." She hesitated a moment, waiting for Dana's reaction.

"Shannon?"

"Yes. She wanted to know if my houseboat was for rent. I told her no. It had been rented. She asked for how long."

"What did you tell her?"

"I told her none of her damn business." Morgan smiled regally.

Dana handed her a cup of tea. Experience had told her she took it plain and strong.

"So?" Morgan came to the galley and looked in the far back corner of the lower corner cupboard. "Aha," She smiled and took out a bottle of brandy. She splashed a little into her tea then held the bottle up to Dana. Dana shook her head. Morgan returned the bottle to the cupboard.

"I wondered who that belonged to," Dana said.

Morgan winked.

"Help yourself, any time."

"I'm sorry Shannon bothered you."

"Why are you sorry? You didn't do anything. And she didn't bother me." Morgan took a sip as if testing her drink. "Very nice tea." She returned to the sofa. "So who is this Shannon person and why is she in or out of your life?"

Morgan asked the question with such kindness and concern Dana couldn't help but answer.

"She's my ex."

"Ex as in girlfriend or ex as in partner slash spouse?"

"Ex as in we lived together for four years but now don't." Dana hoped that was enough information to soothe Morgan's curiosity.

"From the tone of Shannon's questions, I think she already knew someone was living on the houseboat, and I'd bet my new Coach purse she knew it was you. She was just calling to have me confirm it. Is that pretty much the picture?"

"I don't know." Dana sipped her tea. She wished she had made herself coffee. This conversation needed coffee and lots of it. Or maybe a shot of Morgan's brandy.

Morgan smiled coyly and held her cup to her lips, watching Dana's face as she drank. Dana felt her eyes boring inquisitively through her.

"Okay, yes. Shannon probably heard I was staying on the houseboat and just wanted to know for sure. My guess is now that she knows, she won't bother you again."

"Sure, she will. She told me she would."

"She did?"

"She said she'd check every now and then to see if it was still occupied. And if I heard you were moving out, she asked if I'd let her know. She tried to make it sound like she was interested in the houseboat but I could tell she was only interested in who was renting it. Is that a fair judgment of good old Shannon?"

"Probably, yes." Dana took her cup to the sink. She wasn't in the mood for tea anymore. "Morgan, may I ask you to do me a favor?"

"What's that?" She sipped slowly, her eyes still on Dana.

"Don't tell her. If I move out, don't tell Shannon. Please. You're right. I'm sure she doesn't want to rent the houseboat. She just wants to know where I'm living. And I'd rather she hear it from me when I'm ready to tell her."

"Honey, I wouldn't think of telling her. That's your business."

"Thank you."

"Is Shannon stalking you?"

"No," Dana quickly replied. "It isn't like that. Shannon's motives aren't sinister."

"If you are at all concerned, I'd be glad to make a call or two. We can certainly have it stopped."

"I'm not afraid of Shannon. She's actually quite a gentle person. She and I were together for four years. Four years and two days to be exact."

"That's long enough to make a dent in the mattress."

"I was the one making the dent. We lived in her apartment in Lacey. I had an apartment in the Capital district but it was too small. It was a great location, cozy, convenient. Sort of like the houseboat. But Shannon's place was bigger."

"So you moved out of your cozy, convenient apartment into her bigger one in BFE."

"Lacey isn't exactly BFE."

"It is if you like living in Olympia." Morgan held up her cup as if toasting those who like city living. "Give me a small apartment in a great location over a barn size place in the sticks any day."

"More tea?" Dana offered.

"Sure." Morgan grinned and came to the galley to doctor it. "I'm going to play detective, if you'll forgive me." She stood leaning against the sink, stirring the brandy into her tea.

"Help yourself," Dana said, knowing she was going to anyway.

"The facts as I see them are as follows. You and Shannon lived together for four years, correction, four years and two days. You moved into my houseboat three weeks ago and live a rather celibate life." Morgan gave a crooked grin. "Don't ask. I have my sources. The marina is a small community."

Dana opened her mouth to object but thought better of it.

"You haven't had contact with your ex, or if you have, it hasn't been very substantial or she would already know where you live and wouldn't be asking me if the rumors she heard are true. Maybe she has followed you or knows someone who has seen you coming onto the dock. Either way, she knows where you are but doesn't want you to know she knows. That can only mean one thing. You haven't told her where you are living and don't plan on it, at least for the foreseeable future. I have to ask myself why. Why would you not want Shannon to know where you live if you aren't afraid of her?" Morgan took a slow sip while she thought. "How am I doing so far?"

Dana sat on one of the stools at the nook table, leaned on her elbow, and smiled.

"I'm listening."

"Okay. She doesn't argue so I'm on the right track. From my experience as a crack detective," Morgan chuckled, "I'd have to conclude the present situation was not Shannon's decision. It was yours. If she was the one who called it quits, you wouldn't mind her knowing where you live. You'd still be yearning for some kind of contact. But if you are the one who walked out and slammed the door, it would be Shannon who is still seeking contact. And my guess is it has something to do with your anniversary. Four years and two days. Too close not to be significant. And it must be more than just a spur-of-the-moment spat. Whatever the reason, you were willing to put four years of living together on the line. You are holed up here in my houseboat, licking your wounds, and waiting for dear old Shannon's memory to fade, something that isn't happening nearly fast enough."

Dana raised her eyebrows as if waiting for more.

"And you want to know how I have been able to make that

observation with limited information, right?"

Dana nodded curiously.

"Easy. If you were successful in putting Shannon out of your mind, you wouldn't care if she knew where you lived. It wouldn't matter to you. You'd be steeled to her. Obviously Shannon can still twang your heartstrings. Why else would you be asking me to help conceal your whereabouts? You still love her and she knows it. What's more she still loves you. Loves you enough to follow you to the ends of the earth to beg forgiveness for her sins."

With that, Morgan drank the last of her tea, a confident smile on her face.

Dana continued to lean on her elbow, supporting her chin in her hand.

"That's it?" she said. "That's the end of your detective work?"

"How did I do? Pretty close, wasn't I?"

Dana smiled behind her hand.

"Well?" Morgan looked up expectantly.

"Don't quit your day job," Dana said, patting Morgan's cheek.

"Where was I wrong? About the anniversary being significant? You walking out had nothing to do with that."

"Actually, that's about the only thing you did have right."

"What was it? A big fight over the other woman? You caught Shannon with someone else?"

Dana scowled, ready to reply just as the telephone rang.

"She wouldn't do that," she said as she raised the receiver to her ear. "Hello."

"Dana?"

"Shannon?" Dana said with surprise.

"Hello, baby."

Dana's eyes rolled up to Morgan. She was watching with an interested little smile on her face.

"Hello," Dana said and moved the receiver to her other ear, away from Morgan, who raised her eyebrows curiously.

"How did you get this number, Shannon?"

"I don't remember. Probably looked it up. What difference does it make?"

"The difference is I don't want it public knowledge."

"I won't tell anyone. Your secret is safe with me, babe."

"I swear," Morgan said, holding up her hand. "She did *not* hear it from me."

"What do you want, Shannon?" Dana didn't want to have this conversation in front of Morgan.

"You know what I want. I want my girl to say this arrangement is ridiculous and she's coming home. That's what I want." Shannon's voice was sweet and sultry. When she wanted to, Shannon could make the skin on the back of Dana's neck stand on end by just saying her name.

"I'm sure you do, but that isn't what we agreed to," Dana said stiffly.

"I didn't agree to anything. You're the one who thinks a separation would be good for us. I don't. I think you should come home and we can talk it over. There's nothing so wrong we can't work it out. I miss your sweet body next to me in the middle of the night." Shannon's voice had become a husky whisper. "I miss the taste of you, baby. Don't tell me you don't miss my hot tongue on you."

"Shannon, please," Dana interrupted, hoping the blush she felt growing wouldn't give away their conversation.

"I bet you're blushing, aren't you?" Shannon cackled.

"I have to go."

"Wait. Don't go."

"I have company."

"Who is it?"

"My landlady," Dana said, wishing she didn't sound so defensive. She should have said it was none of her business but that would only create another sore subject. Shannon was naturally inquisitive and the less said the better.

"Watch out for her, Dana. She'll be after your ass."

"I doubt that." Dana tried to keep the conversation benign, but she knew Morgan was lapping up every word and expression.

"I have to go. I'll talk with you later." Dana wished she hadn't said that. Now Shannon would be calling her every day, several times a day.

Morgan dug in her pocket and pulled out her jingling cell phone. She read the number on the screen, smiled, and stepped out onto the deck to answer it.

"Shannon, you promised you wouldn't interfere," Dana said after Morgan closed the door. "You said I could have three months to think things over."

"I don't understand why you need three months. Why can't you think things over here at home?"

"A separation means we are separated. I can't think with you there, looking over my shoulder every minute."

"What better place to think about our future than right here with the person who loves you. Let me help, Dana. Let me give support. The day you left, Christ, it broke my heart to see you crying, Dana. I know you're upset. I just think we need to spend some time together to work this out. I love you, baby."

"I know you do, Shannon." Dana swallowed back the lump in her throat. "That's why I'm giving us the benefit of the doubt and trying a separation instead of just calling it quits."

There was a long silence.

"Is that what you want, Dana?" Shannon's voice quivered. "Is that where this is heading?"

"I don't know." Dana leaned her shoulder against the refrigerator and closed her eyes. "I just don't know."

"Tell me one thing. Do you love me?"

"Shannon, please."

"Tell me, damnit. Do you love me?" she insisted.

Dana could see Morgan laughing from the deck, still involved in her own conversation. She was standing at the railing, flipping her hair, and posturing as if she was flirting with the person on the other end of the phone. She seemed confident in her existence and for that Dana was jealous. Morgan threw her head back and laughed wickedly.

"You bad girl, you," Morgan said then gave a lusty groan.

"Dana, are you there?" Shannon said impatiently.

"Yes. I'm here." Dana leaned her forehead against the refrigerator door. The stainless steel was cool and comforting.

"Do you love me, baby?"

"Yes," she finally replied. "I have to go." Dana hung up the phone. She stepped into the bathroom to blow her nose and splash water on her face. She didn't want Morgan to see how much Shannon had gotten to her.

"Dana? You here?" Morgan called from the living room.

"Just a second." She checked her looks in the mirror. Her eyes were red and her face was pale. Maybe Morgan wouldn't notice. "Sorry about that phone call," she said, coming out of the bathroom with as much confidence as she could muster.

"I swear, honey. I didn't give her your phone number. I didn't even tell her you were the one living on the houseboat."

"I know you didn't. Don't worry about it. I think she tried to call this morning. Actually I'm surprised it took her until today to get it."

"Sounds to me like Shannon still loves you. Or at least she still lusts after you. From what I could tell, she wants you back."

"Yeah." Dana turned to wash out the cups.

"Is that why you're here? Are you trying to decide if you want her?"

"Something like that."

"If you'll excuse the pun, there are a lot of fish in the sea. If you don't like the one you caught, throw it back and wet your hook again." Morgan chuckled at the innuendo. Her cell phone rang again. "Oh, God. It's Sharon. I've got to go. I told her ten minutes. I don't want her to start without me." She winked and then gave Dana a hug and a kiss on the cheek, before hurrying out the door and up the dock.

41

Chapter 4

If Dr. Jamie Hughes thought she could get the upper hand, forcing her money on Dana, she had another think coming. The more Dana thought about the fifty dollars, the more determined she was to return it. She would march right up to her, offer a polite thank you, slap the money in her hand and say no in a tone that left no doubt she could pay for her own key replacement. Dr. Hughes would have no choice but to accept. The professor's scientific knowledge and big vocabulary were not going to intimidate her. At least that was the plan.

According to Dr. Hughes, she spent the academic school year teaching advanced biology courses at Capital State University in a small town fifteen miles south of Olympia. She spent the summer doing research. Dana assumed that meant at the university as well. An online check revealed Dr. Jamie Hughes had an office in the science building.

Dana entered the campus just after two. It was elegantly landscaped with thick stands of trees separating the buildings, much like the New England colleges nestled in the Berkshire Mountains. Meandering sidewalks lazily criss-crossed the manicured lawns. A majestic bronze statue of a war eagle with a lightning bolt clutched in its talons stood proudly on the front lawn. The mathematics and science departments were housed in twin brick buildings on opposite sides of the common. Dana climbed the steps to the science building behind several teenagers on a guided tour of the university.

"Built in 1952, Phelps Hall houses the university's biology, chemistry and physics departments. Capital State University was the first privately owned university in Washington to have a scanning electron microscope," the guide announced, leading the group down the hall. Dana could hear her listing the faculty achievements as they disappeared around the corner.

"Can I help you, miss?" a woman asked as she descended the marble staircase to the first-floor lobby. She was carrying a stack of mail.

"Dr. Hughes's office?" Dana asked.

"Dr. Jamie Hughes? Second floor. Room two-forty-one. Up the stairs, turn right, second to last door on the left. If she's not in her office, try the last door. I saw the light on in her lab when I left her mail." The woman gave a polite smile then continued down the hall.

The second-floor hallway was dimly lit. Dana's steps echoed on the marble floors as she passed empty lecture halls and laboratories. A janitor was kneeling next to a floor polisher, changing the pad.

"Good afternoon, miss," he said kindly.

"Good afternoon."

"Are you looking for Dr. Hughes?" he said, slipping a pair of pliers into his back pocket.

"Yes. Two-forty-one?"

"That's her office, but she's in there." He pointed to a door directly across the hall. "SEM room."

"Oh." Dana didn't know what SEM meant and whatever it was, she wasn't sure if she should interrupt Dr. Hughes at work.

"Scanning electron microscope," the janitor said, seemingly reading the doubt on Dana's face. "You can knock but she probably won't hear you." He laughed.

"Is it a loud machine?"

"No. But sometimes she gets so engrossed in her work she wouldn't hear a freight train bearing down on her. I can run the polisher while she's reading a scientific magazine and she never bats an eye. Says she doesn't hear it. Come on. Let's see if she's at a stopping spot." He wiped his hands on a rag then knocked on the door. When no one answered, he knocked again then opened the door a crack and peeked in. "Dr. Hughes, you've got a visitor."

Dana stood behind him, nervously waiting for Jamie to appear but there was no response.

"Dr. Hughes," he said, raising his voice. "Visitor," he practically shouted then knocked again on the open door. "Dr. Hughes."

"Oh, Harley. I didn't hear you. What did you say?" Jamie said from somewhere inside the room.

"You've got a visitor, Dr. Hughes. Shall I have her wait in your office?"

"Yes. That'll be fine. Who is it?"

The janitor looked back at Dana.

"Miss Robbins," she said.

"Miss Robbins," he repeated through the opening in the door.

"Who?" It sounded like Jamie didn't remember her. Dana couldn't decide if that was good or bad.

"Oh, Dana Robbins?" Jamie said.

The janitor looked back and Dana nodded.

"That's the one," he reported.

"Have her wait in my office. I'll be right there."

The janitor showed Dana to Jamie's office then went back to his polisher. It was several minutes before Jamie crossed the hall. Time enough for Dana to read every certificate, diploma, chart and poster in the office. Dana was beginning to think Jamie had forgotten her when the office door opened and she stepped in.

"Miss Robbins." She placed a box of microscope slides on the desk and then offered Dana her hand. "What brings you to academia?" Jamie was dressed casually in well-fitting jeans, a white polo shirt and boat sandals. She didn't look anything at all like Dana expected a college professor to look.

"Did I interrupt something?"

"No. Just printing some test results. I had to wait for the printer to catch up."

"I thought the SEM was a microscope."

"It is. Scanning electron microscope." Jamie pointed to the color photograph on the wall. It looked like a group of orange pod-shaped bowls with blue electrical cords plugged into them. "We can print images from it."

"Very nice." Dana liked the abstract shapes and bright colors in the photograph even if she didn't know what it was. "What is it?"

"Fibril secretion from the Piriform glands of a *Micrathena gracilis*."

Dana stared at it then looked back at her curiously.

"Silk being secreted from the spinneret of a Spiny Back Spider," Jamie clarified.

"That's a spider?"

"A very small part of one, yes. The fibrils are bundled together to make the strand of silk. Those are actually *Glandula aciniformes*, the glands that produce the threads for encapsulating the spider's prey."

Dana wondered if that was a direct reference to predators and prey or just a convenient coincidence.

"The female Spiny Back Spider is a fickle creature. She doesn't know whether to copulate with her mate or eat it. Now, what can I do for you, Miss Robbins?" Jamie sat down at her desk and motioned for Dana to take the chair opposite.

Dana pulled the fifty-dollar bill from her purse, smoothed it and placed it in front of Jamie.

"This is yours. I don't want it. I'm returning it to you in person so there's no misunderstanding."

Jamie leaned back in her chair and locked her hands behind her head as if she was keeping them as far away from the money as possible.

"I thought we settled that the other night."

"No, we didn't. You walked away before I could give it back. I am not a charity case, Dr. Hughes. I don't need your money."

"I didn't say you were. I was just trying to ease the burden a little."

"And I appreciate that. Really, I do. But I can't take this. I barely know you. I can't accept fifty dollars from a person I just met."

"You'd take it if I drove my car into yours."

"That's different."

"I don't see they are that dissimilar. I was merely offering reparation for your loss."

"Are you also then accepting a share of guilt?" Dana asked, raising an eyebrow.

Jamie adjusted her glasses and cleared her throat.

"Okay, I feel marginally responsible for your keys ending up in the bay."

"Thank you. But you were probably right. I shouldn't have been waving them around like that. Setting them on the railing was inviting disaster."

"So it's agreed. You'll keep the money and replace your keys," Jamie said, pushing the money across the desk toward Dana.

"No, it's not agreed." Dana pushed it back. "You keep the money. If you ever smash your car into mine, then we'll talk about it."

"Now look, Miss Robbins." Jamie bristled.

"It's Dana and save your breath, Dr. Hughes."

"It's Jamie, and this topic has become far more protracted than necessary. Take the damn money and forget it."

"No," Dana said stubbornly.

Jamie dug in her pocket and pulled out a money clip.

She counted out twenty-five dollars, slapped it on the desk and thrust it toward Dana.

"There. Half. You pay half the mailbox key. I pay half. Agreed?" Jamie's furrowed brow told Dana she wasn't going to budge. This was the best she could do.

"Okay," Dana said finally. "Agreed." She picked up the money and slipped it in her purse.

"Have you told her yet?" Jamie asked, pocketing the fifty.

"Told who what?"

"The one who gave you the key chain. Have you told her it was lost in a fit of overblown exuberance?"

"No. I haven't talked to her about it."

"It looked like a nice gift. It's too bad it's gone." Jamie went to the small refrigerator in the corner and looked inside. "Can I offer you some iced chai tea or maybe a yogurt drink?"

"No, thank you. I just finished lunch." Dana was thirsty, but neither of those sounded good.

"Is it lunchtime already?" Jamie said, looking up at the clock on the wall. "Two o'clock. That can't be right."

"Yes, twenty after two," Dana checked her watch.

"I thought it was about eleven."

"Don't you wear a watch?"

Jamie looked down at her bare wrist then rubbed it as if checking for a watch.

"Yes, sometimes." She scanned the desk. "Do you see a square watch with a black leather band? I don't remember where I left it."

Dana looked under a stack of papers.

"This?" she said, pulling it out.

"That's it. Thanks," she said, buckling it on her wrist. The uniform tan on Jamie's arms told Dana she didn't wear it very often.

"Didn't your stomach tell you it was lunchtime?"

"I got busy on the microscope and lost track of time. Are you sure I can't get you something? I can run downstairs to the pop machine if you want a soda."

"No, thanks anyway. Maybe I should go and leave you to your work."

Jamie checked the refrigerator again. She spied a bottle in the back and pulled it out.

"How about some Saki? One of my students gave this to me when she finally passed advanced MB."

"Advanced marine biology?" Dana said.

"Yes. She took it twice and finally squeaked through with a C minus."

"Sounds like a tough course."

"Not if you read the textbook and come to class. Studies show perfect classroom attendance can be worth an entire grade point, perhaps two, to a student's overall grade. That course is a prerequisite for the summer internship in Australia studying the Great Barrier Reef. She wants to be a marine photographer."

"Have you been there? The Great Barrier Reef?" Dana said, her eyes widening.

"Yes," Jamie replied, reading the label on the bottle. "I'm not sure but I think this is supposed to be served hot."

"I think so, but no thank you. No Saki for me."

"Dr. Ito has an article coming out next month on crystal formations. It'll be her first publication. Maybe I should give this to her as a congratulatory gift." Jamie slid the bottle back in the refrigerator. "Wait." She pulled out a bottle of water and handed it to Dana. "How about a bottle of spring water? Of course, for all we know it was bottled from some city's tap water. But at least it's cold."

"Thank you." Dana hated to turn it down after all the effort. She opened the bottle and took a drink. She wondered how long it had been lurking in the back of the refrigerator behind the Saki and specimen bottles.

Jamie went back to her desk and began rummaging through the drawers.

"Three crackers and a package of Tic Tacs," she said, giving up in disgust. "I'll grab something later, I guess."

Dana remembered the granola bar she had dropped in her

purse yesterday morning. She quickly dug it out.

"How about this?" She held it up proudly. "It isn't much but maybe it will ward off starvation."

"I don't want to take your last granola bar."

"It isn't my last one. I have more." Dana passed it across the desk.

"Are you sure?"

"Absolutely. Help yourself."

"Want half?" Jamie said, opening the package.

"No. You eat it all. And don't argue," Dana teased.

"Thanks." She took a bite then began reading the ingredients on the wrapper. "Not bad. Oats, molasses, nuts, soy, yogurt."

"That brand isn't bad."

"Then there's monoglycerides, lactic acid, high fructose corn syrup, glycerol, partially hydrogenated coconut oil, calcium lactate." Jamie continued reading the fine print.

"Do you know what all that stuff is?"

"Yes. The monoglycerides are—"

"Don't tell me. I don't think I want to know. They're all probably terrible for me. I'll drop dead before I'm forty from ingesting protein bars."

"I doubt it." Jamie ate the last of it and tossed the wrapper in the trash. "That really was pretty good and the ingredients aren't terrible. Thank you for lunch."

"Thank you for the H_2O," Dana said, glad to show Jamie she wasn't a complete idiot.

"You're welcome. By the way, I didn't mean to be nosy."

"Nosy about what?"

"The key chain. It's none of my business if you tell whoever it is about losing it. I guess I was just feeling a little guilty."

"That's okay, and don't heap so much guilt on yourself. It was just one of those things that happen. Anyway, I overreacted. I'm sure Shannon will understand." Dana didn't intend to drop her name. It just slipped out.

"Shannon? Is she the other heart in the engraving?"

"Yes."

49

"Is she the one you were seeing before you moved into the houseboat?"

"Yes."

"Fairly recently?"

"It's been three weeks," Dana said. "Three and a half, actually."

"And you haven't spoken to her since?" Jamie's questions were right to the point, something Dana wouldn't have thought she wanted to answer but they were phrased so simply it seemed easy to reply.

"Twice. Three times if you count yesterday."

"So the interlocking hearts haven't been completely severed."

Dana looked down at the strap of her purse where she normally clipped the key ring. Jamie had asked a question she didn't know how to answer.

"You still have some contact with her, right? That's why you said she's going to kill me."

"Shannon's very observant. I'm sure she'll notice I don't still have the key ring."

"So you and Shannon haven't completely cut things off?"

"It depends on your definition of completely." Dana squirmed a little in her chair.

"I'm making you uncomfortable. I'm sorry. I guess it's the scientist in me. I'm trained to ask questions, to dig for all the answers. Sometimes I forget not all topics are any of my business. Just tell me to shut up."

"I think I did that the other night." Dana smiled shyly.

"Oh, right. You did. And it was probably completely justifiable, given the circumstances."

"It's just I'm not sure how to describe my relationship with Shannon right now."

"That bad?"

"Not bad, exactly." Dana thought a moment. "Strained, maybe."

"That's why you preferred not to answer questions about it at the party."

Dana nodded, wondering how she got this far into a discussion about her personal problems with a stranger. She didn't know if it was her need to talk about it, or Jamie's understanding and insightful questions. Whatever it was, Jamie was a very intelligent woman and Dana found herself comfortable enough to discuss her inner feelings.

"Shannon and I are separated. That's why I rented the houseboat. I needed a quiet place where I can do my work and have time to think. I just wasn't prepared to talk about it with strangers. Does that sound snooty?"

"No. It sounds perfectly natural to me. If I was in your shoes, I probably would have told the girls to mind their own business."

"But I like them. They're very sweet. I didn't want to make them mad at me first crack out of the box."

"They liked you, too. And of course, Ruth Ann and Connie have adopted you. They may not know everything about your personal life but they've taken you in as a lost sheep. Bev and Kathy like schmoozing with a celebrity. Whether you want to admit it or not, Ringlet makes you a celebrity. And Christy," Jamie said, then smiled slightly. "Christy likes you in the Biblical sense."

"I noticed." Dana blushed. "Every time I turned around Christy was staring at me."

"She's harmless. She was just testing you."

"Did I pass?"

"Yes, you did. You were polite but gave no sign of encouragement. I don't think she'll be drooling on your welcome mat. Although I'm sure she'll be glad to amend that if you feel the need for her company."

"Thank you, no. She's nice but not my type. She's a little too direct for me."

Jamie chuckled.

"That's Christy's trouble. She's too direct for most of the women in Olympia. She's run through the majority of the available women like a red tide, and all she has to show for it is a terrible pick up line and a well worn little black book."

"Did she try that pick up line on you?" Dana said curiously.

"No, I'm proud to say. She didn't. My formaldehyde cologne must have worked."

"I think she's intimidated by you. They all are."

Jamie looked at her with a skeptical frown.

"I don't think so," she argued.

"Absolutely they are. All of them. Me too, I guess."

"That's ridiculous."

"Is it? You are a college professor. You have a PhD in biology. You do research. You use a vocabulary most people can't pronounce, let alone understand. We lowly drones are easily intimidated by intellectuals like you."

"That's ridiculous," Jamie repeated, adjusting her glasses nervously.

"Did I embarrass you, Dr. Hughes?" Dana thought Jamie's fidgeting was cute. The intelligent scientist was crawfishing over a compliment and it was adorable.

"Dr. Hughes," a woman said from the doorway. She was holding an opened shipping carton. "I think the part you ordered is here."

"The rectifier for the electrophoresis?" Jamie said, looking up as if she was thankful for the distraction.

"Yes, I think so."

"I'll need to check the invoice on it. They sent the wrong one last time."

"I better go, Dr. Hughes," Dana stood up, smiled, and offered her hand. "Thank you again for solving that little matter successfully."

"You're welcome," Jamie said. She stood up and shook her hand warmly. "If the fiscal responsibility becomes larger than the settlement, please do not hesitate to contact me."

Dana realized she meant the price of the key and chuckled.

"I'm sure it won't, but thank you." Dana started up the hall, leaving Jamie to her visitor.

"Miss Robbins?" Jamie called from the doorway.

"Yes?" She turned around.

"Let me know if I can be of any further assistance. Sometimes discussing a problem with an outside observer can help bring the situation into focus."

"I'll remember that."

Chapter 5

Dana had just snuggled down beneath her comforter when she heard a tapping at the door. At first she thought it was the wind blowing the rigging on a nearby sailboat. She was often awakened by the metal connectors tapping against the mast. But when it got louder and more persistent, she realized it wasn't a sailboat. She rolled over and squinted at the alarm clock. Six thirty.

"Go away," she muttered and burrowed deeper.

"Aunt Dana, wake up," a distraught voice called. "Please." It changed to a whine.

Dana frowned and closed her eyes, wresting one more moment of peace from the night.

"Aunt Dana!" The voice was dripping with mournful pity.

"Shouldn't you be home sleeping, Juliana?" Dana said, opening the door while she pulled her robe over her shoulders.

Juliana Robbins was twelve and petite for her age. She was a perfect little reproduction of her Aunt Dana from her strawberry blond ponytail to her button nose. Although she didn't yet have Dana's pleasing figure, she did have her expressive blue eyes and it was evident Juliana was upset about something so severe that it couldn't possibly wait until eight o'clock, or even seven.

"What took you so long to answer the door?" she said, pushing her way inside.

"I was in bed, asleep." Dana closed the door and followed her into the living room. "What is so important it couldn't wait until a decent hour?"

"Dad is a big fat liar," Juliana said, enunciating each word for maximum dramatic effect. She crossed her arms and waited for Dana's reply.

"I'm sure there's more." Dana sat down on one of the stools to wait for further information. She blinked herself awake and yawned.

"He told me he would do something, something very important to me. In fact, he promised. And now, when it comes down to the moment of truth, he says no. He won't do it. It's not fair!" Juliana's lip stuck out like a toddler who had just lost a pacifier.

"What is it Steve won't do?" Dana had to tread carefully. She didn't want to commit her support until she had all the facts. The last time she blindly took Juliana's side was over a sleepover on the beach with four other girls without a chaperone. Dana was a seasoned veteran of her niece's wars. With luck, Juliana would outgrow her dramatics by the time she bloomed into womanhood. If she didn't, woe to whoever she dated.

"Last Christmas Dad told me to find something we could do together. Just the two of us. He said it could be anything. His dorky idea was going to the zoo. We did that when I was seven." Juliana made an ugly face.

"What did you pick?" Dana knew where this was going. Juliana undoubtedly chose something absurd like skydiving or being shot out of a circus cannon. The one thing Juliana didn't seem to have was any of Dana's practicality. At least not yet. She was impulsive and dramatic, but then again she was twelve.

"Haley Sloan and her mom did it last year and she's only ten."

"Did what, Juliana?" Dana demanded, cutting to the chase.

"Sailing. You know, those little boats we see in the harbor. They have a Daddy and Me class. They teach you everything you need to know, and they even provide the life preservers. The classes last a week and it isn't that expensive. Dad told me to find something to do that cost less than three hundred dollars. The sailing lessons are only two hundred dollars. That's a whole hundred dollars less." Each detail seemed important. "And I can swim. That's the only requirement. You have to be able to swim in case the boat tips over. Dad can swim, right?"

"Right."

"I did just what he said. I found something for us to do together and it doesn't cost too much. Now he won't do it. He chickened out. He's a big fat liar," Juliana repeated, concluding her arguments for the prosecution and flopping down on the sofa.

Dana scratched her upper lip, hiding a smile behind her hand. This could probably have waited until later in the day, but since she was here, Dana had to deal with it. She had been the mother figure in Juliana's life since she was a baby. Steve, Dana's older brother, was a single parent, having secured sole custody of Juliana soon after she was born. The pregnancy was an arrangement made to provide Steve, a lifelong gay man, with a child. The mother had no interest in raising a child and happily accepted the ten thousand dollars Steve paid for what he called uterus rental. He was a good parent and a dedicated father. As a trust lawyer handling estates for gay and lesbian couples, he could provide his daughter with a comfortable lifestyle but was wise enough not to spoil her with excesses. Dana suspected this was a conflict over just such an excess.

"Two hundred dollars is a lot of money, Juliana. Maybe you need to find something else you and your father can do together.

How about hiking? You like to do that."

"That isn't the reason he said no," she grumbled.

"Sailing could be dangerous."

"That isn't the reason either. He said he doesn't have time to do it."

"How long are the lessons?"

"Three hours a day for just a week. Five days." She held up five fingers.

Dana had to admit it didn't sound like a terribly long commitment. Three hours a day wasn't much longer than a movie on HBO. There had to be more.

"What exactly did Steve say?"

"He said forget it. No way."

"Juliana, why did your father say no?"

"He said he couldn't justify the time off. Those were his very words, justify the time off. Can you believe it? He couldn't justify the time off for his own daughter."

"What time of day are these lessons?"

"One to four, Monday through Friday."

"One o'clock in the afternoon?" Dana had just found the chink in Juliana's defense.

"Yes. It's not as if it's all day. Just the afternoon."

"Juliana, your father works. He spends every afternoon at his office, in meetings or in court. You can't very well ask him to take off five days to go sailing."

"Half day. Not all day."

The telephone rang before Dana could reply.

"Hello," she said, suspecting it was Steve.

"Is she there?" he said with an understanding tone.

"Yes."

"Is she still pissed at me?"

"Yes."

"Did she tell you why?"

"We were just getting to that."

"Tell her I'm sorry. I wish I could take this week off but I've got meetings every afternoon and I can't get out of them. If she

57

had given me a little notice, maybe I could have juggled things around but she just sprang this on me last night."

Dana looked over at Juliana. She was sinking down on the sofa, smirking as if she knew the truth was coming out.

"Dana, tell Juliana I'm sorry. I really am. I don't want her mad at me."

"I will, Steve. Don't worry about it. She'll be fine. She knows you love her."

"God, yes. Tell her daddy loves the heck out of her."

"Let me talk with her."

"Thanks Dana. I don't know what I'd do without you."

"You'll owe me one, brother."

"Yeah, well, I'll owe you a lot more. I have no idea how I'm going to handle it when she's old enough to date."

"One crisis at a time," she said with a chuckle.

"I'll come pick her up in thirty minutes. Is that long enough?"

"Don't bother. I'll fix her some breakfast then bring her home. Do you have your house key, Juliana?"

She nodded.

"Thanks sis. You're a sweetheart."

"Talk with you later," Dana said and hung up.

"He isn't going to do it, is he?" Juliana said in full-blown pout.

"No, he isn't. And I think you know why, don't you?"

"Yeah, he's a big fat liar."

"Juliana Robbins, that isn't the reason and you know it." Dana sat down next to her on the sofa and gave her a disapproving stare. She swept a lock of hair from Juliana's face and tucked it behind her ear. "Your father loves you very much. He wishes he could do fun things with you but he can't take off that much time from work on such short notice. He has responsibilities. Tell me what would happen if you skipped a whole week of school?"

"Dad would kill me."

"Besides that." Dana smiled. "What would happen in the classroom?"

"I'd miss a lot of stuff but that's different. It's summer. I won't miss anything."

"What do you think would happen to your grades if you missed a whole week of classes?"

Juliana lowered her gaze and didn't answer.

"You'd have trouble catching up, wouldn't you? You'd be so far behind you couldn't keep up with the rest of the class. It could take you weeks and weeks to learn everything you missed. If you didn't catch up you might even flunk a class or two. A week's worth is a lot of time to be away from your work."

"I've never been absent a whole week," Juliana complained.

"I know, sweetie. You're a very good student. You're very responsible. And your father is just as devoted to his job as you are to school. Being a student is your job. Being a lawyer is his job. A week away from the office could put your father so far behind it would take him months to catch up. In fact, he might lose some of his clients altogether. If he didn't keep his appointments they might think he isn't responsible enough to be their lawyer." Dana took Juliana's chin in her hand. "I know you wouldn't want him to lose a week's worth of clients, would you?"

"No," she mumbled softly. "But why did he tell me he'd do something with me if he never intended to do it?"

"Sweetheart, your father would have loved to go sailing with you. He said so. But you sprang it on him at the last moment. If it had been evening classes or weekends he'd love to do it with you. You just have to give him some notice so he can plan for it."

"This is the only Daddy and Me class they have open. All the night classes are full. They don't have classes on weekends."

"But you do understand why he had to say no?"

"Yes. Daddy explained all that stuff, too."

"Why didn't you believe him? He never lies to you."

"Because I want to take sailing lessons," Juliana said, her eyes welling up with tears.

"Can't you take them by yourself? I've seen kids your age going out in those little boats all by themselves. He'd probably let you do that."

"I want someone to go with me. I don't want to do it by myself." She looked up at Dana woefully. "Would you go with me?"

"Honey, I'm not your daddy." Dana brushed away the tears trickling down Juliana's cheeks.

Juliana suddenly brightened.

"It doesn't have to be Daddy and Me. It could be Mommy and Me! You could be my mom. Dad always said you're like a bonus mom to me. You can tell them you're my mom and they'd let you in. Dad can tell them it's okay. Please, Aunt Dana. Please. It starts today. Please, please, please." Juliana grabbed Dana's hands and squeezed. "You know how to swim. I saw you at the beach last summer."

"Honey," Dana started.

"Dad will pay for it. I'm sure he will. You and I can take the lessons together. It'll be fun. And it'll be right here in the harbor by your houseboat. Convenient, huh, Aunt Dana?"

"Juliana." Dana chuckled, trying to find room to work in a word or two.

"Dad won't mind. He trusts you. I heard him say so."

Dana laughed out loud.

"That's good to know, but Juliana."

"You don't have an office to go to. You work right at home and I heard you say sometimes you work at night so this won't interfere." With puppy dog eyes so big and vulnerable and the expectations of youth so innocent, how could Dana possibly say no? And Juliana was right. Dana worked odd hours. She worked every day but never on a set schedule.

"They start today?" Dana asked with a furrowed brow.

"Yes. Monday through Friday. One o'clock to four o'clock. Right over there at the Yacht Club dock." Juliana pointed out the window. "You could walk," she added as if that was the clincher.

Dana made little puff noises through puckered lips as she thought about it.

"Please," Juliana begged, jumping up and down anxiously. "It'll be fun. You and me on a sailboat. I'll let you drive the boat."

"Are you sure you call it 'driving a boat'?"

"What else could it be?"

"I don't know but I think we are about to find out," Dana said. Juliana immediately squealed with joy and threw her arms around Dana.

"Thank you, thank you, thank you."

"But remember, we have to run it past your father and the instructors. If anybody says no, you promise to accept it without a big fit. Promise?"

"Oh, I promise. But it'll be great. You'll see." She grabbed the telephone and punched in her home number. "Dad! Guess what? Aunt Dana is going to take the sailing lessons with me. She said so. It was her idea."

Dana rolled her eyes and then went to get dressed. From Juliana's end of the conversation it sounded like Steve approved but wanted assurances she hadn't pressured Dana into something she didn't want to do. At this point, it didn't matter. Juliana was ecstatic. Steve was off the hook as a big fat liar and Dana was about to learn which end of a sailboat was which.

"Dad said that was great. He said to tell you thank you from him," Juliana said, watching Dana comb her hair in the bathroom mirror.

"No problem, honey. Like you said, it will be fun." Dana took a deep breath, trying to suppress her fears. "Do we have to go over there and sign up ahead of time?"

"No. Dad said he would do that. He can call them and pay for it over the phone."

"I'll pay for it, Juliana. Your father isn't paying for my sailing lessons. It'll be my treat."

"Dad said you'd say that."

"Well, I'm going to. He's not paying."

"He said to tell you tough toenails, whatever that means."

Dana groaned disgustedly.

"Steven," she grumbled, going to the telephone. She dialed and waited. It took five rings for him to answer.

"It's all paid for, Dana," he said, as if expecting her call.

"You are not paying for my sailing lessons. I'll pay for this and you can pay when you and Juliana do something together."

"Too late, sis. I called and paid by credit card. You and Juliana have the last spot in the class."

"Steven!" Why did everyone feel the need to underwrite her finances? First Jamie. Now Steve. But that was her brother's way. He had always been very generous. When he was eight and Dana was six, he shared his Popsicle when hers fell in a puddle. He was more than generous. He was protective.

"Say thank you, Dana and don't bitch about it," he said.

"Thank you." She realized she couldn't win.

"And remember Dana, you've never been on a boat before. This will be a new experience for you as well as Juliana."

"I have too. I've been on Ruth Ann and Connie's boat and what about my houseboat?" Dana argued.

"They're both moored to the dock. I'm talking about an actual moving boat."

"A boat's a boat."

"Fine. Have it your way. Be sure and take a Windbreaker. Have you got a hat?"

"Yes, I have a hat, Steve." His maternal side was showing.

"Make sure Juliana wears her life vest and sunblock. At least SPF thirty. Forty or fifty would be better. There's half a dozen bottles of it in the medicine cabinet in the hall bathroom."

"Okay."

"And don't let her do anything stupid like stand up and get knocked overboard by the boom."

"What's the boom?" Dana asked. Just the name sounded dangerous.

"The pole at the bottom of the sail. It's attached to the mast and swings back and forth depending on the wind direction. You have to watch the boom swing. Duck."

"I'll remember that."

"Call me tonight and let me know how you did."

"Juliana will tell you."

"Juliana will either be excessively exuberant or distraught

with disappointment. There's no in between with her. It's triumph or tragedy. At least with you, I can get some details. And she wouldn't tell me if it was too dangerous. You would."

"Don't worry, Steve. I'll bring her home alive. I promise."

Chapter 6

"Dr. Hughes?" a woman said, tapping on Jamie's open office door. "Did you want to see me?"

"Oh, yes, Hanna. Come in." Jamie finished typing a sentence into her computer and saved the file. "Did you pass your scuba class?" She began searching through the stack of papers on her desk.

"Yes. Two weeks ago." Hanna was a blond twenty-two-year-old graduate student who spent the summer working in Jamie's laboratory. She and three other students were offered science credits and a small stipend to run tests, prepare reports and help gather samples.

"Good. I have a little job for you, if you're interested."

"Is it diving with you, Dr. Hughes?" Hanna said enthusiastically.

"I need to collect some algae samples in Budd Bay." Jamie

spun her chair around and continued searching through a box of folders on the table behind her desk. When she didn't find what she was looking for, she went into the laboratory attached to her office. Hanna followed. "It will be a fairly shallow dive along the west shore. Thirty feet or so," she said, rummaging in a desk drawer. "Nothing too complicated."

"And you want me to go along?" Hanna smiled.

"It'll just be a short dive." Jamie grimaced and perched her hands on her hips as she scoured the room. "Have you seen those reports I received from the state lab?" she said, not really expecting Hanna to know. "Ah, there it is." She went to the lab table and picked up a large brown envelope. "They're going to dredge a section of West Bay to open up the channel and I want to check the toxin levels in the algae before they stir things up. Like I said, it won't be anything huge. Just a couple hours."

"I'd love to go," Hanna replied. "When?"

"This afternoon." Jamie flipped through the papers in the envelope.

"Whew," Hanna groaned, wrinkling her nose. "Your lab sure smells, Dr. Hughes." She peered into a jar of green sludge.

Jamie looked up from what she was reading, took a whiff, and coughed.

"I guess I need to open a window." There was a pungent odor of formaldehyde and dead fish.

"No kidding," Hanna agreed, gagging on the stench. "How long has it been since you aired this out?" They each opened a window.

"I don't know. Am I supposed to do that?" Jamie's humor was dry. She could tell a joke and keep a straight face better than anyone she knew.

"Yes. And this would definitely be a good place for a Stick Up."

"What's a Stick Up?"

"You know. Those air freshener disks. You stick them on stinky stuff like litter boxes and garbage cans." Hanna placed a lid on the jar of sludge. "Or fish parts."

"Never heard of them. Where do you get them?"

"Everywhere, Dr. Hughes. Grocery stores. Drug stores."

"Sounds like something you'd get from a computer store."

"No. Not disk as in computer disc. Disk as in round plastic container." Hanna held up her hand to show the shape. "They come in lots of different fragrances."

"Fragrances? Whoever heard of computer parts with a fragrance?" Jamie frowned then finally smiled, letting Hanna know the hoax was over. She pointed to the plastic disk stuck to the side of the laboratory table. "Maybe I need to change it. What do you think?"

"Yes. Seriously." Hanna waved her hand in front of her nose.

"Who was your scuba instructor?" Jamie led the way back into her office, still reading over the papers in the envelope.

"Donna Greenlee."

"She's very good. Very knowledgeable."

"Yeah but she's kind of stuck-up. She wouldn't let us use her cart to get our stuff down to the boat."

"Let me guess," Jamie chuckled. "Donna made you carry your own gear."

"Yes."

"She does that to all her students. Do you know why?"

"Because she's stuck-up."

"Come on, Hanna. That isn't a very scientific observation. Try again. Why would Donna require her students carry their own equipment down to the dock?" Jamie tossed out the question then took her seat, leaving Hanna to ponder her response.

"I don't know," she said, scowling in thought. "That crap weighs a ton. Maybe she wanted to know if we were strong enough to carry it."

"Exactly. If you can't carry your own weight, she wants to know that. She wants to know if she has a weakling in the class. It's better to know that before you get forty feet down."

"Oh."

"Don't you think your appraisal of Ms. Greenlee should be based on her ability to instruct, not her chosen means of student evaluation?"

"You mean since I got my certificate and passed the class I shouldn't bitch?"

"Pretty much."

"So, Dr. Hughes," Hanna said, fiddling with the test tube rack on the corner of Jamie's desk. "Do you have room for me on the McNeil Island trip?"

"I'm sorry, Hanna. I would have been glad to have you dive with us but we had to move it up. They're having a boat race in the harbor and we wouldn't have been able to dive. Didn't you see the notice on the bulletin board? We went last week."

"Are you kidding me?" Hanna slumped in her seat. "I missed it? Dr. Hughes, no! I didn't see any bulletin," Hanna pleaded. "Are you sure?"

"Hanna, I'm sorry. The notice was e-mailed to all my students."

"My computer is broken." She clutched her hands to her head. "I haven't checked my e-mail in weeks. My dad's suppose to fix it before the fall semester starts. I can't believe that stupid computer cost me a trip to McNeil Island."

"I have a trip scheduled for September. Are you interested? We're going to dive off Hazel Point in Hood Canal. It's the graduate marine eco class but I think I'll have room if you want to tag along."

"Yes," she said instantly, energized at the idea. "Put my name on the list."

"You'll probably need a dry suit. Can you rent one?"

"No problem. That's what I told my folks I wanted for Christmas and they said okay. I'll just tell them I need it in September instead of December. Do you know when in September?"

"I'm not sure. Around the twelfth. I need to check the tidal chart. I want to dive during a minus tide."

"Are we staying on the boat overnight? Will I need a sleeping bag?"

"No. No sleeping bag for this trip." Jamie chuckled. "The

Prism is not a houseboat. It's a research boat. We're staying in a motel. I'll provide protein snacks, test kits and anything you'll need to preserve specimens. You'll be responsible for your motel, meals, tank refill and anything else you want to take. I can let you know who else is going in case you want to split a room with one of the girls."

"What are we diving for?"

"Salmon. We are going to study the oxygen levels of the spawning *Oncorhynchus keta*, Chum salmon as they enter the canal."

"Isn't that where they had the big algae bloom a few years ago that killed all the fish?" Hanna offered.

"Yes. And we're going to see if we can chart the changes in the oxygen levels."

"Is there anything else, Dr. Hughes?"

"No, I guess that's all. I'll meet you at the West Side Marina about one."

"Thanks for asking me," Hanna said then left Jamie to her work.

Jamie was already in her black wet suit and loading equipment onto the boat when Hanna pulled into the parking lot next to the marina.

"Bring your gear onboard and we'll get going," she said as Hanna descended the stairs to the dock, loaded down with an air tank and two large tote bags.

"I only have one tank, Dr. Hughes. Will that be enough?"

"It should. If not, I've got an extra one you can use."

As soon as Hanna stowed her gear, Jamie released the lines and shoved off. The twenty-six foot gray metal boat had a center mounted pilothouse that provided protection from the rain and had been specially equipped for Jamie's research. It had twin inboard engines, a rear diving platform with two winches, both rigged with heavy cables to lower and raise equipment. Extra tanks, capture nets, a diving cage, an inflatable boat with a six horsepower outboard and an array of tools were strapped to the deck. Gauges, meters, test kits and storage bins were all crowded onboard, making the craft a small but efficient floating laboratory. They motored out of the marina and headed down the shoreline, well within the mouth of Budd Bay.

"That's where they're going to dredge," Jamie pointed out a quarter mile stretch of beach.

"How many samples do you want to take?" Hanna said.

"Depends on what we find. Fifteen, twenty. Maybe more. I want some microscopic species as well as macroscopic ones. Green algae, blue, red. Whatever we can find. Diversity. Anything in this area. Get into your wet suit and let's go take a look."

Jamie dropped anchor and began unpacking what she would need for the dive. Hanna pulled off her sweatshirt and shorts. She had on a two-piece green swimsuit that looked more suited for tanning than for scuba diving. Jamie couldn't help but notice her young and perky breasts, her tiny nipples visible through the fabric. Jamie was an old hand at getting in and out of her wet suit and strapping on her tank. But Hanna was new at it. Jamie was ready and waiting on the diving platform, checking her gauges and regulator, as Hanna was just zipping her wet suit.

"I'm sorry Dr. Hughes. I guess I'm a little nervous. I'm not used to doing this," she said, going back to her tote bag for her fins.

"Hanna, are you forgetting something?" Jamie said, pointing to her own mask.

"Oh, right." She went back to get her mask. "Sorry."

"Take your time."

"I'm ready."

"Check your mouthpiece."

Hanna hung her mask on her wrist and took a breath through her mouthpiece.

"Okay."

"Do it again," Jamie said, pinching off Hanna's nose. Hanna tried again. "Get anything?"

"No." She looked surprised.

"You might want to turn on the valve."

"Oh." Hanna giggled, obviously embarrassed.

"Relax, Hanna. This is just like any other dive. We're going to take a look around, collect some samples and head back up. If you have trouble, remember the hand signals."

Hanna nodded.

"Stay close. Steady breathing. Watch your gauge. If I give you the thumbs-up, ascend. We'll use a net in the cage for the collection bags." Jamie flipped a switch and lowered a metal cage into the water. "Ready?"

"I think so."

"You'll do fine. Hold your regulator when you enter the water so it won't smack you in the face. Go ahead. You first." Jamie always had her students enter the water first. She didn't want a novice jumping on top of her. She knew adrenaline could cause an error in judgment. Hanna held her mask against her face with one hand and her regulator with the other as she stepped into the water. Jamie waited for her to come to the surface and give the okay sign before following. Hanna was right. She was nervous. Jamie could tell by her breathing. She took two breaths for every one Jamie took. But that would come with experience.

They combed the bottom, searching for algae specimens. Jamie knew just what she wanted and filled over a dozen bags while Hanna combed the edges of the collection field, coming up with only a few. Finally, Jamie signaled for them to ascend. She waited for Hanna to climb the ladder before tossing her fins aboard.

"That was fun," Hanna said enthusiastically. She sat down on the storage bin to unbuckle her tank.

"What's your tank gauge read?" Jamie said, unhooking her weight belt and tank. "Mine reads half."

"Gosh," Hanna gasped, checking her gauge. "I used all that? It's almost empty."

"Slow steady breaths, Hanna. You have to be in control of your breathing or you're going to run out of air halfway through a dive. If we were deeper and you needed to ascend in increments, you would have been in trouble."

"Sorry, Dr. Hughes."

"That's okay. You did fine. As soon as I collect a couple of surface water samples, we can head back to the lab."

Hanna looked up as a shriek echoed in the distance. "It looks like that little sailboat is really hauling ass." The sailboat was heading right toward them. It was a small craft and was leaning at a steep angle, perilously close to tipping over as it skated closer.

Jamie looked up from the equipment locker.

"Tack! Tack to port!" she shouted but the boater didn't seem to hear.

"It's a woman and a kid!"

"Let it out! Luff your sail!" Jamie went to the front of the boat and waved her arms as the little boat continued to bear down on them.

"They must be in one of those beginner's classes," Hanna pointed to the other similar boats darting back and forth across the harbor.

"I know her!" Jamie said, scrambling to put on her glasses. She squinted at the woman at the tiller. "Dana, let out your sail!" she screamed.

"What?" Dana sounded frantic.

"Release the rope."

"I did but it's all tangled." The closer the boat got, the more terrified Dana and the little girl looked. "What should I do?"

"Lay it over," Jamie shouted, cupping her hands to her mouth. "Lay it over NOW!"

"How?"

"Lean the way the boat is leaning. Both of you. Lay it down on its side right now, Dana," she demanded.

Dana tugged at Juliana's life vest, pulling her to the low side of the boat. Just as Jamie predicted, the twelve-foot sailboat splashed onto its side and coasted to a stop a few yards from Jamie's boat. The child slipped beneath the water but immediately bobbed to the surface, her life preserver doing its job. She grabbed onto the boat, seemingly none the worse for the dunking. However, Dana was trapped under the sail. Jamie could see her thrashing to get clear of it. Acting on instinct, she dove in and swam over to help.

71

She lifted the sail with one hand and pulled Dana free with the other.

"Hang onto the boat," Jamie said, pushing Dana against the hull.

"Are you okay, Juliana?" Dana coughed and sputtered.

"Yeah." Juliana seemed more stunned than anything else.

"The rigging was tangled around the mast. Once we got going, we couldn't move it," Dana explained. "Juliana, make sure your vest is tight. And don't let go of the boat."

"Where is your life vest?" Jamie asked.

"I don't know. When I hit the water it came off." Dana choked and coughed out the seawater she had swallowed.

"There it is, Aunt Dana," Juliana said, pointing a few feet away.

Jamie retrieved it and helped Dana get it over her shoulders.

"Buckle the strap," she said, holding it in place while Dana worked the belt.

"No wonder it came off. The buckle is broken." Dana held up the strap with the broken end.

"Hanna, toss me that red life vest. The one under the seat in the pilothouse," Jamie shouted, treading water and holding Dana's damaged vest closed. Hanna tossed it as far as she could and Jamie swam for it. She helped Dana change, making sure she was buckled securely into the new vest. "I'm going to untangle your rigging. But first I need the two of you to hold hands and let go of the boat. I don't want the hull to hit you in the head. Your vests will support you. Okay?" Jamie tread water easily, keeping herself afloat without relying on the boat. "It'll just take a minute. I'm right here if you need me."

"Okay," Dana said hesitantly, looking over at Juliana. "Are you okay, honey?" Juliana nodded and took Dana's hand, clinging to her desperately. They released the hull and floated a few feet away.

Jamie untangled the rigging and straightened the sail before guiding them into position behind the boat.

"Hi, Juliana," Jamie said, trying to calm the child's fear. "I bet this is your first time in a sailboat, right?"

"Yeah." Juliana was doing a frantic doggy paddle with a firm grip on Dana's hand.

"Sooner or later everybody tips the boat over. It's no big deal. Usually you learn how to right the boat a little later in your class. My name is Jamie and I'm going to teach you how to stand your boat back up."

"Okay." She spit a mouthful of water, struggling to keep her mouth above the rolling waves.

Jamie noticed Juliana fighting against the life preserver, not trusting its support.

"Don't fight your life vest, sweetie. It'll hold you up just fine. It has sufficient buoyancy to keep your head above water. Just relax. Easy slow leg kicks are all you need to stay in place." She reached down and guided Juliana's legs into a simple kick. "Like this. Just like a frog. In and out. You're wearing an expensive life vest. Let it do its job."

Juliana reached for Jamie's shoulder, her eyes were huge.

"Are you sure?" she said with a nervous twitter in her voice.

"I'm sure." Jamie smiled confidently, taking her hand and squeezing it. "That's what I'm doing and I'm not wearing a life vest." She looked over at Dana whose face was nearly white. "That goes for you too, Dana."

"I am. I am." There was near panic in her voice.

"Are you okay?"

"I'm just peachy." She coughed out a splash of seawater. "My brother will never forgive me. I told him I'd take care of Juliana. First time out and I crash the boat and dump us in the harbor."

"Relax, Dana. Juliana is fine. She's not hurt, are you, kiddo?"

Juliana shook her head as she bobbed through the waves.

"And you didn't crash the boat. You did exactly the right thing. If you hadn't laid the boat over, you would have collided with my boat. Sailboats don't have brakes like a car. You have to know how to abort the run. I assume this is one of those week-long sailing classes, right?"

"Yes."

"They would have had you intentionally lay the boat down at least once before the week is over anyway. You need to know how to right your craft, Juliana." Jamie kept talking, hoping to reassure them and calm their fear enough to climb back aboard.

"Can we do that then and get out of the water?" Dana said.

"Sure. Juliana, I need you to put your feet on the centerboard and grab onto the side of the boat. Can you do that?"

"I think so."

"Do you feel the centerboard?" Jamie helped position Juliana's feet on the board that extended down through the bottom of the boat and into the water.

She nodded.

"Stand up on it. Put your weight on the board. The boat will tip back toward you so hold onto the side." It did, leaving Juliana suspended in mid-air with her rear pointed out into space. "Now step back on the centerboard. The mast will come up out of the water. When it does, I want you to swing your leg over the side and climb in the boat."

Juliana continued to hold onto the side and bob up and down with the boat, her eyes apprehensively large.

"It'll tip over on top of me."

"No, it won't. Just swing your leg over like getting on a horse." Jamie held the tiller, helping stabilize the rocking.

"Go ahead, honey," Dana said reassuringly. "Do what Jamie says. Swing your leg over."

"Aunt Dana, you do it."

"Go ahead, Juliana. You can do it. This is part of learning to sail. Do what Jamie told you." Dana paddled out of the way and smiled encouragement. "One, two, three, step."

Juliana took a deep breath and bobbed her rear in the air to gain momentum. Finally, she took a step back on the centerboard and lifted her leg as the sailboat righted itself. She scrambled over the side and sat up, a relieved smile on her face.

"All right, Juliana," Jamie cheered. "Good job. Perfect the very first time. Now, pull the tiller hard to port."

"Where?"

"Pull it all the way over and hold it there until Dana gets on board. I need you to move to the other side when she climbs in. You will be the counterbalance."

"How am I supposed to get in there? We don't have a ladder." Dana said as Jamie reached over and floated her into position.

"You don't need a ladder. I'll help you. Hold the side."

"I can't get up there!"

"Yes, you can. Of course, if you'd rather, we could go looking for your key ring," Jamie teased.

"Very funny." Dana grabbed onto the side of the boat.

"Now throw your right foot over the side."

"My foot?" Dana looked back at her in horror. "How am I supposed to get my foot all the way up there?"

"Like this," Jamie said, cupping her hands under Dana's bottom and heaving.

Dana came out of the water long enough to hook her foot over the lip of the boat. Jamie temporarily dipped below the surface of the water but came right back up, wiping the water from her face. Dana was left hanging from the side of the boat by two hands and one foot like a stuffed cat suction cupped to a car window.

"Pull yourself up," Jamie said.

"I can't. I'm stuck."

"Lean the other way, Juliana. Here she comes."

"I told you, I can't," Dana argued.

"I'm going to push. You pull."

"No, no. Don't push."

"Get ready."

"No, Jamie. Don't push!"

Jamie placed her hands on Dana's bottom.

"No, I can do it myself," Dana insisted.

"Pull."

"Don't push!" Dana sounded shrill and frightened.

"Pull, damnit." Jamie pushed Dana up, kicking furiously to keep her own head above the water.

"Ouch," Dana squealed, struggling to get her leg over the side.

Jamie took a deep breath and gave a big push. Her face once again submerged. Her hands slipped into Dana's crack, but the force was enough to vault Dana over the side.

"Pull yourself in," Jamie said, spitting water.

Dana rolled into the boat and sat up.

"Oh, my gosh," she gasped.

"Are you all right?" Jamie asked, holding onto the side to catch her breath.

"My bathing suit," she said, her eyes huge.

"What bathing suit?"

"I've got a bathing suit on under my shorts."

"And it's up your butt, right?" Jamie grinned.

"Yes. Seriously up there." Dana wiggled in her seat.

"Sorry about that. My hands slipped."

"Take your shorts off and pick it, Aunt Dana," Juliana said, dutifully holding the tiller.

"No. I'm not going to take my shorts off and pick it." Dana leaned back and forth, obviously trying to relieve her wedgie.

"You may have to do what Juliana said. Scientifically speaking, sometimes the only way to extricate an impactment is to pick it." Jamie winked at Juliana.

"I am not going to pick it in public," Dana said stoically.

Jamie laughed and shook her head.

"What are you doing out here in the harbor?" Dana said, obviously happy to change the subject. She continued to daintily fidget with her bathing suit.

"Collecting algae samples. You didn't mention you were going sailing."

"I didn't know I was until this morning. This is my niece, Juliana Robbins."

"We met," Jamie said, reaching over and patting Juliana on the leg. "How are you doing, Juliana? Are you okay now?"

"Yeah. I'm a little cold but I'm okay."

"You might check around and see if you can find a shorty wet suit. It'll keep you warmer if you have to lay the boat down. You too, Dana."

76

"Maybe we won't have to lay the boat down again. We've done it once. That's enough." Dana pressed her hands through her hair.

"That was fun, Aunt Dana. Can we do it again?"

"No. Not today."

"Next time you feel the boat going too fast to control it, luff the sail. Let the sheet out."

"And what does that mean?" Dana looked up at the top of the sail.

"Let go of the rope that controls the boom, the pole at the bottom of the sail." Jamie reached up and wiggled the boom. "It's like taking your foot off the accelerator. The boat will slow down and usually will right itself if it is heeling one way or the other."

"What do we do now?" Dana held the end of the rope, waiting for instructions.

Jamie held onto the boat and kicked her feet to slowly turn them toward open water.

"Put the tiller amidship, Juliana."

"Like this?" she said, pulling it to the middle.

"Exactly. Dana, pull the main sheet, the rope in your hand, until you feel the wind start to fill the sail." The boat lurched forward, dragging Jamie along for the ride.

"Now what?" Dana said, leaning forward as if poised for what came next.

"Now, have fun." Jamie let go and dropped into the water as they floated away. "Watch out for the boom. It's going to cross the boat."

Dana and Juliana ducked as the boom swung across and extended out the other side. The sail filled with wind and sent them cruising back to the middle of the harbor.

"Thank you, Jamie," Dana called, waving her arm.

Jamie waved back, then swam back to the boat and climbed in. Hanna was there waiting, watching the sailboat as it drifted away.

"Do you think they know what they're doing?" Hanna said doubtfully.

"Sure. And if they don't, they'll learn. That's why it's called a class, Hanna." Jamie patted her shoulder and went back to work labeling the samples.

Chapter 7

Dana and Juliana walked the four blocks from the houseboat to the Yacht Club for their Tuesday afternoon class. It was a warm afternoon with gentle breezes under a cloudless blue sky. All Juliana could talk about was how they had to lay the boat over and how she was the one who righted it. She had picked up many of Jamie's nautical terms and proudly used them as if she was an experienced sailor. When Juliana mentioned capsizing the boat to her father and how much easier it would have been to right the boat had they been wearing shorty wet suits, he wasted no time in buying them matching suits. At least he tried. As Dana expected, she and Steve spent fifteen minutes at the marine store arguing over who would pay for her outfit. Dana won but only by using her feminine wiles. She threatened to tell Steve's new boyfriend he was afraid of any insect smaller than a breadbox and that he slept with a light on until he was twenty.

The store clerk had laughingly told Dana she didn't need to wear underwear with the shorty. The all-in-one zip up neoprene suit fit like a heavy girdle, holding everything in place from knees to neck. Dana was sure the decorative seam design would leave a permanent imprint on each breast, looking something like a racing stripe down her front and up her butt in the back.

"You're not going to wear that hoodie, are you, Aunt Dana?" Juliana said.

Juliana's shorty was black with a wide pink stripe down each side. Her figure had not begun to round so it fit in one straight shot down her trim little body. Dana's shorty was black with a lavender stripe and to her shock and embarrassment, fit all too well.

"Yes, I am. I can see every lump and bump through this thing." At least it didn't give her a wedgie, she thought.

"It looks dumb," Juliana whispered, after looking at the other sailors congregating for the class.

"But it covers that second slice of pizza I had last night," Dana whispered back. "I didn't know these things were so revealing."

"Jamie wore one."

"Yes but she has the right shape for it and she's used to wearing one." Dana had to admit Jamie looked good in hers.

"I can't wait until I have boobs like yours," Juliana said without whispering, turning a few heads. Dana felt the adults (and one teenage boy with roving eyes) sizing up her bosom.

"That's nice, honey," she said, clamping her hoodie closed over her chest as she blushed.

"Dana and Juliana Robbins," the instructor said, referring to her clipboard. "The boat you were in yesterday has gone in for repairs to the rigging. We're going to put you in a faster boat today. It handles about the same as a Lido. It just isn't as wide and the draft is shallower. It's called a Laser," she said, pointing to what Dana thought looked like an oversized surfboard with a sail.

Dana had seen some of the more experienced sailors zipping across the water in Lasers and from what she could tell they had only two speeds, fast and faster. If the Laser was a car, it would be a two-seat convertible that squealed around corners on two wheels.

The sail was hanging limp in the breeze, but Dana could almost hear it calling to her like a Muse… "Come to me, Dana. Come sail with me. But be afraid. Be very afraid."

"Are you sure you don't have anything wider?" she asked, swallowing hard.

"Oh, boy," Juliana said, practically jumping out of her shorty. "That's way way cool, Aunt Dana."

"Sorry, ma'am," the instructor said. "That's the only thing we've got unless you want to go out in an Opti." She pointed to the stack of tiny pale blue boats overturned on the dock for storage. They weren't much bigger than a bathtub.

"Wow." Juliana was standing on the dock, looking down at the Laser. It was clear she wasn't going to settle for the bathtub boat.

"Yes, Juliana. That's way way cool," Dana said, gulping down the fear that knotted her throat. "Put on a life vest. Pick a big one from the rack and buckle it tight. Maybe you should take two."

The instructor tethered the boats together like a parade of elephants holding trunk to tail and pulled them out into the middle of the harbor. After a few words of advice, the string of little boats was set free to begin their afternoon odyssey. Dana had a death grip on the tiller while Juliana manned the ropes controlling the sails.

"Aren't we going a little too fast?" Dana said, adjusting her course to slow their speed.

"No. Go faster."

"I don't think there is enough wind for that." *From my lips to God's ears*, she thought.

"Look. Isn't that Jamie?" Juliana pointed to the boat anchored just offshore.

"Yes, I think so," Dana replied, ducking down to see under the sail.

Juliana stood up and waved her arms over her head.

"Jamie. Hey, Jamie," she yelled.

"Sit down, Juliana," Dana gasped as the boat began to heel to port. "Sit down right now."

Juliana dropped down but kept waving.

"Jamie, over here!"

Jamie looked up and waved.

"Hey, Juliana," she shouted. "How are you doing?"

"We're in a Laser today. It's faster." Juliana grinned.

"I see that." Jamie gave a thumb's up. "Is that Dana back there?"

"Yes. She's steering. I'm operating the sail."

Dana stuck her head under the sail and waved.

"Hello," she said, keeping them on a straight course.

"Pull your mainsheet tighter, Juliana," Jamie said.

Juliana gave a tug, filling the sail and increasing their speed.

"Dana, pull the tiller a bit to port," Jamie added.

Dana did it, adding even more speed.

"Not too much, Juliana," Dana said. They skimmed across the water, the wind whistling through the top of the sail.

"Give another tug, Juliana," Jamie shouted.

"No, that's enough," Dana said, holding her breath.

Juliana grinned and gave a tug. The sail billowed full and strained against the mast.

"Juliana!" Dana clamped both hands on the tiller.

"That's it," Jamie encouraged.

Like riding a carnival ride, Dana was too nervous and breathless to speak. She held onto the tiller, frozen in place as they sailed past a nearby boat and bore down on another.

"Let out the rope, Juliana," Dana pleaded.

"Do I have to?" she said regretfully.

"Yes, you have to."

"There. I did." Juliana had only released an inch or two of line, making little difference in the boat's speed.

"Juliana Robbins!"

"Don't let it out, Juliana," Jamie shouted. "Keep it tight."

Juliana pulled it back snug.

"You aren't helping," Dana yelled in Jamie's direction.

"You're doing fine. You could go a little faster if you'd steer a bit further to port." Jamie had to shout to be heard.

"NO!"

"YES!" Juliana insisted.

"No," Dana said sternly. "This is fast enough."

"No, we aren't, Aunt Dana. This is fun. It's better than go-carts."

Juliana leaned into the wind, her ponytail flying and her cheeks pink. She grinned and giggled with each slap of the bow against the water. Dana bravely held their course, her knuckles white against the tiller. Finally, she eased the tiller and turned to avoid running into the marina.

"That way, Aunt Dana." Juliana pointed back toward the middle of the harbor but the wind didn't cooperate. The sail fluttered and flapped against the mast, unable to fill. Dana took the opportunity to regain the feeling in her fingers. Juliana pulled at the ropes and boom, trying to find wind but they floundered in a dying breeze. They made their way slowly back to Jamie's position.

"I think you lost the wind," she said as they came within shouting distance.

"Yeah," Juliana grumbled, still working the ropes. "It's a bummer."

"Anyone can sail in a strong breeze. It takes a good skipper to sail in light air." Jamie sat on the side of her boat, her wet suit unzipped to the waist revealing an orange swimsuit top. Dana noticed it supported her bustline like a push-up bra.

"Light air is fine with me," Dana said, sitting comfortably for the first time since they left the dock.

"Aunt Dana is a wuss."

"I am not. This is only our second time out. I'm entitled to be a little cautious."

"Do you know how to sail, Jamie?" Juliana asked eagerly.

"A little," Jamie said.

"I like going really fast. It makes my stomach jiggle."

83

"It makes my stomach turn over," Dana muttered. A large sailboat had motored into the middle of the harbor and raised its sails, propelling the craft toward open water.

"Wow. That's cool." Juliana watched as the boat sliced through the wind.

"He's on port tack," Jamie said.

"The wind on the left?" Dana said, trying to remember the terms.

"Yes and sail on the right. That's how you sail up wind even in light air. Work back and forth across the wind, taking what you can find."

"Have you ever sailed a Laser?" Juliana seemed consumed with Jamie's knowledge of sailing.

"Yes, many years ago."

"Did you tip over like we did?"

"Many times." She chuckled. "I was a slow learner."

"How old are you?"

"Juliana, that isn't polite to ask," Dana quickly said.

"I don't mind. I'm forty-five, Juliana."

"Wow. That's old."

"Juliana!" Dana scowled.

Jamie burst out laughing.

"She's right. I am old."

"Forty-five isn't old," Dana said.

"I'm twelve. I'll be in seventh grade this year."

"Good. You'll enjoy that. You'll probably have Andrea Larson for science if you're going to North Junior High."

"You know her?" Juliana seemed amazed that Jamie knew anyone in her world.

"Sure. I'm a science teacher, too."

"At the junior high?"

"No. I teach at Capital State University." Jamie smiled at Dana as if acknowledging Juliana's curiosity. "I teach advanced marine biology."

"What's that?"

"The study of plants and animals that live in or around water."

84

"Wow." Juliana's eyes widened. "Like sharks and stuff?"

"Yep. Like sharks and stuff."

"Juliana, will you leave Dr. Hughes alone already?"

"No problem. Maybe someday I'll have Juliana in one of my classes. By the way, I need to apologize for yesterday, Dana."

"Apologize for what?"

"For sticking my hands up your bottom."

"Oh." She blushed.

"It was an accident, I assure you."

Dana noticed the little sailboat was drifting closer to Jamie's research boat.

"Juliana, pull that rope. We're getting too close. We need to turn around."

"I got it," Jamie said, using a pole to snag the bow and point them in a new direction. "Pull the boom to the other side and straighten the tiller."

"I wish Jamie was in the boat," Juliana muttered, adjusting the rope. "She'd go fast."

Jamie chuckled then gave them a push with the pole.

"Thanks," Dana said, steering them into open water.

"Have fun."

"Bye, Jamie," Juliana said, waving big.

"Bye, Juliana." Jamie saluted with a grin then went back to work.

Wednesday promised to be warmer. The breeze was intermittent but the harbor was filled with day-sailors out to enjoy an afternoon on the water. The students were eager to join the bigger boats in the bay. Dana felt comfortable enough to go without her hoodie. She allowed Juliana to man the tiller while she handled the ropes. They spent the first hour fighting with the sail and the other boats in their path. Their spirits weren't dampened when they realized the other boaters were having the same trouble. The little spurts of wind encouraged them.

"Let's head over there," Dana said, swinging the boom to the other side. "There are too many boats on this side of the harbor."

"Do you think Jamie will be out there?" Juliana pushed the tiller and changed their course.

"I don't know. I can't see her boat."

"Maybe she can help us find some wind." Just then the sail billowed and the boat lurched forward.

"There you go," Dana said happily. She trimmed the sail, testing how snug to keep the sheet. They bobbed along, making slow but steady progress.

"I don't think she's out here," Juliana said disappointedly.

Dana squinted into the afternoon sun, catching a glimpse of a boat further up the shoreline. It seemed to be anchored and from the look of it, it could be Jamie's boat. Dana pointed and Juliana steered toward it.

"Jamie?" Juliana called as they got closer, but no one answered. The boat seemed empty. "Jamie, where are you?"

"I don't think she's there," Dana said, moving to the other side for a better view.

"What are those bubbles from?" Juliana asked, leaning over the side. "Do you think it's a whale or something?"

"I think those are air bubbles from a scuba diver. Jamie does that. She must be underwater."

"She scubas?" Juliana declared, obviously impressed with another of Jamie's talents.

"Yes. That's what the black wet suit she was wearing is for. I imagine a lot of marine biologists scuba dive. They can get a closer look at what's going on in the ocean."

"Wow. Scuba diving." Juliana's eyes lit up at the thought.

"Don't get any ideas, young lady. I am *not* taking scuba lessons with you."

"Oh, heck," she groaned.

A blast of bubbles broke the surface and Jamie's head popped up. She removed her mouthpiece and pushed her mask to the top of her head.

"Hi, sailors," she said.

"Hello," Dana released the rope until the sail fluttered and fell limp.

"Hi," Juliana said, leaning over the side with a wide grin of fascination.

"How's it going today? Did you capsize or run aground?" Jamie teased, grinning up at the child.

"Nope. There are too many boats out here. We get going and have to turn to keep from hitting someone."

"Some days are like that. I like your wet suit," she said to Dana. "Makes sailing easier, doesn't it?"

"It took a little getting used to," Dana replied, unconsciously checking her zipper. "I noticed people in the bigger boats don't wear them."

"They are less likely to capsize. The little boats have a more transient center of gravity." Jamie swam to the ladder on the back of her boat and climbed onboard.

"Did you catch anything?" Juliana asked, watching her every move.

"I wasn't fishing. I was collecting algae samples." She removed her bulky tank and weight belt, then held up a mess pouch full of tiny baggies.

"What's algae?" Juliana asked.

"Photosynthetic marine organisms."

"Oh." That seemed like more than enough information to quell her curiosity.

Two blasts of the instructor's whistle told Dana they had ten minutes left and should begin steering for the marina.

"Will you be diving tomorrow?" Dana asked.

"Maybe. If I am, it will be further up toward the bulkhead." Jamie pointed toward the pile of concrete and rocks extending into the water. "I want to get a few samples from there."

"What are you doing with the algae?" Dana asked, wondering if she would understand Jamie's answer.

"I'm charting oxygen saturation in the algal flow. I'm collecting samples on either side of the fish ladder next week. It can be an indication of salmon migration habits through the fish ladder."

"We went there," Juliana said. "Last year our class saw fish jumping up the ladder."

"Exactly. And we want to keep them coming back. How are things with you and the key chain lady?" Jamie asked in Dana's direction.

"Quiet," she replied, tossing a glance at Juliana then back at Jamie as if to say she'd rather not talk about it in front of her niece.

"Quiet is good, I hope."

"Yes. Thanks for asking."

Another blast of the whistle meant time was up.

"We have to go," Dana said, looking across at the line of small sailboats heading up the channel toward the Yacht Club. "Maybe we'll see you tomorrow."

"I'll look for you. You'll be the Laser going forty knots. Right, Juliana?" Jamie smiled and winked at her.

"Yeah!"

Thursday, day four of the lessons, alternated between misty cool and partly cloudy. The sailing class spent their afternoon in the bay coaxing minimum speed out of a nearly windless sky. Dana and Juliana wore rain jackets most of the day, flipping the hoods up and down against the occasional rain. Dana was ready to call it a day when a puff of wind scooted them across the harbor, lifting their spirits.

"I thought Jamie was going to be out here," Juliana said.

"Me, too."

"This is a bummer. I hate it when there's no wind." Juliana pulled the sail one way then the other, trying to find propulsion.

"Did you know Christopher Columbus spent an entire week in the middle of the Atlantic Ocean without even a breath of wind? They had to just sit and wait for a breeze to keep them going. But he didn't give up. I think waiting for the wind is all part of sailing."

"I bet Christopher Columbus wished he had his iPod to play." Juliana grinned.

"I'm sure he did," Dana laughed.

"Hey, I wonder if everyone on Christopher Columbus's ship all blew at sail at once if it would move."

"I don't know. But I doubt it."

"I'm going to ask Jamie. She'd know. She knows all that scientific stuff."

"Probably so." Dana had to agree. Jamie *did* have a great deal of experience and knowledge about a broad range of subjects. She hadn't yet found a topic about which Dr. Hughes didn't have a well of factual information.

"I bet Jamie went to school forever. She's smarter than anyone. Except dad, of course," Juliana added proudly. "Dad is the smartest person in Olympia. Then Jamie's second."

"Smarter than Mrs. Grover, your sixth-grade teacher? I thought she was the smartest person you ever met."

"Dad's smarter. So is Jamie. Mrs. Grover is smart but she doesn't know about sailing and law stuff. And don't tell anyone, Aunt Dana, but Mrs. Grover is biased."

"Biased?" Dana didn't think that word had entered Juliana's young vocabulary yet. "Biased about what?"

"About a lot of stuff. I heard dad talking to her on the phone."

"Oh, really?" Dana held her breath, afraid Juliana was about to confess her first brush with homophobia.

"When he hung up he said a bad word and called her a Republican," she said disparagingly.

Dana burst out laughing.

"That's okay, Juliana. We have to be tolerant," she said through a snicker, relieved it wasn't something terrible.

"What's a Republican, Aunt Dana?"

How in the world was Dana going to explain Republicans to a twelve-year-old?

"It's a political affiliation. It has to do with your beliefs in how the government should be run."

"Dad said we're Protestant. It's on my passport."

"No, that's religious affiliation."

"Don't Republicans believe in God?"

"Sure they do. Most of them, anyway. Political and religious affiliation aren't the same. At least, they aren't supposed to be," Dana muttered under her breath. She wondered how she got into a conversation about politics with a twelve-year-old. Just then a gust of wind filled the sail and hurled them toward the middle of the harbor. Juliana pulled the sheet down snug and held onto the side as they picked up speed.

"LOOK!" Juliana squealed and pointed. "There she is. There's Jamie."

"Where?" Dana bobbed back and forth to see around the outstretched sail.

"Over there on the other side."

Jamie's research boat sat anchored off the point.

As they moved closer they could see someone sitting on the side of the boat.

"Jamie," Juliana called.

"I don't think that's Jamie."

"That's her boat."

The woman on the boat looked up from her magazine. It wasn't Jamie and it wasn't the blonde with her on Monday, either.

"Where's Jamie?" Juliana asked unabashedly.

"Dr. Hughes?" the woman said.

"Yes," Dana said, looking over the side for signs of air bubbles. She assumed if Jamie wasn't on the boat, she was diving for samples.

"She had to go in to have her tanks filled. Something about the valve. She should be back soon. Are you Dana and Julie?"

"Juliana," Dana said. "Yes."

"She said to tell you she'd be back. I think she wanted to ask you something."

"What?" Dana said.

"She didn't say." The woman shrugged. "Oh, she did say for you to try a tight sail on a port tack this afternoon. Something about light air."

"Do you sail?" Juliana asked.

"No. I'm just her lab assistant. I don't do any of this stuff," she said, pointing to the scuba equipment hanging on racks around the deck.

Dana guessed she was barely twenty and a college student. Judging from the fashion magazine she was reading and her glittered fingernail polish, she didn't have much interest in marine biology. She did look good in her hip hugging jeans and skin-tight top though. Dana waited for a few minutes, checking her watch and scanning the harbor for Jamie's dinghy. Finally, she gave up.

"Juliana, I think we need to spend more time sailing, not sitting. What do you say?"

Juliana gave a last look toward the marina where Jamie would have gone.

"Okay. I guess so," she said reluctantly.

"Will you tell her we were here?" Dana said to the assistant who was applying a layer of sunblock to her face.

"Sure."

They steered back into the middle of the harbor, both of them occasionally looking back for signs of Jamie. But the instructor's whistle blew without a glimpse of her or her dinghy.

"Could we wait a little while longer?" Juliana said, squinting out toward the point.

"We better not. Everyone else is heading in. Maybe she'll be out tomorrow," she said, heading for the Yacht Club. She could see disappointment on Juliana's face. She had to admit she was just as disappointed. Dana gave a last look toward the point then headed for the dock.

Chapter 8

Jamie stood at the laboratory table reading a report while Lindsay, one of her lab techs, waited expectantly for her to finish.

"You're assuming Trichodesmium?" Jamie said, flipping the page and reading more.

"I think so, Dr. Hughes."

"Blue-green algae instead of green. Not Chlorella?" she said, rereading the first page.

"It could be, I guess." Lindsay shrugged, something that brought a smirk to Jamie's face.

"Let's try again. This time remember you're looking for starch as well as carotenoids, Lindsay." Jamie handed her the papers and headed for her office. "Rerun your sample and see what you get. You may be right, but let's make sure."

"By the way, Dr. Hughes. You wanted to know when it was

one o'clock."

"Is it one already?" Jamie looked at her wrist but she wasn't wearing her watch.

"Actually, it's almost three. I reminded you it was one a couple hours ago. Were you supposed to do something?"

"Three?" Jamie scowled as she checked the time on her cell phone.

"Was it important, Dr. Hughes?"

"Yes, and I'm late. Lock up when you're finished, Lindsay. I'll see you Monday morning. We'll run the proteins through the electrophoresis and see what we get." She rushed into her office, grabbed her keys and headed for the parking lot. It was Friday, Dana and Juliana's last day of sailing classes. She wanted to be there to congratulate them on their success. She drove up highway five and into downtown Olympia but was stuck in traffic behind a slow procession of logging trucks.

"Come on," she said, impatiently drumming her fingers on the steering wheel as she waited through three light changes. She zipped into a parking place then trotted toward the Yacht Club dock. She got there just as Dana and Juliana were inching their way up to the platform.

"Good afternoon, ladies," she said, striding up to them.

"Hello," Dana said, grabbing the dock cleat.

"Toss me your line."

Dana tossed the bow line up to her and waited while Jamie tied them to the dock.

"Hi, Jamie," Juliana said, grinning broadly. "We passed."

"Good for you," Jamie said, offering her a hand and pulling her ashore. She then extended a hand to Dana, helping her onto the dock. "So sailing classes were a success?"

"I think so," Dana said, removing her life vest and tossing it on the pile. "We didn't crash and only capsized that once."

"Dad said maybe I can take junior sailing classes next summer."

"And will you be taking junior sailing classes next summer, Dana?" Jamie said.

"No. I don't think so. These little boats are better suited for younger sailors." She smoothed her flyaway strands of hair.

"Lots of adults race the Lasers. They have quite a following."

"They'll have to do it without me." Dana unzipped her wet suit a few inches.

"Aunt Dana said her butt was sore," Juliana said, beaming brightly. "But not mine. Maybe I'll be a Laser racer."

"If you do, I'll come watch," Jamie offered.

"I'll be the one on the shore, covering my eyes." Dana gave Juliana's ponytail a tug. "You scare me sometimes, missy."

"Fast is fun," Juliana said gleefully.

"Fast is fun, Juliana," Jamie agreed. "But swift is safe."

"Huh?" Juliana wrinkled her nose.

"Fast suggests reckless uncontrollable speed. Swift means successfully using the wind and the conditions to your best advantage. You can be a swift sailor and win more races."

"She means you shouldn't take chances that might hurt yourself or someone else," Dana explained.

"Why didn't she just say that?"

"I thought I did," Jamie said, frowning in thought.

"Dr. Hughes was giving you an analytical explanation, sweetheart."

"Do you have a Laser, Jamie?" Juliana asked hopefully.

"No. I agree with your Aunt Dana. Lasers are better left to younger sailors."

"How come you are always talking about sailing if you don't have a sailboat?" There was a childish skepticism to Juliana's question.

"She told you, honey. She took lessons when she was younger." Dana was obviously embarrassed over the accusatory tone to her niece's curiosity. "Don't be rude," she whispered in Juliana's ear.

"That's okay. She's right. I shouldn't offer advice without current hands-on experience. And as luck would have it, I can do just that."

"You have a boat?" Dana asked.

"A small one, yes."

"I saw your boat. It's not a sailboat," Juliana said. "It's a motorboat."

"Most sailboats have some kind of motor to maneuver in and out of the harbor. Some are inboard. Some are outboard." Jamie said, pointing toward a sailboat returning after a day of sailing.

"But they have sails. Your boat doesn't have sails." Juliana watched as the skipper eased the boat into the slip.

Jamie took a quarter from her pocket and handed it to Juliana.

"I'll bet you this quarter my boat has sails."

Juliana looked down at the quarter in her hand.

"I win then. I get to keep the quarter. I saw your boat. It doesn't even have a mast. How can it have sails without a mast?"

"I think she has you on this one, Jamie," Dana said with a chuckle.

"I don't think so. What you saw was the research boat I use. That is provided by a grant to the science department. My boat is moored at Boston Harbor." She pointed past the mouth of the harbor.

"You have a sailboat?" Dana asked just as Juliana was about to ask it first.

"Yes. I haven't been out on her yet this summer, but she's still there. They keep cashing my checks for the slip rental."

"I don't see it," Juliana said, squinting at the horizon.

"What? You don't believe me?" Jamie chuckled.

"Juliana is a doubting Thomas of the first order," Dana said, winking at her niece playfully.

"Do you want to see it?"

"Yes," Juliana said instantly. "I won't believe you until I see it."

"Okay. Tomorrow."

"Oh, boy! Can I go on it? Will you take me sailing?"

"Juliana, she meant she'd show it to you. Not take you out on it," Dana said.

"I don't see why not," Jamie said.

"Jamie, you don't have to do that. You know how kids are."

"It's okay. I don't mind. I should take her out once in a while to get my money's worth out of the slip rental."

"But that's asking an awful lot."

"She said she didn't mind, Aunt Dana."

"You ask your father if it's all right first." Jamie wagged a finger at Juliana's growing enthusiasm. "He has to approve."

"Oh, he'll say yes. I'm sure he will. I know he'll let me go. Won't he, Aunt Dana?"

"I have no idea. We'll have to see if he thinks you should go out on a big sailboat."

"You're coming too, Dana," Jamie said in her direction.

"Me?"

"Absolutely. I need two mates to help man the missen."

"Should I know what that means?"

"Help with the rigging."

"I *know* I don't know anything about that. We just scooted around the harbor in a tiny boat like a water bug. We didn't learn anything about missen rigging."

"You'll do fine. Sailing is easy once you get the hang of it."

Just then a woman in the returning sailboat stumbled and nearly fell over the side of the boat. She grabbed the railing to keep from falling into the water. One of her shoes splashed and immediately sank out of sight. Dana gulped.

"I see that."

"If you can handle one of those little boats, this should be a piece of cake. And there's much less chance we'll have to lay the boat over." Jamie smiled at Juliana. "Unless you really want to."

"NO!" Dana said, her eyes huge. "No capsizing the boat. Once is enough."

"Agreed." Jamie smoothed the top of Juliana's hair. "We'll have to keep her upright, kiddo."

"Will you teach me how to raise a big sail?" Juliana said eagerly.

"Absolutely. You'll be my first mate."

"And you can be Aunt Dana's date."

96

"Juliana," Dana laughed, trying to cover her embarrassment.

"Well, she could," Juliana argued. "You aren't living with Shannon anymore."

"I know but—"

"Are you a lesbian, Jamie?" Juliana asked as if it was a standard question.

"Juliana Robbins!" Dana gasped. "You don't ask people that."

"Why not?"

"Yeah, why not?" Jamie teased, laughing wildly.

"Because you just don't."

"As a matter of fact, Juliana, yes, I am," Jamie said. "But skippers don't date their crew members. It's a rule of the sea."

"Oh," Juliana replied dejectedly.

"I'm sorry, Jamie," Dana said apologetically.

"Don't worry about it. How are you going to know these things if you don't ask? How does nine o'clock tomorrow morning sound? Boston Harbor Marina." Jamie took out a business card and handed it to Dana. "Call me if you need to change the time."

"Thank you for inviting us sailing, Jamie," Juliana said, taking Jamie's hand as they walked along.

"You're welcome, kiddo."

"Yes, thank you for the invitation," Dana agreed.

"I'm parked over there." Jamie pointed. "I guess I'll see you in the morning."

She waited at the curb while Dana keyed in the security code and opened the gate. Dana waved and followed Juliana down the gangplank. Jamie returned the wave then headed to her car.

Chapter 9

It didn't take much convincing for Steve to agree to the outing. Once Dana explained Jamie was a marine biologist at the university who spent the summer scuba diving on a research grant, he could find no reason not to allow it. Dana wondered if it was Jamie's PhD that impressed him most or that she was gay.

"Have fun you two but don't be a pain in the neck, Juliana. Dana is in charge. If she says no, it's no. No whining," he said when Dana came to pick her up.

Dana packed hats, sunblock, snacks and a few bottles of water. She slipped a small sketch pad in the tote bag just in case anything sparked an idea for Ringlet. She often carried one with her, never knowing what might inspire a single cartoon or even a series of panels. Jamie was already on the boat cleaning and getting things ready when Dana pulled into the parking lot across the street from Boston Harbor Marina.

"Hello," Jamie called, waving them down to the dock. She was standing on the deck, unsnapping the canvas cover over the mainsail.

"Wow. Is this your boat?" Juliana ran down the finger pier to where Jamie's boat was moored.

"Do I get my quarter back?" she said, helping her onboard.

"No," she giggled.

"What did you buy with it?"

"Gumball. A red one." Juliana opened her mouth to reveal a glob of gum.

"She's not into saving yet," Dana said, trying to figure how to get the tote bag and herself onto the boat.

"Give me your bag before you step over. It's kind of awkward." Jamie took the bag then offered Dana a hand as she climbed over the chrome railing.

Jamie's boat was a sleek vessel for its size. Thirty feet long, bright red with white mast and trim. A row of five small portholes lined each side of the cabin. The mahogany hatch was pushed open, revealing a compartment below deck. It contained a small galley, a bench long enough for a bed and a booth for dining. It also had two narrow doors in the forward part of the cabin Dana assumed were closets.

"Juliana was right," Dana said, peeking through the hatch. "This is definitely a wow. I didn't expect you to have a *sailboat* sailboat."

"What did you expect?"

"I don't know. Something with scientific instruments and a big bookshelf full of textbooks, I guess. This is nice."

"I do have a spare tank and regulator in the forepeak and a portable spectrometer in the storage compartment. Do you want me to get them out?"

"No, that's all right."

"What's that mean?" Juliana asked, leaning over the railing and studying the name on the side of the hull.

"Can you read it?" Jamie continued to get the boat ready to sail.

"Carpet Ventum," she said awkwardly.

"*Carpe Ventum.*"

"What's Carpe Ventum mean?" Juliana asked.

Jamie raised her eyebrows at Dana as if asking if she knew.

"Seize the wind?" Dana offered.

"Very good."

"My high school Latin teacher would be so pleased." She chuckled.

"Latin, the language of science," Jamie said proudly. "With a little Greek thrown in for flavor."

"Don't be too impressed. My vocabulary is pretty minimal. About the only other thing I remember is *veni, vidi, vici.* I came, I saw, I conquered."

"Julius Caesar. Forty-seven B.C."

"No one told me Latin was a dead language when I signed up for it as my foreign language credit."

"Didn't you use Latin in biology class?"

"Should I remember that?"

"Scientific names all come from Latin."

"Is bug a Latin word?" Juliana asked with a giggle.

"No. But *Lumbricus terrestis* is. That's an earthworm."

"What's a fish called," Juliana said, as if testing her.

"There are hundreds of kinds of fish. *Carcassius auratus* is a goldfish."

"How about a dog, like Ringlet?"

"Are we going to spend the day talking Latin or are we going sailing?" Jamie asked, obviously amused with Juliana's curiosity.

"Sailing!" she cheered.

"Good. Put your stuff down below and help me cast off."

"Okay." Juliana put the tote bag in the cabin then scrambled back up on deck.

"By the way, Ringlet is a *Canis lupus familiaris,*" Jamie said, untying the forward line. "Can you get the stern line? Just toss it on the dock. That one stays here."

"How about me? What can I do to help?" Dana said.

"I need you to hold the tiller."

"Me?"

100

"Yes, you. You took sailing classes didn't you?"

"Yes, but this is three times as big. I could steer right into something."

"No, you won't. Just hold it in the middle."

Dana held the tiller as she was instructed, watching the sides of the boat as they bobbed back and forth in the slip. Jamie turned the key and started the engine. It belched a bit of blue smoke then chugged into service, slowly inching them away from the dock. Jamie scurried around the deck, coiling rope and stowing the fenders that cushioned the sides of the boat.

"Um, Jamie?" Dana said, nervously gripping the wooden tiller as they motored past the other boats. "Do you want to take this?"

"You're doing fine. Steer for the green buoy. Keep it off your starboard bow," she said without looking up. "Put this on, Juliana." Jamie handed her a life vest.

"Aw, do I have to? This boat is bigger than the Laser."

"Yes, ma'am. You do," she said emphatically even before Dana could say it.

Juliana put it on then sat cross-legged on the top of the cabin, watching as they eased out of the marina.

"Here's one for you," Jamie said, bringing Dana a vest. "You're welcome to wear it but you don't have to," she added quietly. "She has to. It's for her safety and it's the law. Adults don't have to wear them, just have them accessible."

"Are you wearing one?" Dana asked.

Jamie pointed to the life vest hanging on a hook by the hatch door. Dana hung hers on top of it.

"Which way are we going?" Juliana asked.

"Up Case Inlet," Jamie replied, snaking her hand to the right then back to the left. "We can't go up the west side of Hartstene Island and around. There isn't enough clearance under the bridge for sailboats."

"I bet you've sailed every inch of Puget Sound," Dana said, adjusting their course as they cleared the last row of boats.

"Some of it."

As soon as they were out of the harbor Jamie turned off the engine and flipped the switch to raise the sail. The electric motor raised the red and white striped sail into place and it immediately filled with air, jerking the boat forward, nearly pulling the tiller out of Dana's hand.

"Watch the boom, Juliana." Jamie tightened the rigging as they began to move toward open water. Juliana stretched out on her stomach with her hands under her chin to watch as they skimmed along. "That's it. Keep on this heading," Jamie said as she fine-tuned the set of the sail. She noticed the whimsical grin on Juliana's face and nodded to Dana to look. "Having fun yet?" she said, straightening the strap on Juliana's life vest.

"Yeah!"

"Good. Want to steer?"

"YEAH!" She scrambled off the cabin and rushed to Dana's side.

"Show her the heading on the compass. It's there by the hatch."

"Are you sure about this, Jamie?" Dana said nervously.

"Sure, I'm sure."

"I can do it, Aunt Dana. I steered the Laser."

"Okay, but." Dana wasn't sure what to warn her about. "Hold it steady. See the compass. Keep the little line on the three." Dana slowly relinquished control to Juliana's eager little hands but she stood next to her, ready to retake the tiller at a moment's notice.

"Can you come help me untangle the jib sheet?" Jamie didn't seem at all concerned that a twelve-year-old was skippering her thirty-foot sailboat.

"Yes, but..."

"She's doing fine. You sound like a mother hen."

Juliana stood proudly, her fingers wrapped firmly around the tiller.

"I'll be right back, Juliana. If you need me, you just call, okay?"

"Okay," she replied nonchalantly.

"She has no fear," Dana said as she made her way along the

railing to where Jamie was working on the forward rigging.

"Someday she may be racing a Laser. It's good to see that kind of courage in a kid."

"She gets it from her dad." Every few seconds Dana looked back to check on Juliana.

"Ouch," Jamie muttered, catching her finger in the pulley and wincing.

"Careful. Are you okay?"

"I'm fine." She shook it then went back to work. "It wouldn't be a day at sea if I didn't pinch or cut something. Would you like to do the honors?" she said, finally freeing the last tangle.

"What?"

"Pull this rope, hand over hand, until the jib is set. You'll feel a tug when it fills so be prepared to hold on."

"Will she be okay?" Dana nodded back toward Juliana, still happily steering their course.

"I'll watch her. Just pull nice and steady. I need to adjust the boom."

Dana unfurled the jib. Just as Jamie had predicted, once the wind filled the sail, the line snapped in her hand, threatening to fly away with her. She hung on and finished unrolling it. She tied it off as Jamie had explained and went back to where Juliana was standing. The boat had picked up speed and began porpoising through the water, slapping spray onto the deck. Jamie adjusted a rope here and a pulley there as if she was perfecting the boat's performance. Dana was impressed with her expertise as a sailor. Her image of a middle-aged biology professor did not include such agility. She somehow expected Jamie to push her glasses against her nose and squint at an instruction manual on how to hoist a sail—in Latin, of course. Instead, Dr. Jamie Hughes scampered about the deck, balancing precariously as she tended the complex web of ropes that kept them on a true and swift course across Puget Sound.

"Juliana, do you see the lighted buoy off your starboard quarter?"

"That's to the right, isn't it?" she said after a moment of

thought.

"Yes."

Juliana stared out the right side of the boat as if searching for anything lighted.

"That?" she finally said, noticing a blinking light off the point of land in the distance.

"That's the one. That's the tip of Hartstene Island. I want you to ease the rudder until you're headed right for it. After you've got the bow pointed toward the light, check the compass heading."

"Okay." With two hands on the tiller, she gradually pushed it over until the bow lined up with the blinking target. "Like that?"

Jamie ducked under the sail to take a look.

"That's it. What's your heading?"

"The compass says forty-three."

"Then that's the heading from Boston Harbor to the tip of Hartstene Island. Forty-three degrees. If the buoy light went out or if fog rolled in you'd know which way to go. And if you add one hundred eighty to forty-three that is what it will read when we come back."

Juliana looked pensive for a minute.

"It'll be two hundred twenty-three," she said brightly.

Jamie nodded and gave her a thumb's up.

They settled into a comfortable pace, the wind pushing them steadily across the sound. Hartstene Island was thickly forested with a narrow band of rocky shore separating the dense woods from low tide. Two dozen sailboats dotted the horizon, skating across the water in one direction then the other as if they had no particular destination in mind.

"What would you like to drink, Juliana?" Jamie said, descending into the cabin. "Coke, lemonade, iced tea?"

"Do you have root beer?" she timidly asked.

"Let's see." She squatted in front of the small refrigerator. "Coke, raspberry tea, 7Up, ah ha," she said, dragging out a brown bottle. "Draft root beer." She popped the top and handed it up to her, but Juliana still had both hands on the tiller.

"Um, I can't hold it."

"You can steer with one hand."

"I better not," she said, looking over at Dana.

"You want me to steer while you drink your pop?" Dana stretched out a hand to hold the soda.

"Yes," she said and let go of the tiller to take the root beer. The boat lurched to the east, the sails fluttering in the wind.

"Juliana!" Dana gasped and grabbed the tiller as it swayed to the side.

"Oops. Sorry."

Jamie laughed and shook her head.

"Forty-three degrees, Dana," she said, returning to the galley.

"Aye-aye, skipper." Dana sat down on the seat and steered easily.

"What would you like? Root beer? I think there's one more? Lemonade?"

"Lemonade sounds good."

It took a few minutes before Jamie returned on deck, carrying two tall glasses with a sprig of mint floating on the top.

"Lemonade," she said, handing one to Dana before closing the hatch door and sitting on top of it.

"Yum, this is wonderful," Dana said after taking a sip. "What brand is this?"

"Dr. Hughes's all-natural, all-organic fresh-squeezed lemonade." Jamie took a long drink.

"You made it? You squeezed the lemons fresh? I just open the bottle and pour it over ice."

"That isn't lemonade. That's a mixture of citric acid, artificial sweeteners and preservatives."

"It tastes like lemonade. Although it isn't nearly as good as this." Dana took another drink. "Ruth Ann was right. She said you were one of those people who knows what's in everything."

"Oh, she did?"

"Yes. What was it she said? Jamie knows why deodorant keeps

you from having BO and why milk curdles one day after the expiration date. She said it in a kind way though," Dana added.

"Ruth Ann calls me up to ask if she should buy grapes from Mexico and why. I think I'm on her speed dial as a consumer reference. Last week she called from the supermarket to ask if the red lines in the tuna steaks were contamination."

"Are they?"

"No." Jamie laughed.

"Then you're a good person to know. A wealth of information at the touch of a button."

"I guess."

"Jamie, look!" Juliana called from her perch on top of the cabin. "Is that a seal?"

"Yes, a harbor seal. Scientific name, *Phoca vitulina*. He's probably looking for lunch."

"What does he eat?" Juliana asked.

"Fish, specifically salmon."

"Me too," Dana said.

"I bet you don't swallow them whole though."

"He can swallow a whole fish?" Juliana made a ghastly face.

"Sure. Slides right down."

"Yuck."

"My thoughts, exactly," Dana added.

"We eat oysters whole. Oysters on the half shell slide right down," Jamie said, poking the mint down in her glass.

"Oh, no, we don't," Dana said, swallowing as if she was seasick.

"What? You don't like oysters?"

"No. They're slimy. Eeeewww." Dana shuddered.

"I take you for a shrimp person. Shrimp cocktail, deep fried shrimp."

"Yes. How'd you know?"

"Just a guess."

Dana studied her, wondering how Jamie knew that she loved shrimp. A trip to Seattle's Pike Place Market wasn't complete without a shrimp cocktail from her favorite fish vendor. She knew about everyday life without sounding pompous about it. Dr. Jamie Hughes was a curiously knowledgeable woman, and Dana realized she was deeply respectful of her insights.

"How far are we going?" Dana said, checking her course and adjusting for drift. "Are we going to turn around at the buoy?"

"I thought we'd head up Case Inlet on the other side of Hartstene Island. The wind should make it a pleasant trip. Just fresh enough to keep the sails full."

"I've heard that expression around the dock. Is 'fresh' a term for wind speed?"

"Yes. About ten to fifteen knots. It's a great day for sailing. Any stronger and we'd be a slave to the boat."

"You mean continually adjusting the sails?"

"Yep. She'll run with the best of them but it's not as relaxing."

"Do you race?" Dana asked.

"Not since I was younger. I don't have the time or the energy for that."

Juliana played around on the deck like a monkey in a tree. First on one side then the other, watching Jamie trim the sails for a smoother ride. Dana steered for the tip of Hartstene Island and the mouth of Case Inlet. She was surprised how easy it was to sail a thirty-foot boat. Compared to the small Laser, she expected to have to fight the tiller for control.

Jamie was a cordial hostess, answering every one of Juliana's questions, no matter how petty and chatting happily with Dana about boats, sailing classes and Ringlet's latest adventures. She was gracious enough not to mention Shannon in front of Juliana.

"How many years have you been doing syndicated cartoons?"

"Six. Ringlet has been a three-year-old Scottie for six years."

"Rather like Garfield the cat. He never seems to age."

"I thought you didn't look at the comics," Dana said.

"I don't. But every year my sister sends me a Garfield coffee mug on my birthday. I have a box full. She seems to think he's funny. Do you want one?"

"No, thank you. I get mugs with Scotties on them from my publisher all the time."

"You can only use so many coffee mugs," Jamie said.

"Dad said you can never have too many coffee mugs," Juliana said, nonchalantly eavesdropping on their conversation. She had finished her root beer and was meticulously peeling the label and depositing it inside the bottle. "Gary said coffee is the instrument of the devil." She looked back at Dana and frowned. "Then he said something else but he whispered it in Dad's ear. It made him blush."

"Who is Gary?" Jamie asked.

"My dad's boyfriend. He's nice." Juliana didn't seem at all shy about confessing her father was gay.

"Gary Finch," Dana said. "Aka, Gary and the Grinders. It's a jazz band."

"Gary plays a mandolin and a twelve-string guitar," Juliana said proudly. "He can play the guitar with his feet."

"I bet," Jamie said. "So your brother is a lawyer and his partner is a musician."

"Boyfriend," Dana clarified. "They're still just dating. Gary hasn't moved in yet."

"Dad says he isn't ready for Gary to move in. He has too many suitcases."

"Too many suitcases?" Jamie asked.

"Yep." Juliana said it as if she knew what she was talking about.

"I believe what Steve meant was Gary has some baggage," Dana said.

"Oh, those kind of suitcases." Jamie winked at Dana as if to signify she understood.

"Look, Jamie. Here comes a big tugboat." Juliana crawled to the front of the cabin to watch.

"He's pulling a barge of some kind," Dana said, easing the tiller to offer clear passage to the cumbersome boat.

"Probably an empty sawdust barge. Looks like he is on his way to the sawmill at Shelton." Jamie adjusted the sail to accommodate the new heading. "Give him plenty of room, Dana. He'll make a wide turn."

"Should we stop?"

"No. Normally we'd have the right-of-way, sailboats over powerboats, but he'd have trouble getting out of our way. We'll give him a clear channel. They watched as the noisy tugboat chugged past, pulling an empty wooden barge. Juliana waved, eliciting several blasts on the tug's horn.

"Can we blow the horn?"

"Go ahead, Dana. Give it a blast."

"Where is it?" she said, scanning the gauges.

"Red button to the left of the ignition switch."

Dana gave a toot. The tugboat captain waved. As they rounded the end of the island and came more northerly, the wind crossed the bow and fluttered through the jib.

"The wind has swung around. That's good news, team." Jamie sprang into action. "Come on, Juliana. Help me raise Old Betsy."

"What's Old Betsy?" Juliana followed her to the small forward hatch.

"Old Betsy is the most gorgeous sail you've ever seen. She's older than the boat and she weighs a ton but she's a proud lady." Jamie pulled a large canvas bag to the hatch opening. "Can you hand me that clip?" she said, signaling the end of a rope dangling against the mast. Juliana grabbed the clip and hooked it onto the grommet on the corner of the sail as Jamie held it up. Little by little they raised Old Betsy, attaching hooks to the corners of the sail as it slipped out of the canvas bag.

"That's the last one, Juliana. Let's hoist her into place."

As Jamie pulled the ropes through the winch and cranked the huge sail aloft, the yellow and white spinnaker filled with air and threatened to take flight from the bow of the ship. Dana and Juliana both watched in amazement as Old Betsy proudly billowed into service. It billowed beyond the tip of the bow like a huge hot air balloon turned on its side.

"She's an old, well-patched spinnaker, but she's the biggest spinnaker this boat can raise." Jamie adjusted the mainsail and boom and Old Betsy doubled their speed. The boat knifed through the water, slapping at the waves and sending spray high in the air. Juliana giggled and squealed as she held onto the railing. The wind around the edges of the sail fluttered through their clothes and hair like a ride in a convertible.

"Wow!" Dana gasped, holding onto the tiller with both hands.

"Absolutely, wow." Jamie made a few minor adjustments to the rigging as if it was good but not yet perfect. All three of them grinned like children on Christmas morning as they raced along. For Jamie, it seemed to be a sense of pride and achievement, solving the mystery of the wind. For Juliana, just plain fun. For Dana, a thrill and a sense of accomplishment at skippering a thirty-foot sailboat on Puget Sound.

"How are you doing, Dana?" Jamie asked, crawling under the boom.

"Great." Dana knew she had a stupid grin plastered across her face, but she didn't care. "I didn't know a sailboat could go so fast."

"Juliana, come sit back here," Jamie called over the rushing wind. She helped her down into the steering cockpit. "Let's see what we can do."

Jamie took the tiller, propped one foot up on the bench, and peered under the edge of the sail. From her position she could trim the sails and steer the boat. She pulled the rope to tighten the boom. "Sit on that side with Juliana," she said to Dana, who obeyed. The boat heeled to port, slicing through the water, and gaining even more speed. The sails and rigging groaned and creaked under the pressure but kept the pace. It was as if Jamie was testing her skills and the boat's capacity to perform. She never seemed completely satisfied enough to give in and enjoy the ride. The collar of her shirt flapped against her neck as if urging her on to an even better performance, stretching her abilities to the limit. Dana could see it on Jamie's face. The boat was challenging her and she wasn't giving in. Jamie set her jaw and wrinkled her brow in concentration, almost oblivious to everything else around her.

"Faster, Jamie. Faster," Juliana said gleefully.

She obliged, cranking the winch a half-turn and stretching the spinnaker seemingly to the limit. Dana's stomach tumbled and fluttered like a luffing sail as the boat responded with an extra surge. The more speed Jamie extracted from the boat, the tighter Dana held Juliana's hand. But Juliana didn't seem afraid. She leaned and bobbed with the rolling action of the hull over the waves, giggling with each jolt. Just as Dana was sure the boat couldn't possibly go any faster, Jamie turned the tiller, heading dead downwind. The boat skipped over the waves and nearly took flight as it raced across the inlet. Dana gasped, unable to catch her breath. She closed her eyes as the wind struck her square in the face. She tried to speak but could only manage a gurgle. Juliana began to laugh and couldn't stop, gulping for breath. Jamie held the course toward the eastern shore, slowly pulling a satisfied smile.

"Jamie," Dana finally managed to say. "JAMIE!"

Jamie heaved a sigh as if pleased then eased the tiller over, relaxing the strain on the sails.

"Aw!" Juliana complained as the boat slowed and turned north.

"Thank you," Dana said, ashamed of herself for being such a sissy.

"How was that?" Jamie asked the grinning Juliana.

"Yeah. That was great." She had the hicups from laughing.

"Definitely fast," Dana said, trying to catch her breath.

"Old Betsy can still haul tush," Jamie said, releasing the tension on the winch. They once again settled into a comfortable speed up the eastern coast of Hartstene Island. "In sail life, Old Betsy would be over a hundred years old."

"I'm impressed," Dana said, trying not to cheer as they slowed down.

"Juliana, we're looking for a dock with a blue sailboat. It'll be on the port side. There will be a staircase up the hill next to the dock."

"Are we stopping?" Dana said.

"Yes. To see an old friend. I thought we'd stop for a few minutes. Maybe I can talk her into fixing lunch."

"No, no, Jamie. Don't bother anyone. I brought snacks and bottled water."

"There it is, Jamie." Juliana pointed.

Jamie motioned for Dana to take the tiller while she lowered the spinnaker. "Give a couple blasts on the ship's horn, Juliana. Let them know we're coming."

Juliana happily lay on the horn, giving several loud blasts. Jamie lowered the mainsail and allowed the boat to drift the last fifty feet. When they were within reach, she jumped onto the dock, guided the boat into place, and then tied the lines.

"Jamie, really. I don't want to show up at someone's house unannounced."

"I do."

Chapter 10

"Jamie!" a woman screamed from the top of the wooden staircase attached to the hillside. "Is that you, sweetheart?" She eagerly bounced down the steps and wrapped Jamie in a hug. She was a gorgeous woman in her fifties with a well-tanned body and a streak of silver running through her brown hair. She wore shorts, a tank top with no bra, and was barefoot in spite of the rustic conditions.

"Dusty, I'd like you to meet some friends of mine," Jamie said, waving Dana and Juliana to the side of the boat. "This is Juliana Robbins, first mate." She held Juliana by the waist and helped her onto the dock. "Ladies, meet Dusty Hooten."

"Hello, Juliana," Dusty said and gave her a hug.

"Hi."

"And this is Dana Robbins, helmsman and second mate." Jamie helped Dana ashore as well.

"Hello, Dana." Dusty smiled broadly and offered a warm handshake.

"How do you do, Dusty? I'm sorry we just popped in on you like this. I told Jamie it might not be a convenient time."

"Of course it's a convenient time. Come on up to the house. I was just about to make lunch." Dusty wrapped an arm around Juliana's shoulders and led her up the steps, chattering all the way about how good it was to see Jamie, how long it had been, and how wonderful it was to have company for lunch. *I have no idea who this woman is, but she's obviously glad to see Jamie*, Dana thought.

When they crested the hill Dana could see a modest, two-story house nestled between tall fir trees. The lower floor was half garage. The upper floor consisted of windows and glass doors that led to a deck stretching the full length of the house. Several rocking chairs, a chaise lounge, table and chairs, and a gas grill lined the deck. A white cat was walking the railing, precariously close to the edge.

"You know better than that, kitty," Dusty called up at it. "Get down before you fall again."

"She fell off the deck?" Jamie chuckled.

"Yes. Stupid cat. She landed in the rhododendron bush."

"Was she hurt?" Dana asked fearfully.

"Not a scratch. She got up, gave a hideous meow and went right back up there."

"Can I pet her?" Juliana said.

"You can have her, cupcake. Be my guest."

"No, Juliana," Dana smiled at Dusty. "She'd take home a piranha if I'd let her."

"Juliana is Dana's niece," Jamie explained.

"Wow. Really? They look so much alike. I thought this was her mother."

"Yeah. Scary, isn't it?" Dana chuckled.

"And someday I'm going to have boobs just like Aunt Dana's," Juliana said proudly.

"Juliana!" Dana blushed and wrapped her arms Juliana,

covering her mouth.

"And so you should," Dusty's eyes twinkled.

"She's twelve. Her horizons are small," Dana said, smoothing Juliana's ponytail.

"Someday you'll have great boobs, Juliana," Dusty said, winking at her. "Just don't be in a big hurry to get them. Take it from me. The best boobs don't come until you're a lot older."

"Or when you least expect them," Dana said.

"Can you believe it?" Dana said. "I'm talking about boobs on an island with a perfect stranger."

"Hey, Jamie. Did you hear that?" Dusty elbowed Jamie in the ribs. "She thinks I'm perfect."

"It's only because she doesn't know you, Dusty."

Dusty led them inside and up the stairs to a large room. The kitchen was at one end with a breathtaking view of Mt. Rainer from the kitchen window. The opposite wall held an enormous fireplace, charred black by years of use. The furniture was casual, a mixture of colors and styles that blended surprisingly well into a cozy and inviting space. Magazines, newspapers and books were scattered about suggesting well-read occupants. The art was modern and diverse, everything from wire sculpture to handmade Chinese dog statues. A wood-planked harvest table with benches on the sides marked the dining room. An oversized wooden bowl of yarn balls and pine cones was the centerpiece. The kitchen had open cupboards filled with colorful Fiestaware dishes and pewter serving pieces. The stainless steel stove matched the enormous stainless steel refrigerator. Both seemed exactly opposite to the rest of the relaxed and eclectic ambiance.

"Bo," Dusty called down the hall. "We've got company."

"Who is it?" a voice replied.

"The Easter Bunny. Who cares who it is? Turn off the computer and get out here."

"You could at least tell me who it is," a gangly teenage girl said, appearing in the hall. She was tall, taller than Dusty and nearly as tall as Jamie. The only resemblance to Dusty was her slender face.

"Hello, Bo," Jamie said, grinning broadly.

"Jamie!" Bo shouted, coming to hug her.

"Is that the best you can do, shorty?" Jamie said, holding on to her. Bo hugged her again.

"What are you doing here? Mom didn't say you were coming."

"She didn't know. We sailed over. It was a surprise. And I want you to meet Dana and her niece, Juliana."

"Hello, Bo," Dana smiled.

"Hi." Bo had a bright smile and gorgeous dark eyes.

"I'm going to make us some lunch. Why don't you show Juliana your room? I'll call you when it's ready. Juliana, the bathroom is the door at the end of the hall. You make yourself at home, cupcake."

"Come on," Bo said eagerly, as if the half dozen years between them made no difference. "Want to play with my Game Boy?"

"Yeah." Juliana followed close on her heels and disappeared behind the closed door.

"We won't see them for an hour or two," Dusty said, washing her hands then turning to the refrigerator.

"Damn, she's sure growing fast, Dusty," Jamie said, motioning Dana toward the bar stools at the end of the counter.

"I know. I can hardly find pants long enough. Thank God it's summer. She can wear shorts. She's grown four inches since Christmas."

"Is her father tall?" Dana asked.

"Her father?" Dusty smiled sweetly. "Her father is a two-timing, good-for-nothing, son-of-a-bitching asshole. But who's keeping score?" She smiled again and batted her eyelashes.

"Oh." Dana didn't mean to pry.

"It's good to see you have gotten past the hard feelings, Dusty," Jamie teased.

"Nothing to it." She gave a flip of her hair. "Now, lunch. Let's see what the fridge has in store for us."

Dana was amazed how easily Dusty turned what seemed to be an ugly past into a harmless joke.

116

"Mom," Bo said, exploding through the bedroom door with Juliana right behind. "Can we have crab? It's low tide."

"Sure." Dusty peeked around the refrigerator door. "Get Juliana a bucket, too."

"Oh, boy. I love crab." Juliana was like a puppy hot on Bo's heels as she trotted down the stairs to the garage.

"Do I need to go help?" Dana asked, knowing Juliana had never been crabbing before.

"No. Bo will show her." Dusty made it sound like nothing more complicated than picking Popsicles out of the freezer.

"Juliana, stay close to shore," Dana called as she heard the door slam.

"Don't worry, Dana. Juliana is in good hands," Jamie said, watching the two girls out the window as they made their way to the stairs that led to the beach. "She'll take care of her. Bo is a certified scuba diver and a junior division sailing champion. That's her blue twenty-four footer at the dock." Jamie nodded toward the glass bookcase full of trophies and ribbons. "Those are hers, too."

"She sails that big sailboat all by herself?"

"Yes and very well, in fact."

"She's driving me nuts, Jamie," Dusty said, grimacing dramatically. "She wants to move up in class. She wants a thirty-foot Catalina or a Hunter. I told her we just got new sails and forestay. Now she wants something else. You've got to talk to her. If she goes bigger she'll have to go older. The competition won't be the same. She'll be campaigning against twenty-year-olds, at least."

"I think it's a good idea. She's ready. Why don't you have her try Stacy's boat? She isn't racing it right now. Keep *Madonna* in case she changes her mind but let her get a taste of a bigger boat."

"Her boat is named *Madonna*?" Dana said.

"Yes. It's the perfect name for a racing sailboat," Dusty said, rolling her eyes. "She's a material girl. There's always something to replace or fix."

"Campaigning a boat is expensive," Jamie said. "It takes money and a lot of time. You really have to be dedicated. But it pays off if you're good enough." She went to the bookcase and looked in at the trophies.

"And Bo's good enough?" Dana asked.

"Oh, yes. She's definitely good enough."

"I don't think she knows just how good she is," Dusty said.

"She'll probably be on the women's cup team as soon as she's eighteen. And the Olympics in three years."

"And you've got her babysitting a twelve-year-old and schlepping crabs?" Dana checked out the window.

"We have to keep her from getting a big head," Dusty said, putting the finishing touches on a salad. While they were talking Dusty had started two pots of water boiling, melted butter and shucked a dozen ears of corn.

"What can I do to help?" Dana offered.

"Nothing," Dusty replied, starting a third pot of water. "It won't be much. I hope you like crab and clams."

"Love them." Dana watched as she rinsed a sink full of fresh clams.

"Dusty attended the School of Culinary Arts in Paris," Jamie said. "The kitchen is her laboratory. If there is a way to cook seafood, she knows it."

"Then maybe I should go help Bo and Juliana with the crab. They may have trouble finding any."

"A quarter says they'll have at least a dozen," Jamie said, digging a quarter from her pocket.

"Don't take that bet, Dana," Dusty warned. "Jamie knows we're sitting on the best crabbing spot in Case Inlet."

"Aunt Dana!" Juliana scrambled up the stairs carrying a plastic bucket. It was so heavy she had to use two hands to carry it. She was barefoot and wet to the waist. "Look! I got six crabs all by myself. Well, Bo helped a little." She set the bucket on the kitchen floor for all to see.

"Good job, Juliana," Jamie said, giving her a pat on the back.

"Juliana, you're dripping on the floor," Dana said, grabbing a paper towel from the holder.

"Don't worry about it, Dana," Dusty said. "The floor is made for that. It's always getting dumped on. You should see the things that get dragged across this floor."

Bo followed, also using two hands to carry her bucket.

"How many?" Jamie said, looking in the two buckets.

"Fifteen," Bo said it as if ashamed.

"BO!" Dusty perched her hands on her hips disgustedly.

"There's five of us, mom," she said. "Three apiece."

"They're rock crab, Dusty," Jamie said, poking around in the buckets. "At least half of them anyway. That's okay."

"What's wrong with fifteen?" Dana asked. "Is that over the limit?"

"Yes," Dusty said.

"No, it isn't," Jamie corrected. "They increased the limit on the red rock crabs and you know it. It's twenty this summer."

"See, Mom. I told you it was twenty."

"I give up." Dusty threw her hands up in surrender.

Lunch lasted until nearly three o'clock. The five women sat on the deck, eating, telling jokes and having a good time. Bo and Juliana sat on either side of Jamie, chattering with her almost nonstop, but she didn't seem to mind. They feasted on cooked crab, steamed clams, corn on the cob, Caesar salad and fresh Marionberry compote. They left the dishes in the sink and all went for a stroll up the beach to walk off the heavy meal. Juliana collected seashells in a pail and asked Jamie what they were. Bo visited with Jamie about sails, new techniques in rigging and changes in the rules. Dusty and Dana talked about teenagers, food and Dusty's online consulting firm. They walked two miles up the rocky coast before turning back to avoid the rising tide. Jamie stopped at *Madonna* so Bo could show her the new sails and how she had rigged them. Juliana sat on the dock, tossing the shells into the water and watching them sink.

"How long have you known Jamie?" Dusty asked Dana, the two of them sitting on the bottom step of the staircase.

119

"We have some mutual friends and met at their boat party two weeks ago."

"I thought maybe you were a teacher at the university. One of those nerdy types like Jamie." Jamie and Bo had gone below deck.

"No. Not me."

"What do you do, Dana?"

"I'm a cartoonist."

"Oh, really? Anything I might recognize?"

"I draw Ringlet. A Scottie with an attitude."

"You mean that one in the magazines? The cute little black dog owned by the lesbian?"

Dana nodded.

"Wow! I love that cartoon. Last week's was hilarious. I thought I'd die when she found a goldfish in her bowl." Dusty threw her head back and laughed. "What's she going to do next week?"

"I submit several at a time but they aren't necessarily sequential. I never know what order they are being used unless I indicate there is a series."

"Is it hard to come up with something new and fresh every week? Do you ever get writer's block like an author?"

"Occasionally. But I usually have enough submitted that it isn't a problem. I try to stay several weeks ahead."

"Okay, Dana," Dusty said with a stern face. "I have to know." She grabbed Dana's arm and scowled at her. "Is she or isn't she?"

"Ringlet?"

"Yes. Is she a lesbian dog?"

"I'll never tell," Dana said with a cheeky grin.

"Oh, come on." Dusty slapped her arm playfully. "Tell me."

"Do you think she's gay?" Dana raised her eyebrows.

Dusty stared deep into Dana's eyes as if looking for the truth.

"She is," Dusty declared then frowned. "Isn't she?"

Dana smiled and shrugged.

"You little stinker."

"How about you?" Dana said, changing the subject. "How long have you known Jamie?"

"Me?" Dusty chuckled and looked over at Bo's boat. "Forever. At least it seems like forever." Dusty seemed lost in thought. As if a chill suddenly washed over her, she crossed her arms to warm herself. "Sometimes it seems like not nearly long enough." She smiled over at Dana as a tear glistened in her eyes.

Dana felt she had asked too much. She had opened a wound Dusty wasn't prepared to face. Asking any more might only be punishment. Dusty stood up and walked to the end of the dock, staring out at a passing sailboat. Dana wished she knew more. Dusty had said just enough to raise her curiosity. She had said enough to make Jamie human and vulnerable just like everyone else.

"It's getting late, Dana," Jamie said, climbing onto the dock. "We better head back. I'd rather not sail into Boston Harbor after dark."

Dusty turned around, her composure once again cheerful.

"You come see us again real soon, cupcake," she said, giving Juliana a hug and kiss on each cheek. "Have fun and keep that life preserver on," she added, tweaking her nose then helping her onto Jamie's boat.

"Thank you very much for the crabs," Juliana said politely.

"Bye, Juliana," Bo waved, still standing on the deck of her boat. "See ya."

"Bye, Bo. See ya."

"It was so nice of you to let us invade your wonderful home, Dusty. And thanks so much for the meal. It was delicious." Dana gave her a hug. Dusty held it longer than she expected. When she released it she was biting her upper lip.

"Thanks for coming," she managed.

"Come visit me sometime, shorty," Jamie said to Bo. "And soon."

"I will."

"Now get over here and give me a hug," Jamie demanded

with a grin.

Bo hopped onto the dock and shared a warm hug with Jamie.

"Good luck with your sailing, Bo," Dana said, shaking her hand.

"Thanks."

Dusty had waited until all goodbyes were said before going to Jamie. She wrapped her arms around her warmly, melting into her shoulder. Jamie closed her eyes and held her, swaying slightly. She placed a tender kiss on Dusty's neck and swallowed hard. Dusty whispered something in Jamie's ear that made her chin quiver. Dusty then kissed her and whispered something else. Whatever it was, Jamie stiffened and frowned at her, as if she didn't agree.

"You come back soon, you hear me, doctor?" Dusty scowled at her then took Jamie's face in her hands and placed a sloppy kiss on her mouth. "And that does not mean in six months." She turned to Dana. "You make her bring you back real soon."

"I will. Thank you."

"Helms alee," Dusty said, touching Jamie's cheek then stepping back.

Jamie climbed on board and turned on the motor. Bo untied the lines and tossed them onto the boat.

"Thanks again," Dana said as they slowly moved away from the dock. Dusty blew her a kiss then waved. Bo and Dusty stood arm in arm at the end of the dock, waving and watching until they had cleared the shallow water and hoisted their sails.

"She's a sweetheart," Dana said, giving one last wave. "Both of them. And what does it mean when Dusty said 'helms alee'?" Dana asked.

"Yes, they are sweethearts. And the helm is the wheel or tiller, the thing that steers the boat. The helmsman says that to announce he's about to turn the boat. The crewmembers have to watch out for the boom as it swings to the other side. It roughly means taking a new tack, going in a new direction. It's one of those expressions like bon voyage or happy landing."

She went to work trimming the sails. She repacked the spinnaker into its bag and stuffed it into the forepeak.

Dana steered south, retracing their route out of Case Inlet. Juliana watched from her perch on the top of the cabin.

"Are we using Old Betsy on the way back?" Juliana asked.

"No. We'll be tacking into the wind. Spinnakers are for running with the wind."

"That'll take us longer to get back, won't it?" Dana said, already feeling the wind battling the sails.

"A little. That's why I wanted to leave when we did. Boston Harbor is a little tricky to get into after dark."

"Will our heading be two-twenty-three?"

"Yes. But not until we get into Dana Passage."

"Dana Passage?" Dana smiled.

"Yes. Didn't you know that's what they call the section between Budd Bay and Case Inlet?"

"No, I didn't know that."

"Is it named after you, Aunt Dana?"

"No," she chuckled. "It's been around a long time before me."

"Are we in Dana Passage now?" Juliana asked, staring out over the bow.

"Not yet. We have to be past the blinking buoy," Jamie said.

Dana was dying to ask about Dusty, their past, and what she whispered. She didn't know Jamie well enough for that. It could be so private that she may never tell her.

Juliana took a turn steering but lost interest as the wind began to fade. The slow progress toward the blinking buoy was pale in comparison to the thrilling ride up the inlet with all sails full and straining. She sat down next to Dana and rested her head against Dana's side as they quietly slipped into Dana Passage.

"Are you tired, sweetheart?" Dana brushed a few stray locks behind her ear. Juliana nodded, her eyes growing heavy.

"Juliana, why don't you go below and stretch out on the bed," Jamie said, patting her on the knee. "I'll need your help later so why don't you take a little nap." She winked at her.

Juliana went below and curled up on the bench. She was asleep almost instantly.

"It's been a long day for her," Dana said.

"She's great. I love curious kids. That means their brains are working."

"Then hers is in high gear most of the time. She's been like that since she learned to talk."

"I bet she's a good student."

"Yes. All A's, so far."

"Did she get that from you?"

"From her father. Steve was valedictorian in high school. He graduated in the top ten percent from law school."

"How about her mom? What's she like?" Jamie asked.

"We have no idea. She gave Juliana up to my brother at birth."

"So she's adopted? It's amazing how much she looks like you considering she isn't related."

"No. She's my brother's child all right. She's a Robbins," Dana chuckled as if that was a moniker she couldn't avoid. "Steve is gay. The woman was artificially inseminated. She didn't want to take care of a baby, so Steve convinced her to give him full custody. He was in the delivery room when she was born. He cut the cord and everything."

"Any second dad in the picture?"

"There was for a few years."

"What happened to him? Was he jealous of Juliana?" Jamie whispered it so Juliana wouldn't hear.

Dana looked up at Jamie in amazement.

"How did you know that? But yes. He was extremely jealous of all the time Steve spent with her. Brad gave him an ultimatum. It was give him equal time or else. Steve thought about it for two seconds and took door number two." Dana smiled victoriously. "Best decision he made since he took Juliana."

"I take it you didn't approve of Brad."

"I approved of him moving out."

"Judge not lest ye be judged," Jamie said, giving her a sideways glance as if referring to the fact she moved out on Shannon.

"He was just using Steve," Dana said.

"Oh. Parasitic relationship."

"Exactly. In the five years they were together Brad worked maybe two weeks."

"In many relationships throughout the animal kingdom, not just humans, one member or the other remains in a domestic role."

"Well, that wasn't Brad. Steve did the cooking and cleaning. And he's a full-time lawyer. Brad was the eater and soiler."

"Steve sounds like a dedicated father."

"He is and Juliana is a sweetheart," Dana said, nodding back toward Juliana. "She'll grow up with no prejudice or bias. Steve wouldn't allow it."

"How about grandparents? I bet your folks spoil her rotten," Jamie said, looking through the hatch at the sleeping child.

"I'm sure they would have done that. They would have loved Juliana." Dana smiled reflectively. "My mother died when I was six. Heart attack. Dad died when I was seventeen. Lung cancer."

"Oh, Dana. I'm so sorry," Jamie said with a concerned frown. "I didn't know."

"That's okay."

"So it's just you and Steve?"

"Yes. He took on the role as parent." She laughed. "He said he would be the mother. I told him it was more like smother. We didn't get along real well those first few years after Dad passed away. We both had to mature a little. Now we're best friends, at least most of the time."

"How about you? All A's in school?" Jamie made a few adjustments to the sails but the wind had died to just a few knots and they were left to slow progress.

"Mostly but I had trouble with a few things."

"Such as?"

Dana grimaced, almost afraid to answer.

"Come on. Let's have it. What did you flunk?"

"I didn't flunk but I got a C in biology."

Jamie laughed out loud and came to sit on the hatch door.

125

"My saving grace was that I could draw pretty fair pictures for my lab notebook. Miss Reece would look over my shoulder and say no shading, Miss Robbins. Stipple," Dana said, wagging her finger.

"Dots on the paper?"

"Yes. Do you have your students do that? Make a zillion tiny dots instead of shading their pictures of amoeba and paramecium? Gosh, I can't believe I remembered those names."

"No," Jamie chuckled. "Sounds a little tedious to me."

"It was. I spent hours tapping my pencil point on the paper to show parts of frogs and flowers."

"A definite waste of time. It's learning about the organism's relationship to each other that's important. Not how you draw them."

"I wish you had taught my biology class. I might have done better." Dana's brain spun out a clear picture of herself as a student to Jamie's as the teacher. *I also might have had a bit of a crush*, she thought. She found herself blushing and was glad that Jamie quickly continued the conversation.

"When you were taking high school biology I was probably teaching undergraduates how to culture cells in a petri dish."

"We did that. We'd dip a wire loop in something nasty then smear it across this brown Jell-O. Then we'd let it grow in an incubator until it had spots on it."

"Then?" Jamie asked as if testing her.

"Then we'd lift off a spot and look at it under the microscope."

"What did you see?"

"I have no idea. Remember, I only got a C. Besides, that was sixteen years ago." Dana relinquished the helm to Jamie and went below to check on Juliana. She was fast asleep. When Dana returned to the deck, Jamie was sitting on the stern, steering with her knee.

"She's out like a light."

"Let her sleep." Jamie reached over and slid the hatch door closed. "So you're what? Thirty-three?"

"Thirty-two."

"How old is Shannon?"

"Thirty-one. And I really appreciate you not mentioning Shannon in front of Juliana, by the way."

"Of course." Jamie smiled and stared out into the distance. "Dana, I think I need to apologize."

"You already apologized for putting your hands up my rear. I forgive you."

"No. I mean last week when you came by my office. My predator prey platitude was completely out of line. I had no business saying things like that. I'm sorry. I was making assumptions I had no right to make."

"That's okay."

"No, it isn't. Sometimes my subjective brain gets me in trouble. Ask Ruth Ann. I'm a little too analytical for my own good. I embarrassed you and I'm sorry."

"Jamie, that's okay. You didn't embarrass me. I appreciate your interest and concern. In fact, I found it..."

"Instrusive?"

"No. Informative. I don't think I've ever had someone use science to explain relationships."

"But I may have been wrong."

"Time will tell," Dana said, letting her eyes scan the horizon.

"I promise to keep my opinions to myself."

"No!" Dana said loudly then remembered Juliana sleeping below. "No," she whispered. "I don't want you to do that. I want to hear what you have to say. I do."

"You're kidding, I assume." Jamie moved the tiller one way then the other, struggling to find enough wind to fill the sails.

"No, I'm not kidding. I want to hear your point of view. It may sound silly but I think you have given me a fresh outlook on things. What was it you said? Discussing things with an outside observer can bring things into focus. Well, you're my outside observer."

"Me? Why me?" Jamie seemed tickled with that idea. "Because

I'm the one who made you drop your keys into the bay?"

"No. And I thought we agreed that was an accident."

"Well, it can't be because I'm a marine biologist."

"Partly."

"You want my opinion because I have a PhD in biology?" Jamie shook her head in disbelief. "Dana, my PhD doesn't make me some kind of super hero. I just happen to know a lot of useless trivia about plants and animals."

"You know much more than that. You have the most amazing common sense."

"That's just life's experiences. If you've been around long enough you see things."

"That's another reason your opinion is important to me. You're older."

"That I am." Jamie smiled ruefully.

"I didn't mean it that way. Gosh, now it's my turn to apologize. I didn't mean you were *old*. Forty-five isn't really old."

"Thank you." Jamie chuckled.

"I meant you are seasoned. Mature." Dana realized that didn't sound any better.

"Older," Jamie said, adjusting her glasses.

"It isn't that old. I'll be forty-five in a few years."

"Did you have trouble with math class, too?"

"Okay. I'll be forty-five in thirteen years but it's not old. Just older. Than me," she quickly added to keep her foot out of her mouth. "Gosh, this is coming out all wrong. I sound like a complete idiot."

"You sound like you think the opinion of an old biologist has merit on topics outside her field of knowledge."

"Yes, I guess that's exactly what I think. Do you mind?"

"I don't mind necessarily. I just think you could find a better, more informed opinion."

"That's the problem. I can't. My brother's opinions are filtered through his legal brain, then recirculated through his parental brain. There isn't much left by the time it gets to me. Juliana is a sweetheart but I really prefer not to get my advice from a twelve-year-old. And then there's Ruth Ann and Connie." Dana raised her eyebrows. "They know Shannon. Everything I tell them will probably end with her."

"How does Juliana get along with Shannon?"

"They really didn't spend a lot of time together, just the two of them. Shannon preferred not to babysit."

"But no big rivalries?"

"No. Nothing major."

"Then Juliana is not a factor in your current situation?"

"If you are tactfully asking if I'm separated because Shannon is jealous of the time I spend with Juliana, no. When we were living in Lacey, I didn't see Juliana as much. Now that I'm on the houseboat Juliana can walk over anytime she wants."

Jamie's cell phone rang.

"It looks like we're back in range," she said, reading the caller ID. "Dr. Hughes here."

The call came from who Dana assumed was a colleague running some kind of laboratory tests. After the initial pleasantries, the conversation became so technical Dana could only recognize one in ten words.

"What pH?" Jamie said, listening intently. "Then try that. Call me if it doesn't work, Shelia. We may have to recalibrate the machine." She said good bye and hung up.

"Sounds complicated," Dana said.

"It really wasn't. Shelia is a graduate student and like most grad students, she's impatient. Some things take time. If the test needs twenty-four hours she can't expect results in eighteen."

"Of course not." Dana had no idea what she was agreeing to, but it seemed like the right thing to say.

"Certain amino acids *will* ionize above pH seven point four," Jamie said nonchalantly, guiding the boat into the mouth of Boston Harbor.

"Absolutely." Dana bit down on her lip but couldn't stop a giggle from escaping. She covered her mouth, hoping to hide her complete ignorance about whatever amino acids were.

"What?"

"Nothing." Dana cleared her throat. Then she laughed out loud. "I'm sorry, Jamie. I have *no* idea what you are talking about. I didn't understand one word of your conversation after you asked about the tests."

Jamie opened her mouth as if to explain then chuckled.

"Next time I'll try not to laugh," Dana said, touching Jamie's knee. "That was rude."

"Amino acids are nothing to laugh at," she smiled. "At least that's what I tell my students." Jamie stood up as they made their way toward the marina. She pushed the button to electrically lower the mainsail. The small jib gave enough propulsion to ease them into the slip. Jamie jumped onto the dock and leaned against the bow to keep it from bumping. Dana went below to wake Juliana for the ride home.

"Thank you, Jamie," Dana said, helping Juliana onto the dock. "We had a wonderful time."

"Yeah. Thanks, Jamie." Juliana rubbed her eyes and yawned.

"You're welcome, kiddo." Jamie patted her head. "You take care. And you too, Dana." Jamie seemed caught between offering a handshake and a hug. Dana solved the dilemma for her and gave her a half hug, one arm supporting Juliana.

"Call me if you need an old biologist's opinion," she called, watching Dana and Juliana walk up the gangplank toward the parking lot.

"I will," Dana said, waving back.

Chapter 11

"Dr. Hughes?" Hanna said, entering the lab.

"Yes?" Jamie replied, squinting through the eyepiece and adjusting the specimen under the microscope.

"There's a call for you. Should I tell her you'll call back later?"

"Is this the only slide you prepared for this sample?"

"Dr. Hughes? The call? Shall I say you're busy?"

"Yes," she said, not paying much attention. "Who is on the phone, anyway?" Jamie asked without looking up from the microscope.

"That woman on the little sailboat," Hanna said, reaching for the doorknob.

"Dana?" Jamie looked up curiously. "Hanna, wait! I'll take that call." She pulled her glasses from the top of her head and went into her office. She waited for Hanna to leave before answering the call. "Hello, Miss Robbins. How's my second mate?"

"Hello, Dr. Hughes. I'm sorry if I took you away from something important. I told Hanna not to bother you if you were busy."

"Not a problem. What's up?"

"Oh, gosh. I did! I interrupted you while you were doing some huge laboratory experiment and now you'll have to run it all over again."

Jamie chuckled.

"Actually, your call was perfectly timed. I'm going to have to rerun a few tests, so you kept me from getting eyestrain staring through the microscope. You rescued me. Now, what can I do for you?" Jamie sat down and propped her feet up on the corner of the desk.

"Jamie, I simply had to call and tell you again how much fun Juliana and I had last Saturday. That's all she talks about. And Dusty and Bo are such sweethearts. I can't believe how nice she was to us. She didn't know us from Adam and she took us in and fed us."

"She thought you were very nice too, Dana. And Dusty doesn't say that about just anybody."

"Will you *please* thank her again for me? She made us feel right at home. It takes a special person to do that on the spur of the moment."

"I will. And yes, she is special." Jamie waited for Dana to reply but she didn't. "Is there anything else?"

"No, no. I'm sorry, Jamie. I took you away from your laboratory long enough. You go back to work." Dana sounded tentative.

"Dana? How are things with Shannon? Anything new?"

Dana hesitated. Jamie suspected something else precipitated the call.

"She called, didn't she?" Jamie suggested.

"She left a message on my cell phone."

"What did the message say?"

When Dana didn't answer, Jamie suspected one of two things.

Either Dana wasn't sure how to tell her or she was too upset to talk about it.

"Dana, you don't have to tell me if you don't want to. It's private. I understand."

"No, wait. I wrote it down so I can read it to you," Dana said. "This is exactly what she said. 'Dana, this is Shannon. I hate talking to your voice mail. I've been calling you for two days. Baby, I really need to talk to you. I promise I won't say anything to make you mad or upset. Just call me. We really need to figure this thing out. I love you, Dana'." Dana gave a long sigh. "I can't go on ignoring her messages and not answering her calls. I feel like a criminal hiding from the law."

"Do you want to talk to her?"

"I don't know. I feel like I owe it to both of us to at least talk to her. But something else tells me no. I need more time to think this over."

"That probably won't be the last message from her, will it?"

"No. I'm sure of that. She has left several. She wants to take me to dinner. She offered to pick me up and take me anywhere I want to go, at her expense, of course, just so we can have a quiet conversation. But I don't know if I can do that. Not yet."

"Okay, here's what you do. Make a list of the pros and cons of why you should meet her or talk to her. Then make a list of why you shouldn't. See which list carries more weight."

"I've been doing that. I argue with myself about it all the time."

"Does Shannon just want to talk?"

"What she wants is for me to move back in with her and give up the idea I need a separation."

"Give in and see it her way, right?"

"She didn't say it like that but yes. She thinks we stand a better chance of solving our problems if we're together. And I gave Morgan a three-month lease on the houseboat for a reason. I want time."

"So Shannon wants you to give up your lease and move back in with her now, even though you decided you needed some time on your own?"

"I assume so, yes."

"What is your first instinct, Dana?"

"To throw my phone in the bay and let it sink to the bottom with my keys." She laughed uncomfortably.

"Is Shannon paying your rent on the houseboat?"

"Absolutely not," Dana said defensively. "I am paying my own rent. I told you before. I am not a charity case, Jamie. I can take care of myself. Shannon didn't even know I was moving out until I did. I knew if I told her what I had in mind she would have tried to stop me. I hinted about it one other time, telling her I wasn't happy with the way we were always bickering. A few days later she booked us on a cruise which didn't help anything." Dana sighed. "She thought that going on a trip would erase the problems."

"What do you see as your core problem?"

"To tell the truth, Jamie, if I knew that, I wouldn't have needed to move into the houseboat. And I wouldn't be afraid to talk to Shannon. I just feel like there is something between us. Something simmering below the surface that I can't put my finger on."

"Dana, can I ask a personal question?" Jamie said in a straightforward tone.

"Yes."

"Is it sexual?"

"Lesbian bed death? No."

"Is either one of you cheating?"

"No. I don't believe in doing that. And I don't think Shannon is unfaithful. At least not that I'm aware of."

"But you're not sure."

"That isn't the kind of problem we're having."

"You feel there is a problem but you don't know what it is. That makes it a little difficult to offer advice."

"It makes it a little difficult to sleep at night, too. Any suggestions? Should I call her back and agree to meet with her or should I stick to my guns? Steve told me I was, and I quote, 'being a chicken shit'. Am I being unreasonable? I trust your judgment, Jamie."

Jamie wasn't sure she wanted that responsibility. She wasn't sure how deeply Dana and Shannon were committed to each other. On the other hand, Dana had made the initial step by establishing her own separate existence, free of Shannon. As much as Jamie didn't want to admit it, she found a growing interest in Dana and didn't want to see her hurt. If Dana trusted Jamie's judgment, she would do her best to offer sound advice. However, Dana might just need someone to listen.

"Dana, listen. Don't make the decision now. Give yourself some time to weigh your options. Try to imagine all the possible consequences. Let's say you decide not to meet her."

"Are you saying I shouldn't?"

"No, just imagine you didn't. What would the repercussions be if you told Shannon no, you couldn't meet with her right now? Then imagine what they'd be if you said yes. You have to remember there are two separate and distinct types of ramifications. Short term and long term. Both represent a completely different set of alternatives. The decision you make and can live with today might not be the one you can live with further down the road."

"You certainly don't make this easy."

"If it was easy, would you have called me and asked my opinion?"

"But now you've given me a whole new set of things to think about. I called with one simple question. You've raised some issues I hadn't even considered."

"The short-term outcome versus the long-term outcome, right?"

"Yes." Dana groaned.

"Okay. I'll tell you what. You give it some thought and call me later if you need a sounding board."

"IF!? If I need a sounding board? Dr. Hughes, that is going to be an absolute necessity. I should have just moved to Alaska and lived on an ice floe with the Eskimos."

Jamie chuckled at her.

"You'll be fine, Dana. You just need to be practical about it."

"Since when is practicality a factor in relationships? If I was practical, I would have joined a nunnery right out of high school and avoided this whole business."

"Are you even Catholic?" Jamie asked, trying not to laugh.

"No."

"Then I think you are on your own to figure this out."

"No, I'm not. I have a very insightful college professor to give me advice."

"Dana, I'm sorry but I have to go. I've got to pick up my clothes at the cleaners by five," Jamie said, noticing the clock on the wall. "I'll be in town later. Give me a call on my cell phone if you need another pep talk."

"Thanks, Jamie."

Jamie hated to cut her off but she knew Dana was capable of making her own decisions. Granted, Shannon was playing on Dana's sympathy by calling against her wishes but this was one of those times when Dana needed to make a stand. And Dana didn't strike Jamie as being unable to do that. If she was, it was time she learned.

Jamie drove across town and picked up her cleaning then stopped at the grocery store. She strolled the aisles, searching for something to call dinner. She was next in line at the deli counter when her cell phone rang.

"Hello, Dana," she said with a laugh. "Any decision yet?"

"Yes. You're terrible. Why did you do that?"

"Do what? Make you think?"

"Yes. You had no business making me think."

"What have you come up with?" Jamie waved the next person in line to go ahead of her.

"I have no idea. I thought I did. I had decided to call Shannon and tell her no, I wasn't going to meet with her. I was going to insist whatever she has to say she could do over the phone."

"Okay. Sounds good."

"But what if I'm being unreasonable? Maybe the only way we can really work things out is by sitting down, face to face, and talking."

"Dana, you are making this way too difficult."

"But you told me to think through every conceivable outcome. Short term, long term and everything in between."

"I didn't mean overanalyze it. Where are you?"

"On the houseboat about to walk the plank."

"I'm hungry. Would you like to meet me for a sandwich someplace?"

"How can you eat at a time like this?"

"Even we primordial sages need sustenance."

"There's a new place downtown near the courthouse. Steve told me about it. He and Gary went there for their six-months anniversary. It's a bar slash grill slash nightclub slash cute place. At least that's his description. Great burgers, if that helps?"

"Bartolu's?" Jamie said.

"Yes and if that is okay, I'll need thirty minutes," Dana said. "I have to get dressed."

"Sure. I'll meet you there."

Jamie drove through downtown, looking for a parking spot close to the restaurant. It had just started to rain. Bartolu's was so new in town that their sign was still a vinyl banner strung between the building's upper floor windows. Two weeks ago the restaurant had been nearly empty, but business seemed to have picked up. Most of the highback booths and intimate tables were occupied.

"Good evening, miss. Table for one?" a woman said, greeting Jamie at the door. The woman was smartly dressed in a black pantsuit, sling back heels, and earrings long enough to be fishing lures.

"I'm expecting someone," Jamie replied, scanning the room for Dana.

"Would you like to be seated while you wait?"

Jamie was about to say she would wait when Dana came through the door, holding a newspaper over her head as an umbrella. She was out of breath and flushed.

"Am I terribly late?" she gasped, shaking the water from her hands.

"Nope. Right on time. You're out of breath. What did you do, run all the way here from the marina?" Jamie joked.

"I'm just a few blocks away. Why drive?" Dana patted the rain from her face.

"Table for two?" the hostess said and led the way to a booth in the rear.

Jamie noticed the woman inspecting them from head to toe. Dana seemed to have noticed as well and allowed her hand to discreetly check the buttons on her blouse.

"Can I bring you anything to drink while you look over the menu?"

"Dana?" Jamie asked, giving the menu a quick scan.

"Iced tea, extra lemon, please."

"Make that two. What is your special tonight?" she asked, pointing to the spot on the menu.

"Spaghetti marinara. That comes with a salad and bread sticks. The soup of the day is chicken gumbo. I'll give you a minute to decide."

Dana ordered soup and a Caesar salad. Jamie ordered vegetarian lasagna.

"Are you a vegetarian?" Dana asked.

"No. But Dean Hansett had their veggie lasagna at our meeting and said it was good. I thought I'd give it a try. Are you a vegetarian?"

"Yes, except for the chicken, fish and beef I eat," Dana said with a straight face. "As a woman of science, I would have thought you'd eat healthy."

"As a woman of science, I don't have time to be that careful. Besides, I like meat. Seafood, steak, barbeque. You name it. The things I like aren't all vegetarian."

"Me, too. But I do like vegetables."

"Which ones?"

"Almost all of them. Broccoli, squash, green beans, tomatoes."

Jamie looked down, smiling at the floor, trying to act nonchalant.

"What?" Dana asked, noticing her expression.

"Technically, tomatoes are a fruit. So are squash and green beans."

"No, they aren't." Dana laughed at her. Jamie didn't smile back. "You're kidding, aren't you? Green beans can't be fruit. They're *green*."

Jamie nodded.

"Okay, Dr. Hughes. Explanation, please."

"Botanically speaking, a fruit is the ripened ovary of a flowering plant, including the seeds. All fruits have seeds. *Vegetable* is a culinary term. Not a scientific one. Vegetables are generally considered all parts of herbaceous plants eaten as food by humans, whole or in part."

"What other vegetables—slash—fruit do you like?" Dana said, carefully squeezing three lemon wedges into her iced tea.

"Anything but lima beans and asparagus," Jamie said without hesitation.

"I agree. Lima beans are disgusting. They look good. Nice color. Nice surface texture, but the interior texture doesn't match the expectation."

"That sounds like an artist talking."

"It's a bean lover talking. Lima beans are the black sheep of the family."

"So…here's the question of the hour. What have you decided to do about Shannon's call? Are you going to meet her?"

Dana took a long slow sip through her straw, as if planning her answer.

"I'm going to tell her." She suddenly gasped, staring at the group of women coming through the door. She sat frozen by what she saw, then lowered her gaze, hunching slightly in her seat.

"Tell her what?" Jamie asked, noticing Dana's expression change.

"Hello, Dana," a woman said, striding up to the table. She gave Jamie a quick glance before concentrating entirely on Dana. Even with rain dampened hair, this was a beautiful woman. The

139

snug top tucked into her low-rise jeans showed off her trim abs.

"Hello." Dana swallowed and looked up.

"Well, what do you know? I didn't expect to see you here." The woman smiled broadly. Jamie watched her carefully. Behind the woman, she could see a small group of other women at the bar who were watching their table. *Probably this woman's friends?* wondered Jamie.

"Caesar salad and chicken gumbo," the waitress said, bringing their order to the table. "And vegetarian lasagna. Will there be anything else?" she asked, awkwardly reaching around the woman standing at the end of the table.

"Could I have a little parmesan cheese, please?" Jamie said. "And she'd like more tea and lemon. Thank you."

"You should have gotten the Cobb salad if you were salad-hungry, Dana. It's great. Lots of veggies and the bacon is nice and crisp. Just the way you like it," the woman said. She paid little attention to Jamie. Her conversation was directed at Dana and only Dana. "That blouse looks good on you." She looked Dana up and down. "And I see you wore those pants anyway." The woman frowned.

Dana clenched her jaw and averted her eyes. She was uncomfortable and Jamie could see it.

"Would you like to join us?" Jamie said. Dana instantly looked up at her as if objecting to her invitation.

When no one introduced her, Jamie stood up and extended her hand to the woman.

"I'm Dr. Jamie Hughes. How do you do?"

"Hello. Doctor? What's your specialty or are you family practice?"

"I'm not a medical doctor. I'm a professor at Capital State."

"So it's a PhD doctor, right?" She shook Jamie's hand firmly.
"Yes."

"Good. I'm glad to hear it. I was afraid Dana was sick or something. I'm Shannon Verick."

"Shannon? Well, well." Jamie looked down at Dana who was picking at the tablecloth. "We were just discussing the differences between scientific analogy and artistic interpretation. Please, join us."

Shannon hesitated, looking down at Dana.

"If you two will excuse me," Jamie said, sliding out of the booth. "I need to find the little professor's room and powder my microscope." She smiled and went in search of the ladies room. She had seen the desperate look on Dana's face as she excused herself but knew they needed a few minutes of privacy, or as much privacy as they could find in a restaurant filled with fifty people. *I don't want to get in the way of whatever Dana needs to say to Shannon. Perhaps this is exactly what she needed. No time to think about it. No planning. No appointment with destiny. Just face to face. Here and now.* Jamie looked back in time to see Shannon sliding into the booth next to Dana. Jamie gave Dana a thumbs up and disappeared around the corner. She was dying to stay and watch but this was Dana's situation. She had no right to interfere.

Jamie took her time in the ladies room. She decided if Dana and Shannon were still talking, she would pause at the bar and ask some question about which wine they should have with salad. But Dana was alone in the booth, administering more lemon to her iced tea. She looked up and smiled at Jamie.

"I thought you fell in," she said as if nothing was wrong.

"I was giving you and Shannon a few minutes." Jamie sat down and started on her lasagna.

"You didn't have to do that. Nothing was said you couldn't have heard."

"I thought the two of you might need a little privacy."

"The conversation was short. She asked if I'd meet her for dinner. I told her I'd meet her for lunch instead."

Jamie took a bite and thought a moment.

"Okay, why lunch instead of dinner?"

"I took your advice and thought of the long-term and the short term consequences. Dinner with Shannon may be short term but it definitely has long-term consequences. It's two or three hours of drinks, talking, waiting for food, eating the food, waiting for dessert, eating the dessert and more talking.

Suddenly, evening leads into night. And the night is what I'm sure Shannon has in mind."

"And you aren't ready for a night with Shannon, I take it?"

"No, I'm not. So I cut her off at the knees. I said lunch, twelve-thirty, at Capital Deli. A nice neutral territory."

"The sandwich place on Fifth?"

"Yes. No mood lighting. No long waits. No back booth with candles on the table. It's boom, boom, boom. Order, eat and be out of there by one, one fifteen at the latest."

"And she agreed to that?"

"She did." Dana stabbed a piece of lettuce. "Not willingly but I told her it was that or coffee at the supermarket's espresso stand." She grinned devilishly.

"Good for you. You made a decision that gives you options. I'm proud of you. If it works out, you can move on to dinner. If not, you left yourself a way out." Jamie shrugged.

"I tried to imagine what you would say if you had been in that situation. You wouldn't have been pressured into anything you weren't comfortable with and that's exactly what I did. I told Shannon I needed time to think things over and insisting I meet her for dinner before I was ready wasn't going to help me do that."

Jamie was proud of Dana. It was a start. If nothing else, she let Shannon know she could make decisions without intimidation. That may have been the best thing she could do for their relationship. Jamie also knew she would have to stay strong. Whatever the problem, Dana couldn't expect to undo it in one day. But progress was made.

Jamie looked around the restaurant for Shannon and her friends but didn't see them.

"Where did Shannon go? Into the lounge with those other women?"

"I think so." Dana pointed to the placard on the table. "Tonight is half price wells."

"Ah. Brings out the upper crust of society when you can get drunk for under five bucks."

"Shannon doesn't drink that much." Dana frowned. "She may have one or two but she doesn't go to bars to get drunk. She's with a bunch of friends, out for a little fun. More often than not, she's the designated driver."

"I'm sorry. I shouldn't have said anything."

Jamie saw something she didn't expect. Dana still had deep protective feelings for Shannon. She may not have chosen to go out to dinner with her, but she wasn't willing to let Jamie run over her either. When she went to bat for her ex-lover, it spoke volumes about her dedication. Shannon was still in Dana's life and in her heart. Jamie was absolutely positive of that. It gave her a whole new insight into how she should handle any advice she offered Dana. *That was something I needed to see*, she thought, and was surprised when her stomach twisted slightly.

"Let me give you a ride to the marina," Jamie said, tossing her credit card on the dinner bill.

"You are *not* paying for my dinner, Dr. Hughes." Dana quickly pulled out a twenty-dollar bill and placed it on the tray.

"Okay, Dutch treat. But it's raining and no one will call you a charity case if you take a ride from me."

"I accept." Dana smiled.

The temperature had dropped. It was raining so heavily they were both soaked by the time they reached Jamie's car.

"I'll have some heat on in just a minute," Jamie said, starting the car. She used a tissue to wipe her glasses as the engine warmed up.

"I've lived in Washington all my life. You'd think I'd learn to wear a raincoat." Dana hunched her shoulders and shivered.

"Are you cold?"

"Yes. Aren't you?"

Jamie reached into the backseat and found a blue chambray shirt. She gave it a shake then placed it over Dana's shoulders.

"Use this until the car warms up."

"Thank you but are you sure you don't need it?"

"Nope. I'm fine." Once they reached the marina, Jamie pulled to the curb next to the security gate.

"Thanks for the shirt," Dana said, handing it back.

"Take it with you. It'll keep you warm until you get down to the boat."

"Are you sure?" Dana said, looking out at the torrent of water running down the window.

"I'm sure," Jamie reached over and held the sleeves while Dana slipped it on. "Good night." Her hands brushed the soft strands of Dana's hair.

"Good night, Jamie." Dana climbed out and looked back in the car before slamming the door. "Thank you for listening."

"My pleasure, Dana. Take care."

Dana closed the door and disappeared into the deluge.

Chapter 12

"Ahoy, the *Kewpie Doll*," Jamie shouted, shielding her eyes from the morning sun.

"Ahoy, your own damn self," Ruth Ann said with a hearty laugh as she came bursting onto the deck. "Come on. Climb aboard." She waved with both hands as if signaling a commercial airliner up to the gate. She was dressed in what the locals laughingly considered standard summer apparel for Washington: sandals, shorts and a navy blue fleece jacket. Connie had a matching fleece jacket, as well as matching shorts and sandals. Many of the things in their lives were matching. Their coffee mugs, fanny packs, TV trays, and even their recliners were identical right down to the guest towels pinned to the armrests. "We didn't expect to see you today." Ruth Ann gave Jamie a hearty handshake and a slap on the back, dislodging her glasses.

"Did I come at a bad time?" Jamie pushed her glasses back

into place with her finger.

"Heck, no."

"Hey, Jamie." Connie grinned from the window where she was washing dishes in the galley. "Coffee? Got a fresh pot."

"I'd love some. I forgot to make any this morning."

"How can you forget to make coffee?" Ruth Ann said, motioning for her to have a seat at the table.

"I got busy. You know," Jamie shrugged. She didn't have much of an explanation. Forgetting to make coffee did sound a little inane, but she often became so absorbed in her work she forgot simple tasks. Burning food in forgotten skillets was just another day at the office for her. She had learned to rely on microwavable dinners. If she forgot them, at least she wasn't risking a fire.

"Milk and sugar?" Connie asked.

"Milk."

"I thought you took sugar in your coffee," she said with a confused look on her face.

"Not me. That must be the other Dr. Hughes you know."

"Your sister takes sugar in her coffee, Connie," Ruth Ann said. "Not Jamie."

"She doesn't anymore. She switched to Splenda. She thinks one packet of that stuff a day is going to make her skinny. HA!" Connie filled a cup and brought it to Jamie on the deck.

"Can I get another cup, too? Thanks, peaches." Ruth Ann gave Connie's rear a pat as she passed.

"You know what the doctor said," Connie warned.

Ruth Ann shot her a pleading look and quivered her lower lip for emphasis.

"Okay. One cup. That's all. I should have made decaf," Connie muttered and went to get it.

"I heard that and don't you dare give me any decaf," Ruth Ann warned. "Decaf coffee is like having phone sex. If you want to get excited, you have to do it yourself."

"Jamie, what brings you down to the marina?" Connie called from the galley.

"Can't a person drop by to say hello?" Jamie said, taking a

seat at the table.

"Sure they can and we're glad you did," Ruth Ann said, joining her. "But you have that look."

"What look?"

"This I-have-something-to-ask-you look."

Jamie leaned forward and looked at her reflection in the glass topped table.

"I don't see any look."

"Okay. No look. Just a friendly visit," Ruth Ann said, patting her leg and smiling warmly.

"Actually there is one little detail I wanted to discuss with you," Jamie said after clearing her throat and adjusting her glasses.

"Ah ha!" Ruth Ann cackled. "I was right, peaches. She wants at ask something," she yelled toward the galley window.

"So you're a Sherlock Holmes. Big deal," Connie replied, carrying a tray of coffee mugs and a plate of banana nut bread to the table. "What can we do for you, honey?" She sat down and hitched her chair in close.

"I need to make a dive here in the marina but there's no moorage available for my boat. I was wondering if I could use your boat as a base for my dive."

"Sure. Where do you want to take it?" Ruth Ann said.

"No, no, Raggie. You weren't listening. She wants to dive off the *Kewpie Doll* right here where it sits, in our slip. Is that right, Jamie?" Connie asked.

"Yes. I need a place to leave my extra tank and gear. And a place to change into my wet suit."

"Sure, you can. What are you diving for? Slimy critters?"

"Something like that." Jamie didn't want to confess the real purpose for the dive. What if she couldn't find what she was looking for? Somewhere in the back of her logical mind she knew that was a distinct possibility. She had made enough dives in Budd Bay to know finding something as small as a key ring made finding the proverbial needle in a haystack seem easy.

"I bet she's diving for buried treasure," Connie said sinisterly.

"There's a pirate ship under Hudson Marina and it's filled with gold and silver."

"That's it." Jamie chuckled and took a sip of coffee, lest she give away her secret.

"When are you going to do it?" Ruth Ann asked.

"Later this morning, about ten or ten thirty. It will be low tide and only fifteen to twenty feet deep. Is that a problem?"

"Nope." Ruth Ann went inside and returned with a key on a lanyard. "This unlocks the dock-side door. Help yourself."

"You won't be here?"

"Connie's having her eyes tested. I have to drive her because they put those drops in and she won't be able to drive."

"You don't mind?" Jamie said, taking the key.

"Hell, no. Make yourself at home. The ladder on the stern folds down but you have to unlatch it at the top first."

"Maybe she needs one of us to be here while she's down there," Connie said, obviously trying to talk Ruth Ann out of going. Connie had been a bus driver for the Olympia transit system for twenty-five years. Jamie suspected, even with her eyes dilated, she trusted her own driving more than Ruth Ann's.

"I don't need anyone here. I can handle it. I may have a very short window of opportunity anyway. Once I stir things up, the visibility will be pretty poor."

"If you see our butter knife…" Connie trailed off.

"I'll keep an eye out for it," Jamie said, finishing her coffee. "I better go. I have to have my tanks filled."

"We'll probably see you later then. We should be back by noon or so," Connie said.

"Maybe you should take a look for Dana's key ring while you're down there," Ruth Ann said casually.

"She'll never find that," Connie argued. "And it's a shame. I heard that little piece of bling was worth a hefty chunk of change. Dana said it was white gold."

"I understand it was a gift," Jamie said, staying noncommittal.

"Uh-huh," Connie said cautiously then looked at Ruth Ann.

"Oh, for Pete's sake. Tell her."

"Tell me what?" Jamie asked.

"Shannon had it especially made for her."

"I knew that. Dana told me."

"Did she tell you Shannon gave it to her as a peace offering when Dana threatened to walk out on her last year?"

"So you know this Shannon person?"

"Yeah. She runs a travel agency over in Lacey. She has booked three of our cruises. She organizes the cruises for several GLBT Web sites."

Jamie knew there was more to be gleaned, but if Dana wanted her to know about her and Shannon, she would tell her. Jamie didn't need to pry and she certainly wasn't going to squeeze tidbits of half informed information from Ruth Ann and Connie. All she hoped to do was retrieve Dana's key ring and return it to her. She was willing to invest an hour or two and a tank of air for that purpose, but Dana's private life was none of her business, and from what Dana divulged so far, it didn't appear she was going to offer much more.

Jamie collected her equipment, had her tanks filled, and headed back to Hudson Marina. Once back on the *Kewpie Doll*, she changed into her wet suit and geared up for the dive. As gently as possible, she slipped into the water, hoping not to disturb the sediment at the bottom. She knew she had one good clean chance at grabbing anything lodged in the soft black silt before raising a mushroom cloud that would obliterate her vision. After that, she would have to wait for the silt to settle again.

It was after one when Ruth Ann and Connie returned home to find Jamie changing tanks. She was frustrated. More than frustrated, she was angry.

"Are you still at it?" Ruth Ann asked.

"Yes," Jamie replied, clenching her jaw.

"Did you find anything good?" Connie came out onto the deck sporting oversized sunglasses.

"Oh, yes. I forgot." Jamie opened the mesh bag attached to her weight belt and pulled out a blackened butter knife.

"Is this yours?"

"My grandmother's silver butter knife!" Connie exclaimed, examining it lovingly. "How in the heck did you find it? We assumed it was long gone."

"It must have fallen point down. It was stabbed into a clump of mussels growing on a cinder block. A little polish should clean it up," Jamie said, stepping over the railing, ready to go down again.

"Thank you, honey," Connie said, coming to the railing to give Jamie a hug in spite of her bulky diving gear. "This means a lot to me."

"You're welcome," Jamie smiled and fitted her mask against her face.

"Jamie, what are you looking for?" Ruth Ann asked with a concerned scowl. "And why?"

"I wish the hell I knew," she said. She put the mouthpiece in place and stepped into the water.

What started out as a Good Samaritan effort to try and retrieve Dana's key ring had turned into a personal crusade. Every time she came up empty-handed made her try again, and again, and again. *You are being pigheaded*, she told herself. *Unnecessarily stubborn and unreasonably foolish. This is not like you. There is no way I am going to find it.* Why hadn't she listened to herself that evening during the party when she explained that fact to Dana? But oh, no. She was spending hours groping around in the muck and mud, hours she should be spending in her lab. She was using up the last of her tanks of air for nothing.

Jamie checked the gauge on her tank. The needle was on red. If it wasn't empty, it was only a few minutes from it. That was it. She had tried her best but much as she hated to, she had to resign herself to failure. She gave one last look across the bottom, then headed for the surface. Suddenly she stopped, hovering several feet off the bottom. She looked down. Something had caught her eye. But where? A microsecond's worth of something. Quickly, she swam back down, her eyes darting back and forth over the rocks, trash, mud and shells.

There, nestled in a clump of seaweed, visible only when the current stirred the wide green blades, was a glimmer of something. Jamie exhaled and took another breath but the tank was finally empty. She felt nothing fill her lungs. She swam toward the object, her lungs demanding oxygen. She took one swipe across the seaweed with her gloved hand. She didn't know if she got it or not but she had to surface and surface *now*. She felt her lungs burning and kicked wildly, propelling herself upward. As her head and face broke the surface, she spit out her mouthpiece and gulped for air. She was almost afraid to look at what was in her hand. It could be the key ring or just a handful of seaweed.

"I thought you'd never come up," Ruth Ann said, looking over the railing.

Jamie took several more breaths before moving to the ladder. She handed Ruth Ann her fins and climbed aboard, her hand still clutching whatever she had grabbed. She slipped out of her tank and dropped her weight belt.

"What the hell are you doing with that? You took all that time just to grab some slimy seaweed?"

Jamie slowly opened her hand, the blades of seaweed laced between her fingers. Nestled in her palm, under the seaweed, there it was. Dana's key ring. It was muddy and covered with green slime but it was unmistakably hers.

"What's that?" Ruth Ann said, staring down at it.

"That, my friend, is a miracle. Pure and simple." Jamie rubbed it with her fingers, dislodging the slimy algae coating.

"That's Dana's key ring, isn't it?"

"Yes." Jamie found her glasses where she had left them on the table and studied the discolored object. A smile grew across her face as she examined it, the keys still attached and dangling from the ring. Dana's initials were still legible, the engraving not yet filled in by the tarnish.

"Damn, Jamie. What a stroke of luck. First you find Connie's grandmother's silver butter knife, then you find Dana's gold key ring."

"Is that what you were looking for, Jamie?" Connie said,

squinting over Jamie's other shoulder to get a look at it.

"Naw, she wasn't," Ruth Ann said then looked up at Jamie. "Were you? Is that what you were diving for all along? Dana's lost key ring?"

"I wanted to give it a try. I felt partially responsible for her losing it. I knew it was a long shot but I had to at least take a look."

"She'll be so pleased you found it. I bet she's pacing the houseboat, waiting for the telephone to ring."

"She didn't know I was going to look for it. I was afraid I couldn't find it."

"You're going to polish it up, aren't you?" Ruth Ann said.

"Yes. It hasn't been in the water that long. It should come clean." Jamie wanted to say it would come clean because it was silver, probably silverplate. But Dana had told them Shannon had given her a white gold key ring. They must have misunderstood and Jamie saw no reason to contradict them.

She was just a short walk to Dana's slip but wanted a chance to polish the key ring before returning it to her. She headed home, placed some water softener and salt into an aluminum pie pan, and added warm water. As soon as it was dissolved, she dropped in the key ring. It instantly changed from dingy black to gleaming silver, shining as if it was new. Jamie was right. It was silver. She called Dana, but the cell phone rang six times before Dana's voice mail answered. Jamie left a message.

"Hi, Dana. It's Jamie. Give me a call when you have a chance. I'd like to talk with you. Nothing terribly important. You might call it interesting though. Talk with you later. 'Bye."

She had just finished hauling her diving equipment up to her apartment when her phone rang.

"Dr. Hughes here," she said, balancing her cell phone against her chin as she carried an armload of equipment into the study.

"Hi, Jamie. It's Dana. I just got your message. What did you need to talk to me about?" There was barking in the background.

"Where are you? On the houseboat?"

"No. I'm walking across Sylvester Park. I walked up to the post office and library. Somebody's dog is having a fit because he can't reach a squirrel up the tree."

"Would it be okay if I met you somewhere? It won't take long but I need to talk with you." She knew she should go ahead and tell her why but she couldn't. She wanted to see her eyes light up and hear that gasp and giggle when Jamie gave her the key ring.

"Sure. But what is it, Jamie? Is something wrong?"

"No. Nothing is wrong."

"Would you like to come by the houseboat? I'll be back soon. Dock A, slip thirty-eight. And then there's the security code." Dana paused. Jamie quickly understood.

"That's okay. I understand. You don't have to give it to me. Maybe we could meet outside the security gate."

"No, it isn't that. I don't mind telling you. I just don't want to say it over the telephone. You never know who is listening."

"Unless you are a fugitive from justice, I doubt your phone is being tapped."

"But there is a group of pedestrians I'm sure can hear every word I'm saying."

"Can you give it to me surreptitiously?" Jamie said.

"Okay. First number. Your age, the numbers added together. Then Juliana's age added together. Got that so far?"

"Yep."

"Finally, the last two numbers on Bo's *Madonna*."

"Nine three one six?"

"Very good, Dr. Hughes."

"See you in thirty minutes."

Jamie checked the key ring to make sure it was polished as well as she could get it then headed to the marina. She punched in the security code and started down the dock. A hanging basket of petunias swung from the corner of the houseboat as it swayed from the wake of a passing boat. Jamie stepped onto the deck and knocked.

"Right on time, Dr. Hughes," Dana said, wiping her hands on a towel as if she had just finished cleaning something. "Come in. And what's this big secret you couldn't tell me over the telephone?" She followed Jamie inside.

"It's not a big secret necessarily."

"It sure sounded like it. Sit down. Would you like a cup of coffee or maybe a glass of juice? I'm sorry I'm all out of soda. I meant to get some at the store but you had me all flustered with your mysterious visit."

"Nothing, thank you." Jamie sat in one of the bar stools next to the little nook table. "I just wanted to do this in person."

"Do what in person?"

"Give me your hand."

"Why?" Dana extended her hand. "Are we now officially engaged?" she joked.

Jamie pulled the key ring from her pocket but kept it hidden. She placed it in Dana's hand and closed her fingers around it. "This."

Dana opened her hand. There was a split second of silence followed with a shriek.

"THE KEY RING?! Oh my, God. Jamie! Where? How?" Dana seemed incapable of forming a sentence. She sunk into a chair and stared at it.

"Lucky. Just plain lucky."

"You found it down there? Down there where you said nothing could be found, not even a ship?"

"Like I said, I got lucky. It landed on a clump of seaweed. It never made it to the bottom. If it had it would have been lost. The sediment was three feet thick. It was so soft it sucked things in like quicksand."

"You did that for me? You went scuba diving for me and my key ring?" Dana clutched it to her chest and grinned. "What a special thing to do for a friend. Thank you," she said and kissed Jamie's cheek.

"You're welcome. I'm glad I could return it. I guess that makes my certification card worthwhile." Jamie looked past Dana at a large cartoon panel leaning against the wall on the back of the sofa. "So, this is where Ringlet lives."

"Yes. She's drying. I just signed it so I can scan it into my computer later."

Jamie went to get a closer look at it. The human in the cartoon was scowling and shaking her ankle, trying to dislodge Ringlet's grip. The dog had her front paws wrapped around her owner's leg, suggesting she had been humping her ankle. The bubble over Ringlet's head read: *I prefer to call it safe sex.*

"Now, that's funny," Jamie said, laughing. "I like it."

"Thank you. Sometimes Ringlet is a little irreverent. My readers seem to like that."

"How many do you submit at a time?"

"Five or six. Sometimes I get on a roll and can have a dozen in a week. But it's been a little slower these past few weeks."

"I'm sure it has but it'll get better." Jamie stroked Dana's arm.

"It has already. I can't believe you did that for me. I never ever thought I'd see it again."

"I polished it up so no one will ever know it spent a few days on the bottom of Budd Bay," Jamie said with a smile. "The engraving is as good as new." Jamie's cell phone rang as she was saying it. "Dr. Hughes here," she said, answering it. "Yes. I left it on the table next to the door. I want it run again. Those results looked hinky to me." Jamie scowled. "All right. Wait. I'll be there in twenty minutes. No, don't start. I'll be right there." She hung up and grimaced. "I'm sorry Dana. I have to go."

"Sounds bad."

"Not bad. They ran some tests for me and I question the results. I want to do it myself this time." She headed for the door. Dana followed.

"Thank you again, Jamie," she said, squeezing Jamie's hand. "You have no idea how pleased I am. You're wonderful."

"Take care of it."

"I will," Dana said. She pulled her into a hug and kissed her on the cheek. Jamie smiled to herself as she slipped out the door. If she didn't stop smiling until she got home, she never questioned it.

Chapter 13

Jamie locked her office door and headed down the hall. As she crossed the parking lot, she pulled out her cell phone and played the message from Dana one more time.

"Hi, Jamie." She sounded anxious. "You must be working in your lab. I don't want to interrupt, but I need to meet with you. How about this evening after dinner? Bartolu's between seven and seven fifteen for a drink. If you can't make it, I'll understand, but I really, *really* hope you can. See you then. 'Bye."

Jamie pushed the button and redialed Dana's cell number, but she didn't answer. It was ten till seven. She placed the cell phone on the console and headed for Bartolu's.

"Hello," the hostess said. "Welcome back. Table for one or are you meeting someone?"

"I'm meeting someone," Jamie said, scanning the room.

"The cute little blonde you were with the other night?" she

asked coyly.

Jamie wasn't going to agree out loud but yes, Dana was a cute little blonde, now that she mentioned it.

"Has she been in yet?"

"No, not yet. I can seat you if you'd like. How about a drink while you wait? Or maybe coffee?"

"Do you have anything in the lounge?" Jamie asked. It was crowded in the dining room and Dana said they weren't meeting for dinner. The message said just a drink.

"Sure. Right this way." She seated Jamie at a secluded table in the dimly lit bar. Two young women sat at the next table, holding hands and whispering to each other over a pair of draft beers. Jamie glanced around the room. Most of the dozen or so patrons appeared to be gay, all of them with a partner. The waitress was a well-tanned blond beauty with big bosoms and tight black slacks. She seemed proud of her ample cleavage and wore a deeply cut V-neck top to show it off. When she bent over to place a paper coaster on the table, Jamie was certain something was going to fall out.

"What can I get you?" She gave Jamie a friendly smile.

"Seven and seven with a couple cherries," Jamie said.

"Would you like an appetizer?"

"No, thanks." Jamie kept an eye on the door. It was after seven thirty. Dana had said between seven and seven fifteen. She was late and Jamie was worried. She tried Dana's cell phone again, but it rang immediately to her voice mail. Jamie nursed her drink, occasionally dialing Dana's number and staring at the doorway. Just as she was ready to head toward the marina to check on Dana, the hostess came through the door, a smile on her face. Dana followed as if she was late to catch a train.

"Jamie, I'm sorry. I'm terribly late and I have no excuse."

Jamie stood up and held her chair. Dana kissed her cheek and smiled.

"Are you all right? I was starting to worry." That was a fib. Jamie had begun worrying when she first heard Dana's message on her cell phone.

"I was working on a set of panels and I couldn't get away. You know how it is. You get going on a project and can't find a stopping place until you're finished. Forgive me." Dana patted Jamie's hand as she took her seat.

"I thought maybe you dropped your cell phone in the bay."

"It didn't ring," Dana said, digging it out of her purse. "Uh-oh." She grimaced, noticing it was turned off. She pushed the button and cowered sheepishly. "I'm sorry, Jamie. I forgot to turn it on."

"And I thought I was forgetful," she said, giving her a little scowl.

"Oh, look," she snickered. "I missed a few calls from Dr. Jamie Hughes. Quite a few calls, I see."

"What did you expect? You leave me a breathless message insisting I meet you this evening at Bartolu's. The only information you offer is that it's for a drink, not dinner and I quote, 'I really *really* hope you can make it.' I was certain there was some earth shaking news about Shannon."

"Well, there is a little. Not earthshaking though."

"About the lunch meeting?" Jamie felt sure this was it. The big important reason for Dana's call. Either the meeting with Shannon went well and they had moved up to a dinner rendezvous, or it went poorly and Dana was back to square one.

"What can I get you to drink, hon?" the waitress said, doing her dip and dangle in front of Dana as she placed a coaster on the table in front of her.

"White wine, please," Dana replied, leaving Jamie hanging over her news.

"I'll have that right out. Can I interest you all in chips and dip or an onion blossom?"

"Do you have crab dip?" Dana asked.

"Absolutely. Anything else?" She looked at Jamie.

"Jamie?" Dana asked.

"No. That's good." She wasn't at all interested in appetizers. She wanted to know about the lunch with Shannon.

"They have oysters on the half shell," Dana said, holding up the table placard. "You like those."

"Okay. Sure. Oysters on the half shell," she said, discharging the order so they could get back to the news about Shannon.

"That's crab dip and oysters on the half shell," the waitress said cheerfully, winking at Dana. "And a white wine. Do you need another seven and seven, miss?"

"No, I'm fine." Jamie covered her glass with her hand.

The waitress left them alone and none too soon for Jamie's curiosity.

"How did your lunch go?" she said, sitting up and leaning into the question.

"Shannon didn't show up. She called that morning and said she had to work. They're doing the last bookings for an Alaskan cruise in two weeks so she couldn't get away."

"Then you haven't talked with her yet."

"Actually, yes, I did."

"But you just said," Jamie started then saw something in Dana's face. "Dana, did you meet her for dinner after all?"

"No. Not yet. But I agreed to meet her tomorrow night. I know. I know. I said I didn't want to do the long dinner thing with her, but we had no choice. She had to work through lunch. She didn't even get a break. She had to order out for pizza. And she'll be working every day for the next two weeks."

"Where are you meeting?" Jamie said, seeing no reason to argue with her. She seemed to have made up her mind.

"Seven o'clock at Trinacera. She said she was hungry for Italian."

For some unknown reason, Jamie wanted to make a nasty crack about eating an Italian. But she didn't.

"Here we are," the waitress said, bringing their order. "White wine."

"You don't approve, do you?" Dana said.

"It isn't my place to approve," Jamie replied, sipping her drink nonchalantly.

"Crab dip with a basket of crackers and oysters on the half shell," the waitress added then left.

Jamie stared down at the raw oysters. The plate was artfully arranged with lemon wedges and a tiny boat of cocktail sauce.

"But you don't," Dana insisted.

"Are you comfortable with your decision?"

"Sure, I am. I wouldn't have made it if I wasn't."

"Then there's nothing to discuss."

Jamie dabbed a little cocktail sauce on an oyster, held the shell to her lips, and let the oyster slide down.

"How can you do that?" Dana said, wrinkling her nose. "Aren't they slimy?"

"They're delicious. Try one."

"I don't think so."

"Come on. Just one. You're a woman who likes to try new things. You never know. You may like them."

"Or I may gag," Dana said, watching her prepare one.

Jamie used the cocktail fork to dab on a little sauce then squeezed a lemon over the top. She handed Dana the shell then prepared one for herself.

"Don't chew it. Just let it slide down. When it passes over the palate, that's the moment supreme." She held her shell up to Dana's as if clinking glasses for a toast. "*Bon appetit.*" Jamie ate hers. Dana hesitantly tipped the shell to her mouth, grimacing as if anticipating foul tasting medicine. As the oyster entered her mouth, she closed her eyes and swallowed, making a gagging sound.

"How was it?" Jamie asked hopefully.

"I have no idea. It went down," Dana replied and burped. "I think."

"You have to admit, it wasn't terrible."

"If that's the best you can say about raw oysters, it isn't much of a recommendation."

"Try another one." Jamie quickly applied the sauce and lemon.

"No, thank you. You enjoy them." Dana covered her mouth as if worried the oyster might come back up.

"Okay for you." Jamie chuckled and swallowed another one.

160

She wiped her mouth with a napkin and took a slow sip from her drink. "I take it your call to have me meet you was to tell me about your change in plans with Shannon, right?"

"No. That's not the reason I called. I wanted to thank you again for recovering my key ring. Having it back represents such a kind thing you did for me. What did they call it in that movie? Beau Gest? Beautiful gesture."

"It wasn't that big a deal." Jamie felt a blush warm her face. She didn't expect Dana to make such a production out of it. That wasn't why she did it, and Dana's lavish thank you was humbling.

"It was to me. That's why I invited you to meet me here tonight. For a thank you drink, on me. Oysters, too," Dana said, raising her glass. "I'm only sorry it couldn't be dinner, but I was on a time crunch today with Ringlet."

"I don't need you to buy me a thank you drink."

"I know you don't. I want to."

"Ladies," the waitress said, placing a second drink in front of each of them.

"We didn't order another drink," Jamie said.

"This one is on the house, from the management," she said, nodding toward the bar as she left.

"Why?" Dana said, looking in that direction.

The hostess who had seated them waved and smiled from the end of the bar.

"Is she flirting with us or do you know her?" Dana said out of the corner of her mouth.

"I have no idea who she is. She must be flirting with you," Jamie said.

Before they could make any more guesses the woman came to their table.

"Thank you for the drinks," Dana said, holding up her wineglass.

"You're welcome. I noticed you two were here the other night." The woman pulled up a chair and sat down. "I'm Janice," she said, offering to shake their hands.

"Hello. I'm Jamie. This is Dana."

"Please don't think I'm being terribly forward but I have a favor to ask. I'd like for you to allow us to photograph the two of you for our Web site."

"Photograph us?" Jamie said, still skeptical.

"Yes. As you probably know, we haven't been open very long. We've hired someone to build our Web site. Most of the restaurants and bars have them now. You have to have one to be included in the Olympia community listings. People want to know where to go for dinner so they look online. People use the Internet more than the phone book. Our webmaster says we need photographs of people in the restaurant to show the ambiance. I noticed you two when you came in for dinner and I thought you were the perfect couple to photograph." She smiled encouragingly. "What do you say? He's in my office right now. It won't take but a few minutes. He has a camera and everything."

Dana looked over at Jamie.

"It's up to you, Dana. I don't mind if you don't."

"I guess so." Dana shrugged.

"Be right back." Janice hurried away, seemingly excited over their agreement.

"I'm a little surprised she asked," Jamie said. "Usually places like this just take candid shots and post them on the Web site."

"Maybe she's new at it and thinks she needs permission. I bet she thinks she has to have us sign a waiver or something."

"We'll probably need to push our chairs a little closer together," Jamie said, scooting hers over a bit.

The woman reappeared, followed by a young bearded man with a camera and a tripod.

"This is Danny," Janice said. "He's our web builder."

"Webmaster," he corrected.

"I think we're ready," Dana said, sliding her chair next to Jamie's.

"No, I don't need you at the table," Janice said, wringing her hands nervously.

"Where then?" Jamie said, looking at the empty barstools.

"On the dance floor." She pointed to the raised parquet floor next to the jukebox. There was no music playing. "We want to show that we have dancing on Friday and Saturday nights."

"What?" Dana laughed. "I thought you meant a picture of us sitting here with a drink in our hand."

"We've got plenty of that kind of shot. What we need is a picture of an attractive couple dancing. And you two are perfect. Right age, right size, right chemistry. They're perfect, aren't they, Danny?" she said in his direction.

"Yes. Perfect."

"See. You two will keep us from looking like a teenybopper hangout or the lobby of a nursing home. I've been waiting for a couple that represented a sophisticated yet casual clientele. Please. It'll just take a few minutes." What started as good logical reasoning had become downright begging.

"No one else is out there," Dana said.

"That's what we want," Danny said. "It's hard to get a clear focus with a lot of background motion."

Jamie instantly envisioned having to strike a pose as if she was doing some wild rock-and-roll dance then hold it for several minutes while Danny focused and checked the lighting. The more the woman talked, the more Dana's expression changed from disbelief to understanding. And the more Dana seemed to agree with the woman's plan, the more worried Jamie became.

"I don't have a good feeling about this, Dana," Jamie said, poking her glasses against her nose.

"Just standing out there. That's all you need, right?" Dana asked, seeming to sense Jamie's concern.

"Yes," Janice said.

"Dancing," Danny said at the same time. "Slow dancing."

"Ahg," Jamie groaned softly.

"One dance?" Dana said, patting Jamie's knee reassuringly.

"Tell you what," the woman said. "I'll turn on the jukebox. It should make it easier for you. You'll look more natural if you're actually dancing, not just posing. And I'll pick up the check for everything. I'll even throw in a couple complimentary shrimp cocktail. What do you say?"

"Shrimp cocktail, Jamie," Dana said, elbowing her in the side playfully as if that should make a difference. "Just for dancing one dance. How hard can it be?"

Jamie furrowed her brow as the woman hurried over to the jukebox and flipped the switch on the back. Danny set up his tripod next to the dance floor, calculating his field of focus.

"I'm a sucker for a shrimp cocktail. It has to be better than raw oysters." Dana pushed her chair back. "Come on, professor," she said brightly. "Pretend you're in your laboratory."

Jamie knew her face had lost its color. It wasn't that she didn't know how to dance but she hadn't done it in years and even then, not very well. Dana was a new friend. Too new to be exposed to Jamie's clumsiness. Underwater she was agile and swift, even graceful. On a fifteen-foot square dance floor, not so much. She reluctantly followed Dana onto the raised floor, standing as close to the edge as possible. Dana stood next to her, awaiting instruction. The music started, something instrumental and light.

"Would you mind taking off the fleece vest?" Danny asked Jamie. "The dark color will blend you right into the background."

"Okay," she said, removing it and straightening the collar of her shirt.

"That's good," Janice said, eyeing her up and down. "Would you mind?" She unbuttoned the top button of Jamie's shirt, took a long look then unbuttoned another. Jamie scowled down at her as she slipped her fingers inside the opening, her fingers brushing against her cleavage as she spread the collar. "Perfect." Janice then turned to Dana. "Could I talk you into removing your ponytail holder, Dana? I think your hair is gorgeous, and it would look so great down."

"Sure, I guess so," she said and pulled it free. She gave her hair a toss, releasing it into a cascade of blond waves. Janice laced her fingers through it, fluffing it over Dana's shoulders.

"Great."

164

Dana's top button was already unbuttoned but Janice couldn't resist opening the top of her blouse slightly to reveal the top of Dana's lace bra.

"I love it," Janice said proudly, as if gloating over what she had created.

"I feel like I'm auditioning to be a pole dancer at a strip club," Dana muttered to Jamie.

"This will be the most expensive shrimp cocktail in history," Jamie whispered.

"One more thing," Janice said, stepping back and looking at them. "Your glasses. Could you possibly dance without them, Jamie?"

"She has to see, doesn't she?" Dana said, as if rushing to Jamie's defense.

"What the heck," Jamie said, removing them and setting them on the table. "I'm practically undressed as it is."

"Will you be able to see where you're going?" Dana asked.

"Maybe." Jamie squinted, forcing her eyes to focus.

"That's encouraging," Dana teased.

"Let's see what we have here," Janice said, turning them to face each other. "Jamie you're taller but that's okay." She placed Dana's hands on Jamie as if Dana was leading. Dana seemed to know what to do and for that, Jamie was glad. "Good, Dana." Janice stepped back and nodded as if that was the cue to begin. Dana instinctively took a step then another, forcing Jamie to follow.

"Closer," Janice said, waving her hands together. "Move closer together."

Their moves were awkward at best. Jamie struggled to keep from stepping on Dana's feet. Dana moved stiffly, her strides unequal. Finally, she stopped.

"I need to start again," Dana said, with an embarrassed frown.

"Wait a minute," Jamie said, switching hands. "Let's try this."

"Okay," Dana said, slipping her hand in Jamie's. She seemed

165

relieved to surrender the lead. Jamie took a step. Dana followed.

"A little closer," Janice said, standing next to Danny as he focused. "Don't look at the camera. Look at each other. Closer. Hold her closer, Jamie," she said over the jukebox.

Dana stepped closer, leaving only a few inches between them.

"Bossy little cuss, isn't she?" Jamie chuckled, finally matching her stride to the music. She pulled Dana into her arms, their bodies pressed together as they moved around the floor. Jamie hadn't danced with a woman in her arms in six years. It felt strange but her fears and clumsiness were fading. It was coming back to her in a rush of emotions. She pulled Dana closer, close enough to feel her heart beat and the breaths rise in her chest. She didn't hesitate as the song changed but kept them floating around the floor as if on a graceful carousel.

"Good. Great!" Janice said as Danny snapped shot after shot, moving with them as if trying to capture their magic.

Dana rested her head on Jamie's shoulder as they moved in time with the music.

"Did you get that?" Janice demanded, shuffling around the floor, pointing out shots.

Jamie closed her eyes and tilted her chin against Dana's forehead. The music swelled dramatically, pulling her deeper and deeper into the fantasy. It was no longer her and Dana dancing. It was someone else. Someone whose face was obscured by the music and by time. Jamie continued to dance, guiding them through billowing clouds of memory.

"That's wonderful, Jamie. Thank you." Janice said, stepping onto the dance floor. "Danny got some great shots. I'm sure of it. Thank you both so much."

But Jamie didn't stop. She moved Dana around the floor, still holding her locked in her arms. Dana followed obediently, matching Jamie step for step. The feel of Dana's body in her arms, the sweet smell of her, was something Jamie couldn't bring herself to give up. Not until the song ended and Janice turned off the jukebox did Jamie realize how totally she had allowed herself to revisit that old memory. She finally stopped dancing but held Dana in her arms for a long last moment before releasing her. Dana didn't say a word. As if she understood where Jamie's thoughts had been, she squeezed her hand then walked off the floor.

Chapter 14

Dinner with Shannon was at seven, but Dana's nerves were frazzled by three. She didn't care about what to wear or how she would look, just what they would talk about. Like other times when she needed an outlet for her anxiety, Dana sat down on the deck with a sketch pad. Ringlet would calm the jitters that had tied her stomach in knots. It only took a few strokes of her pen to have the pup's impish face smiling up at her. She had drawn the black Scottie hundreds of times, and amazingly, each time it brought a smile to her face as Ringlet's personality took shape. She thumbed through the notepad she carried in her purse for ideas she had jotted down. Nothing caught her interest.

She looked out toward West Bay Marina where Jamie kept her research boat and wondered what she was doing. Scuba diving? Collecting samples? She smiled and sketched two fish on the pad. She sketched Ringlet's human, a slender, working class, attractive lesbian with big round eyes and short hair. She ate healthy, lived clean and didn't smoke. Dana hadn't given her a name since the cartoon was drawn from Ringlet's point of view. For the first two years Ringlet's sex was ambiguous, but Dana's publisher suggested she make a commitment one way or the other. Ringlet was a girl with just enough tendencies to suggest she too was gay. But it was Ringlet's independence and feisty curiosity that sold the cartoon.

Suddenly, she had an idea. Flipping to a clean page, she began to sketch.

Ringlet stood at a window, her front paws on the sill. Her human stood behind her, also looking out the window, both of them watching the moving van backed into the next-door neighbor's driveway. A dream bubble over the human's head showed her imagining a voluptuous woman moving into the house. A dream bubble over Ringlet's head showed her imagining a sexy poodle moving into the house. Both Ringlet and her human looked love starved and interested in whoever was moving in next door.

She finished the details and reviewed it. *Curious. They're both curious*, she thought. She looked out over the marina, in the direction of Jamie's ship. Her cell phone rang just as she signed Robinette to the corner.

"Hello, Shannon," she said, reading the caller ID.

"Hi, babe." Shannon sounded happy. "What are you doing?"

"Working," Dana had another idea but it was slowly dissipating. She began an absentminded sketch of Ringlet, hoping the idea would return.

"I thought I'd see if you want to meet me a little earlier. How about six thirty? I called and changed the reservation. They're booked up but said they could work us in. I asked for that table in the front window. The one we always get."

The one that makes me feel like a fish in fishbowl, Dana thought. She closed her pad. She knew she wasn't going to get anything else done today. Shannon never seemed to care when she interrupted Dana's work. But it was her own fault. She's the one who answered the call.

"Six thirty at Trinacera," Dana said, wondering why Shannon bothered to change it for just thirty minutes.

"I'll pick you up around six."

"Shannon, I don't need a ride. It's four blocks. I'll walk over."

"I don't mind. It's practically on the way," she insisted.

"It's not on the way and I want to walk. I'll meet you at Trinacera at six thirty," Dana said emphatically. She could think of several reasons to stick to her guns on this one. First of all, it didn't take thirty minutes to go four blocks. Second, she wanted to be on her own to come and go as she saw fit. And mostly it was just because she said so. Shannon grumbled something under her breath then agreed and hung up.

Dana rounded the corner onto State Street at precisely six thirty on the dot. Trinacera was a small restaurant run by a Sicilian gentleman, Eugenio, who did all the cooking from recipes he kept in his head. The best meals were the ones customers allowed him to create rather than ordering off the menu. It was a secret only a few locals knew but for them he created more than simple dinners.

Shannon was already waiting inside when Dana opened the door and stepped in. Shannon was dressed in what Dana suspected were her work clothes. Brown slacks set stylishly low on her hips and a yellow sweater with the sleeves pushed back, a color that accented her rich brown hair. Dana had always thought Shannon was an attractive woman. Even in jeans, she turned heads. She carried herself with confidence and professionalism. In her line of work, that perception was important.

"I knew I should have picked you up," Shannon said, checking her watch.

"I'm not late. Six thirty-two is not late."

Shannon kissed Dana's cheek then turned to the hostess.

"Reservation for two. The name is Verick. The window table for six thirty," she said.

The window table was the only vacant table in the restaurant. Shannon held the chair for Dana then took her seat across the table.

"We'll have a bottle of Tivoli Chianti," she said, turning up their glasses.

Dana had begun reading the menu. She had eaten at Trinacera many times but always labored over what to chose. Everything sounded delicious.

"I don't know if I want a calzone or something with pasta," she said, reading everything. "What did we have the last time? Something marinara?"

"You didn't like it, remember? You said it was too spicy."

"I thought that was you."

"Why don't you let me order for you like I always do? It takes you forever to decide."

Dana paused and looked up at her.

"I like to read the menu," she said.

"It hasn't changed in five years, babe." Shannon set her menu on the edge of the table. She reached across and adjusted Dana's collar then let her eyes scan down over her. "Where did you get those earrings? Are they new?"

Dana felt her ears. She couldn't remember which earrings she was wearing.

"They aren't new. These are the ones Steve gave me a few Christmases ago."

"You look nice. I like that outfit on you. Baby blue is definitely your color." Shannon leaned forward. "And I like that bra," she whispered.

Dana looked down to see if her bra was noticeable.

"You can't see my bra," she said.

"I can't see it but I like what it does for you." She grinned. "Are you chilly, baby cakes?" She winked.

"Actually, yes, I am." Dana crossed her arms over the table as much to warm herself as to discourage Shannon from staring at her nipples.

The waitress brought a bottle of wine to the table. Shannon tasted it, giving her blessing for Dana to try it.

"That's good," Dana said, enjoying a sip. "Very smooth. Good choice, Shannon."

"Have I ever missed when it came to wine?" She took a drink then refilled their glasses. "Remember that time we went to Portland and ate at Sarge's Steakhouse? We had that terrible California wine." She laughed loudly.

"The one that had a head on it in the glass?" Dana said with a snicker.

"Yes. That crap tasted like cat piss."

Every time Shannon used that expression, Dana wanted to ask how she knew what cat piss tasted like. Shannon had become quite a culinary expert—to a limited degree. She knew what the specialty was at many of Olympia's restaurants. She could choose an appropriate wine for any meal. And Shannon knew what Dana liked and didn't like, even when she wasn't sure herself.

"I remember the manager blamed it on the glasses. He said they had beer residue in them." Dana wrinkled her nose. "Either way, it was nasty."

"Like they'd use wineglasses to serve beer. Anyway, I got our dinner free. Remember?"

"Yes, but I hated to do that. I would have settled for a different wine."

"It was a drop in the bucket. He'll never miss it. I heard him tell someone to pull all that wine off the shelf. He knew it was bad."

"What can I get you ladies this evening?" the waitress asked, setting a basket of bread bowties on the table.

"She'll have Tagliatelle with prosciutto and mushrooms. I'll have Rigatoni Pomodoro with Italian sausage," Shannon said. "Salad. Right, babe?"

"Yes, please." Dana closed her menu. That sounded good. Not something she considered but good.

"Would you like an appetizer?" the waitress said, claiming the menus.

Dana wondered if they had oysters on the half shell. She didn't like them but Jamie did. Curious little food, she thought.

"No. That's all. Just the two salads." Shannon turned her

attention back to Dana. "You'll love the Tagliatelle."

"Is it penne pasta or spaghetti?" Dana sipped her wine, wishing she had read what that was.

"Fettuccine." Shannon waited for Dana to take another sip of wine then filled her glass.

"I don't need anymore," she said, moving her glass out of Shannon's reach.

"Smooth, isn't it?"

"Yes, very." Dana repositioned her napkin over her lap and straightened her silverware. She was waiting for Shannon to start the conversation in a new direction. She would be just as happy to continue with small talk but knew Shannon had something else in mind.

"How do you like the houseboat?"

"I like it. It's very restful. It's sort of like a floating cabin."

"I've been giving some thought to looking for a cabin somewhere in the mountains. Maybe up on the peninsula. Nothing fancy. Kind of a getaway cabin. It would be a great place for you to work. Away from the noise and crowds. Something by a stream with a dynamite view. Dorothy and Lynette have one over by Quinault. They've got hiking trails all over the place."

"Sounds lovely."

"They've invited us to go up there with them. I told them I'd talk with you about it. Maybe in the fall."

"Perhaps."

"The first weekend in October might be nice. What do you say?" Shannon said it as if the plans were already in the works.

"We'll see, Shannon."

"I thought you liked cabins."

"I do. I'm just not ready to commit to it. I'll need some time to think it over and see where I am with my work."

"Like you needed some time to think about us?" Shannon said, looking straight into Dana's eyes. "Babe, this is crazy." She reached over and took Dana's hand, squeezing it softly. "You don't need time to think about us. You just need to come home to me. I love you. With all my heart, I love you. You know that. I don't know how else to show you. What haven't I provided?"

"That has nothing to do with it. It isn't about things."

"Then what? What can I do to get you back home where you belong?"

"Shannon, it isn't about you."

"What is it then?" she demanded.

"It's about me."

That didn't salve Shannon's curiosity. There were no gray areas to her reasoning. If Dana had an issue with their relationship, she wanted to know the exact day and date of the problem. She would explain it and resolve it. Cut and dry. But Dana didn't know what was wrong. At least not so she could put her finger on it. That was what the time on the houseboat was supposed to help her figure out. Time alone without Shannon's smile and touch to cloud her feelings. That's what she told herself. That's what she had told Morgan and Jamie. Even Steve and Juliana understood she needed a change. The precious time she needed to put things into perspective had somehow disappeared in the reality of her life. Shannon had called, asked her to dinner, and she agreed. How had she ended up across the table from Shannon, when she had been firmly committed not to? Dana had no idea. It seemed so easy when Jamie explained it. Why hadn't she listened more closely to her analytical reasoning?

"Dana?" Shannon snapped her fingers in front of Dana's face. "Earth to Dana. Dinner is here."

"Sorry. You know me when I get an idea for Ringlet." Dana fibbed, looking down at her plate, trying to focus.

"Oh yeah, that reminds me." Shannon stabbed one of Dana's mushrooms with her fork and took a bite. "This is great." She took another. "I have an idea for you. It's really funny. Have you got a notepad?"

"I'll remember. Tell me," Dana encouraged cheerfully, twirling a bite onto her spoon. Shannon had offered several ideas for cartoons and Dana appreciated her efforts but so far nothing sounded useful. Dana didn't tell her that. As far as Shannon knew, each and every one of her ideas had been added to Dana's in process file, awaiting development.

"You've got to write this down so you get all the nuances."

"Okay. One second." Dana took a bite then opened her purse and pulled out her pad and pen. "Shoot."

Shannon took a bite and a sip of wine while Dana sat holding the paper.

"Now, Ringlet and her owner are standing on the dock waiting to board the huge cruise ship. Those string streamers are flying everywhere. People are waving and cheering. The ship's horn is blasting. The whole departure scene. Ringlet has this really disgusted, pissed off look on her face."

Shannon looked over to see if Dana was taking notes. Dana jotted down a few things.

"Good. I got it," Dana said.

"And here's the kicker. Ready?"

"I'm ready."

"Ringlet has one of those steamer trunk stickers stuck right on her ass. You know the ones they used to put all over luggage fifty years ago. It's right there on her ass, big as day." Shannon laughed. "Can you believe it? A luggage sticker on the damn dog."

"That's good, Shannon." Dana gave a supportive chuckle. "Very funny."

"Did you get the description I gave you?"

"Yes. Cruise ship."

"Departing cruise ship."

"That's cute." Wouldn't Ringlet and her human already be onboard if the streamers were flying, Dana thought. And why would the sticker, something that isn't used anymore and her readers probably wouldn't understand, be on her ass? But Dana appreciated her effort.

"What have you got Ringlet doing this week?"

"She just finished obedience school. It was a four-part series."

"Did she graduate?"

"Sure," Dana giggled. "Not happily but she passed. She

graduated in a dunce cap with a tassel on the front. How's your work going? Did you get your quota for the Alaskan cruise?"

"Not yet, but I will. There's always a few who wait until the last minute, hoping for a discount. But I've never missed a quota."

"I'm glad things are going well."

"I didn't say things are going well," Shannon said loudly, pouring the last of the wine in Dana's glass. "For things to be going well, I'd need you to say you're finished with this houseboat nonsense and ready to move back home with me."

"Shannon, please," Dana whispered when the customers at a nearby table turned to stare. "Let's talk about this later. Not here."

"All right. Okay. We'll talk about it later."

"Thank you."

The rest of dinner was innocuous small talk about Juliana entering junior high school in the fall and Shannon's plans to expand the travel agency. Dana ate slowly, enjoying the food and the conversation. Shannon refrained from anymore insinuations about her decision to move into the houseboat. She paid the check and left a generous tip, refusing to allow Dana to pay for any of it.

"I ate too much," Shannon said, opening the door for Dana.

"Me, too. But it was good."

"It's always good here. Did you like the fettuccine?"

"Yes. Very delicious. Thank you. But I'm uncomfortable with you paying for my dinner. I really wish you'd let me pay for my own."

"No." Shannon took her arm and led her to the corner. "Let's head over to the boardwalk. I need to walk off that dinner."

They strolled along the boardwalk, past the marina and the little café where Dana sometimes sat to sip coffee and work on her sketches, past the observation platform and beyond the last access to the parking lot. The end of the boardwalk narrowed to a few feet wide where it looked out over Budd Bay. Dana rested her hands on the railing and stared out at the blinking buoy lights. She couldn't help smile, remembering how she had steered Jamie's boat toward just such a buoy off the tip of Hartstene Island.

"Isn't it a magnificent evening?" she said, closing her eyes and taking a deep breath. "I love the way the water looks when there's no wind. It looks just like ice. Like you could slide right across it."

"Ruth Ann said you came to her Lakefair party on their boat," Shannon said, kicking at a pebble. "Did you have a good time?"

"Yes. They're nice people."

"I'm still trying to talk them into going on this Alaskan cruise. They went last year but this one is going to be better. If you have a chance, mention it to them."

"Okay. Look, Shannon. There's a harbor seal." Dana pointed at the dark head moving through the water.

"That's an otter," Shannon said, giving it a disinterested glance.

"I think it's a harbor seal," she said, squinting at it. Dana remembered hearing Jamie explain the difference to Juliana. "It doesn't have external ear flaps."

"Whatever," Shannon laughed. "So, who else was at Ruth Ann's party? A bunch of their retired friends?"

"No one retired. Just a few of their friends I'd never met before."

"You didn't meet anyone interesting, I hope," she said with a chuckle.

"Interesting? Actually, I did. You met her."

"Who?"

"Dr. Jamie Hughes. The professor."

"Oh, her," Shannon dismissed her as insignificant.

"She's doing research in Puget Sound, something about oxygen saturation. I don't understand it but it sounds very interesting. It has something to do with what little fish eat before big fish eat them."

"Survival of the fittest."

"Jamie called it a food web. Microscopic organisms eaten by

algae eaten by small crustaceans and fish eaten by bigger fish then animals like seals and otters and so on." Dana smiled, surprised that she remembered the order.

"I've heard all I need to hear about that professor for one night." Shannon stood behind Dana, placing a hand on the railing on either side of her. "I don't care about microorganisms. This is our evening." She buried her face in Dana's hair and breathed in. "I noticed you still wear the perfume I gave you." She nuzzled her neck.

"Yes." Dana closed her eyes, feeling the warmth of Shannon's breath against her skin.

"What is it called?"

"Night Rapture."

"I like it on you. It's very sensual." Shannon's lips brushed Dana's neck. She eased the ponytail holder out of Dana's hair then combed her fingers through it. "Don't ever cut your hair, babe. There's nothing so incredible as the feel of your hair through my fingers," she whispered.

Dana had to admit she loved to have someone play with her hair. Ever since she was a child, the feel of fingers through her hair was a pleasing sensation. When Shannon did it just right, it made Dana shudder all over.

"You like that, don't you?" Shannon said, working her hands through the silken strands. She tugged slightly until Dana moaned. "You like me to play with your hair."

"Yes," she sighed, leaning back.

Shannon filled her hands with Dana's long hair and rested Dana's head on her chest.

"Tell me how much," she said, pressing a kiss against Dana's neck.

"I love it when you do that. I love to feel your hands in my hair." It was the truth. Dana couldn't hide the fact her hair was a source of arousal. And Shannon knew it.

"I want my hands in your hair, Dana. I want my hands all over your body." She turned Dana around and kissed her. "I need you," she insisted, taking Dana in her arms and devouring her mouth in a demanding kiss. Dana melted into Shannon's arms, just as she had always done. She fit perfectly against her chest, Shannon's familiar embrace strong around her. Dana folded her arms around Shannon's neck and leaned into the kiss.

"Come home with me tonight, sweetheart," Shannon whispered, holding her close.

Dana's mind was in a whirl. It had been months since she last lay in Shannon's arms, the smell of their lovemaking thick around them. Months since they had put their bickering aside and found sweet satisfaction in each other's touch and taste. Shannon's arms were still warm and inviting. Her kiss still enticed Dana beyond all reason. Standing there on the boardwalk, the moonlight shimmering across the bay and Shannon's whisper calling her to bed, it was hard for Dana to think clearly. She couldn't think of a reason not to go with her. At that moment she couldn't remember why she moved out in the first place. Giving in to Shannon had felt right four years ago and it felt right tonight.

Shannon slipped her arm around Dana's waist and headed them back up the boardwalk.

"I can't wait to feel you against me. I'm going to make you sorry you waited so long," Shannon said, nuzzling her. Dana closed her eyes as they walked along, guided by Shannon's purposeful strides.

"Remember the time we drove over to Ocean Shores?" Shannon said. "I made a reservation at that hotel with a view of the beach and the breakers coming in."

"Last fall," Dana replied.

"It was rainy. I drove right out onto the beach at low tide and we watched the sunset."

"Yes, I remember."

"We were making out in the car. You always were a sucker for romantic settings."

"It was raining so hard we couldn't see out the windows most of the time." Dana remembered being thankful for the heavy rain since theirs wasn't the only car on the beach.

"God, you were hot that night, babe. I couldn't get enough

of you."

Dana opened her eyes as a shudder shot up her spine. Yes, she remembered that evening. In spite of the chilly temperatures and nearby cars, Shannon had talked her out of her clothes and down on the seat for over an hour of lovemaking. Even though Dana pleaded with her to return to the room, Shannon insisted she couldn't wait. But yes, it was good sex. Sex with Shannon was always good. She was a passionate and generous lover. The first time Dana slept with her had been one of those nights she had always dreamed of. The candlelit room had glowed. Rain fell softly against the window. Between bouts of the lovemaking, they sipped wine and confessed their innermost secrets.

"Damn. What am I thinking?" Shannon chuckled. "We've got the houseboat right there." She pointed over the railing at the marina below. "I should be glad you rented the damn thing. What's the code for the gate?"

Dana was still lost in her memories, the thought of them pushing her along blindly. She punched in the code and Shannon opened the gate.

"Key?" Shannon said as they descended the gangplank and headed down the dock toward the houseboat.

Dana handed her the key, the new one Morgan had given her.

"Where's your key ring?" she asked, stepping onto the rear deck and unlocking the door. She pushed it open and followed Dana inside.

"Oh, I forgot to take it," Dana said, noticing the key ring hanging on the hook behind the door. "I grabbed the single key. It was easier to slip in my pocket." She didn't know why she had taken the single key instead of the key ring. One of those mindless habits, perhaps. "Excuse me for a minute," she said and stepped into the bathroom. When she came out, Shannon was standing on the deck looking out at the city lights.

"Beautiful, isn't it?" Dana said, joining her.

Shannon wiped her hand along the railing, turned, and sat on it.

"Do you really like living here?"

"Yes. It's fun. Very inspirational for my work."

"Isn't it a little confining?" Shannon crossed her arms and stared inside at the rooms.

"Not really. It's cozy. I love to sit out here in the evening and watch the sailboats come in from a day of sailing. Sometimes I eat my dinner out here."

"I'm talking about inside. Not outside. Sure, it's wide open on the deck. All you've got is railing around you and a roof over your head. Inside, you've barely got room to stand up."

"That's just in the loft. It's really quite roomy for a houseboat. I've got plenty of room for my desk. The sofa becomes a bed when Juliana stays overnight. And the galley—" she began but Shannon interrupted.

"The galley?" she said with a sarcastic smirk. "Have you gone nautical?"

"Kitchen. Galley. It's the same thing. Anyway, it has everything a house kitchen has. Sure the appliances are apartment-sized but most of the time it's just me. And the loft has a low ceiling for a reason. It's to lower the center of gravity and reduce the sway."

"Who told you that? The landlady trying to talk you into renting it?" Shannon frowned.

"Jamie told me. She said many stationary houseboats have loft bedrooms. They're intended for sleeping so the ceilings can be lower to reduce sway and keep a more pleasing profile."

"Jamie again. The old professor must be a whiz at Trivial Pursuit."

Dana smiled to herself. Shannon was right. Jamie had even admitted being full of useless trivia.

"By the way, how did Jamie know you have a low ceiling in the bedroom?" Shannon asked suspiciously. "Has she been on the houseboat?"

"Yes."

"When?"

"A few days ago. She came by to return something." Dana caught herself. She didn't want to admit she had lost the key ring, even if it was only temporary.

"Return what?"

"It was nothing. Just something I left at Ruth Ann's during the party."

"What?" Shannon insisted.

"My key ring. Jamie was nice enough to return it."

"You left the key ring at Ruth Ann's? The one I gave you? The gold one?"

"I just forgot it."

"For two weeks? They just live over there," she said, nodding her head across the marina. "Why didn't you go get it the next day? Hell, Dana. Why didn't you go back and get it that night?"

Dana knew she had boxed herself into a corner. If she said she just forgot to go get it, Shannon would think she didn't care about it. One fib might grow into a string of lies she couldn't defend.

"I couldn't go get it, Shannon. I couldn't get it because it was at the bottom of the bay."

"WHAT?!"

"It got knocked overboard. It was an accident but it fell off the railing of Ruth Ann and Connie's boat during the party."

"What was it doing on the railing?"

"I was showing it to Jamie and I set it on the railing. It was a wide board and I didn't think it would get knocked off. And before you say anything else, yes, I'm well aware how stupid that was. I wasn't thinking. And for that week when I thought it was lost, I felt terrible about it."

"Who knocked it off?" Shannon stared at her.

"We both did. I mean, both of our hands grabbed for it at the same time and we both missed. Before we knew it, it plunked into the water and sank."

"What's that? A bogus replacement?" Shannon pointed at the key ring hanging on the hook. "A cheap imitation?"

"No. That's the one you gave me."

"Yeah, right. I'm not stupid, Dana. I know what happens when you drop something into the bay. The bottom is nothing but mud. I remember when we went crabbing off Cooper Point. We were ankle deep in mud."

"That's right. Jamie told me it was nearly impossible to find anything once it went overboard but she found it."

Shannon smirked skeptically and kept her arms crossed.

"She did," Dana insisted. "She scuba dives. She went down and found it. She said it landed in some seaweed and tarnished. Since it hadn't been in the salt water that long, it polished up beautifully. You saw it. It looks just like new."

"Jamie said, eh?" Shannon wasn't happy and Dana knew it. "Seems like this Dr. Jamie whatever her name is sure hangs around a lot."

"Hughes. Dr. Jamie Hughes. And she doesn't hang around a lot. But yes, she was there at the party on the boat. And Shannon, I'll forever be grateful to her for finding the key ring and returning it to me," Dana said, touching Shannon's arm affectionately. "If she hadn't, I wouldn't have it today."

"If she hadn't knocked it overboard, it wouldn't have been on the bottom of the bay to begin with."

"Please don't look at it that way, honey," Dana moved against her. "It was an accident and she recovered it for me. That's the important thing."

"I can't help wonder why you put it on the railing in the first place."

"I know. I know. It was a dumb thing to do. I kicked myself a million times about it." Dana rested her head on Shannon's shoulder, trying to console her anger. "I promise I'll never do that again. I'll never ever treat it so carelessly."

"It sounds like you expect me to be thankful you met this Dr. Hughes."

"I just don't want you to be mad. I shouldn't have mentioned anything about it. I can see it upset you and I'm sorry. The key ring was a gift and I didn't take care of it. Forgive me." Dana heard her own voice saying those things, and dimly wondered about the decisions she'd been trying to make.

"Promise me you'll take care of it. I didn't get it at a dime store, you know."

"I promise."

"And promise you won't have Dr. Hughes here on the houseboat again."

"What does that have to do with the key ring?"

"Promise."

"I'm not sure that's relevant, Shannon."

Shannon wrapped her arms around Dana, trapping her in a hard embrace.

"It is because I love you. Whatever problems we have are our private business. We'll work them out. The two of us. We don't need Ruth Ann or Connie or your brother. And we certainly don't need that professor. You said it yourself. You said you needed to be alone and I respect that. You shouldn't let anyone interfere. If you do need to talk to somebody, the logical person should be me."

"I know what you're saying, but it isn't like that. Jamie isn't interfering. She isn't like that at all."

"So she won't be here hanging around the houseboat again?"

Dana didn't agree. To agree meant denying a source of support and encouragement. She may not be the answer to all Dana's problems but having Jamie's advice was not something she wanted to surrender. Jamie had the art of gentle reason. Shannon did not.

"I can't promise that, Shannon. I don't expect her on the houseboat but I can't promise she'll never come by."

Shannon gave Dana a disappointed glare and stormed inside.

"I'm sorry. It doesn't mean anything but I can't be positive," Dana said, following her. "She's doing research in the harbor. If she stops by to say hello, what am I supposed to do? Tell her she can't come in?"

Shannon took the key ring from the hook and examined it.

"All right. You can invite her in. In fact, tell her thank you for me for recovering this." She placed the key ring in Dana's hand.

"Tell her I appreciate it."

"I will." Dana rehung it.

"Let's not talk about her anymore. She has nothing to do with you and me." Shannon collected Dana's hands and kissed them. "Let's talk about us."

"I thought we were."

"Let's talk about something else," Shannon said, wrapping Dana in a hug. "How about let's talk about what we came down here for? Better yet, let's not talk at all," she whispered, nibbling Dana's neck. "I can't wait much longer. Why don't you show me your loft?" She cupped her hands around Dana's bottom, rubbing herself against her.

"Shannon," Dana said, trying to push away. "Stop."

"Why?" Shannon slid her hand down to Dana's crotch, fondling her mound through her slacks.

"Please, stop," she said and stepped away from Shannon's grip.

"My God, babe. You've got me all hot and then you shut me down. What's going on here? I thought we were going to make love."

"Please don't ask me," Dana said, standing stiffly.

"I thought we decided this is what you wanted." Shannon whispered, kissing Dana's neck as she cupped a hand over her breast.

"I know it sounded like that, but I can't. It isn't the right time. Please," she said. She shoved Shannon's hand away and went to the window.

"I don't understand."

"I know you don't. I'm sorry but please, if you love me, don't force this."

"Is that the problem, Dana? Is that why you moved out? Are you not satisfied with our sex life?" Shannon grabbed Dana's arm and turned her around.

"No. It isn't the sex."

"Then what?" Shannon said, raising her voice.

"I don't know," Dana replied as tears filled her eyes. "I just don't know."

"You don't know what's wrong, but you know we can't fuck. How am I supposed to understand this? How can I help if you won't tell me what I should do?" Shannon stared at Dana.

"I'm sorry!" Dana began to cry. She turned away, burying her face in her hands. As she sobbed, all Dana could hear was the door slamming behind Shannon.

Chapter 15

Jamie knocked on the door of the houseboat, expecting Dana to answer with her usual warm smile. When no one answered she knocked again. The miniblind moved and she heard the lock being turned. The door opened a crack and an eye appeared in the opening.

"Hello, Jamie," Juliana sniffled.

"Hi, Juliana." Jamie expected her to open the door and let her in, but she didn't.

"Aunt Dana isn't here." Her voice was weak and vulnerable.

"Are you okay, Juliana?" Jamie squinted through the crack. Juliana's eyes were red and swollen. She'd clearly been crying.

"I can't let you in. I'm not supposed to be here."

"Dana doesn't know you're here?"

"No. You won't tell her, will you?"

Jamie immediately assessed the situation. Something was

wrong. Juliana was upset and had fled to her Aunt Dana's for refuge but no one was home.

"That depends on what's wrong. Why don't you tell me why you're hiding out in Dana's houseboat? Then, we can decide how much of it she needs to know." Jamie leaned closer and whispered through the opening. "Maybe we can figure it out together."

Juliana sniffled and slowly opened the door just enough for Jamie to slip through. The houseboat was dark and smelled stuffy. All the blinds were drawn. Juliana was wrapped in a blanket. The pillow on the sofa told Jamie she had been napping. Her hair looked like two otters had been fighting in it. Tearstains streaked her cheeks. Wadded tissue littered the floor next to the sofa. The head of a stuffed animal peeked out the top of the blanket that Juliana kept clutched around herself. Jamie thought it must be pretty severe if whatever was wrong warranted a stuffed animal for comfort. Juliana stood by the front door, the blanket wrapped up around her neck, exposing only her eyes, nose and the top if her head. She looked frightened.

"Shall we open a couple of windows? I'm sure Dana wouldn't mind," Jamie said, raising the blinds over the table.

"NO! Don't," Juliana said, covering her face with the blanket.

"Why not? It's stuffy in here." Jamie raised one window a few inches and waved her hand in front of it, encouraging an exchange of air.

"I don't want anyone to know I'm here."

"Juliana, are you playing hooky?"

"No. It's still summer vacation."

"Then what's the big mystery? Are you supposed to be doing something you don't want to do?"

"No," she whined. "Do you know where my aunt is?"

"No. I thought she'd be here. She left her jacket at my office and I was returning it." Jamie hung the jacket over the bathroom doorknob. "Do you need her? I could call her on my cell and see where she is." She unhooked her cell phone from her waistband.

"Don't do that," Juliana insisted.

"I could just tell her you're here and find out when she'll be back. I won't say anything else," Jamie said, hoping to reassure Juliana she was on her side.

"She'd just freak out and rush home to see what's wrong."

"Okay. I won't call her, at least, not yet. But you're going to have to give me a reason why I shouldn't. I'm your friend, Juliana. If you've got a problem and your dad or aunt aren't around to help you, I'll be glad to listen. I'm a pretty fair listener. At least that's what my students tell me." Jamie winked.

"You can't help." She peeked over the top of the blanket. "No one can." She started to cry again.

"I can try to help." Jamie draped an arm around Juliana's shoulders and held her as she cried. "Come sit on the sofa and tell me what's wrong. You might be surprised. You're smart and I'm older. Between the two of us, we might be able to figure it out." Juliana cried even harder, burying her face against Jamie's side. "Oh, sweetie," Jamie cooed, wrapping her in a bear hug. "Don't cry. It can't be that bad."

"It is," Juliana said, muffled against Jamie's shirt. "It's terrible. It's worse than terrible." She continued to sob, her tears and nose making a wet spot on Jamie's shirt.

"Let's sit down and decide just how terrible we're talking about here." Jamie guided her to the sofa and sat down, Juliana still clinging to her side.

"The worst kind," she said, wiping her nose on the blanket.

From her personal memory of being twelve, Jamie had made a mental list of possible catastrophes Juliana might be facing. Massive pimple breakout. A best friend moving away. Allowance reduction. Being grounded. At twelve, surely it couldn't be a problem with her love life.

"Could I have a hint?"

"It's way too bad to tell you," she said dramatically.

"Here's how you do it. Pick a word to describe the problem. Just one word. The absolute worse thing you could say about it and spit it right out. That way you've got the bad part out of the way. For instance, if the problem was about a boyfriend, you just say Mike or Josh or whatever his name is. Just spit his name right out there. Now, I'm going to count to three. When I get there, you say the word and we'll take it from there. What do you say?" Jamie smiled encouragement.

"Okay," Juliana said meekly.

"Here we go." Jamie kept an arm around her for support. "One, two, three."

"Even if it's really, really bad, you won't hate me?"

"I promise." Jamie held up her hand as a pledge.

"Okay. I'm ready." Juliana hunched her shoulders as if bracing herself.

"One, two, and three."

"Cancer," Juliana said then turned her face up to Jamie. "I've got cancer, Jamie." She said it as if the weight of the world was on her young head.

"WHAT?!" Jamie gasped.

"It's true. I've got cancer. It's the really bad kind. Libby's mom has cancer. She has to wear a bandana because all her hair fell out. My hair has already started to fall out." Juliana's chin quivered as she told her fate.

"Does Dana know about this?"

"No one knows yet."

"Who told you you've got cancer, Juliana?"

"It's one of those things you just know," she said fearfully.

"Juliana." Jamie combed her fingers through the child's tangled hair. "Just because you are losing some of your hair doesn't mean you have cancer."

"Oh, I know."

"What makes you think you have cancer?" The fear Jamie felt with Juliana's first statement was fading. The word cancer held a powerful sense of dread. She didn't want to belittle Juliana's problem but Jamie was beginning to think the diagnosis was just a little premature.

"I just know it, Jamie."

"How long have you had the symptoms?" Jamie decided to try a different tack. "A long time or just a few days?"

"Not very long."

"How long?"

"Since last night."

"That recent? Sweetie, where is your cancer? All over or in just one place?"

"My stomach." Jamie could tell even through the blanket, Juliana was holding her lower gut.

"Juliana," Jamie said, locking a flyaway strand of hair behind her ear. "Have you been throwing up and had diarrhea?"

"No. That just means you have an upset stomach. This is worse. Way worse."

Jamie had eliminated the most obvious ailments. There was another possibility. Diagnosing this would open a box of questions she wasn't sure she was the right person to answer.

"Sweetie, did it start with cramps way down low in your tummy?"

"Yes. Really bad ones."

"Then you got out of bed and there was blood on the sheets?"

Juliana looked up at Jamie with terrified eyes and trembling chin.

"Yes. There was blood everywhere. Tons of it. I'll probably need a trans, trans, trans-something."

"Transfusion?"

"Yes. Libby's mom had one. That's where they give you more blood from somebody else. But it doesn't hurt. Libby said her mom was listening to her iPod and writing Christmas cards while she had one."

Jamie bit down on her lip to keep from smiling her relief. What Jamie suspected Juliana had was a very rude and early introduction to her menstrual cycle.

"Juliana, I don't think you have cancer. In fact, I'm sure of it," she said confidently.

"Yes, I do, Jamie. My whole insides are leaking out."

"I think what you are experiencing is your first menstrual cycle. You're a little young. It usually starts around thirteen or

191

fourteen but some girls start early. And your first time can be a shock."

"You mean my period?" Her eyes widened.

"Yes."

"I know all about that. We had a movie in school about it. But mine is much worse. The teacher said we would lose about two tablespoons of blood. I've lost way more than two tablespoons. I'm telling you, it was gallons and gallons. It was everywhere." She extended her arms from under the blanket and broadcast them.

"Sweetie, has anyone talked with you about starting your period? Told you what you need to do?"

"Dad brought me some panty liners you stick on the inside of your underwear. He put the box under the sink in the bathroom. That's how I know this is not just my period. I'm bleeding way too much for panty liners. I'd need a whole box."

"Are you wearing anything now?" Jamie asked, resisting the urge to check Dana's couch.

"Not those tiny liner things. They're useless."

"What then?"

"Don't tell but I'm using one of Aunt Dana's hand towels. I used three from home. I threw them away. I don't want anyone to get my cancer."

"Juliana, you do *not* have cancer," Jamie said, intercepting another onslaught of tears. "You have started your period. That's all. I know it seems like you're going to bleed to death sometimes but you really haven't lost that much blood. I don't want to go into details but take it from me, a veteran of many a monthly campaign, you are just doing what all women do. I know it's gross and messy. But it will get easier."

"You still have your period? I thought old people didn't do it anymore."

"Sure." Jamie chuckled. "I'm not that old. And I bet your Aunt Dana has them too. Most women have them until they're fifty or so. It's one of those cruel jokes of nature. Even when the factory is abandoned the plumbing still works."

"You mean I'll bleed like this for forty years?" Juliana gasped in horror.

"No. It won't always be like your first one." Jamie saw no reason to scare the child. "You'll have some months when you barely know you're having a visit from your friend."

"Friend?"

"That's what some girls call it." Jamie wasn't going to tell her what that meant either. She would leave sex education to her family.

The rattle of the doorknob caught their attention. The door opened and Dana stepped in, gasping in surprise.

"Hello," Jamie said.

"Hi, Aunt Dana."

"Hello. Should I be expecting company?"

"I stopped by to return your jacket," Jamie said, standing up. "You left it in my office that time you came to see me."

"Oh," Dana said, staring down at Juliana. "Honey, what are you doing here? Are you okay?"

Juliana looked up at Jamie.

"Juliana would like to have a little talk with you. She isn't feeling well and could use a bit of support."

"Are you sick?" Dana dropped her purse on the sofa and felt Juliana's forehead. "Do you have a temperature? You look pale."

"She doesn't have a temperature. That isn't where the problem lies."

"Do you have a stomachache?" Dana asked, sitting next to her on the sofa and stroking her face. Juliana nodded feebly. "Did you eat something that didn't agree with you? Let me see if I have some Pepto-Bismol." Dana headed for the bathroom.

"Maybe you should see if you have any Midol instead," Jamie said, smiling down at Juliana.

"Midol?" Dana asked curiously then looked over at her niece. "Juliana? Oh, my gosh. Midol?" Dana rushed back to the sofa and took Juliana's face in her hands. "You've started your period?" Dana made it sound like she had just won an Olympic medal. "When?"

"Last night," Juliana said only slightly less than tragically.

"Oh, honey." She wrapped her in a hug. "That's wonderful." Dana held onto Juliana but rolled her eyes up to Jamie and grimaced as if to say this was a surprise.

"I have to go," Jamie said, opening the door.

"You don't have to leave," Dana said.

"I'm interviewing a new lab tech in an hour." She checked her watch. "By the way, Juliana may need to discuss adequate and appropriate feminine supplies."

"Thank you, Jamie," Dana said. "I appreciate your help and concern. Juliana does too, don't you, honey?"

Juliana peeked out of Dana's hug and nodded.

"Thank you, Jamie," she said.

"You're welcome, kiddo. Anytime." She gave her a wink. "And Dana, drop me an e-mail and let me know how things are going with your dilemma." She smiled then left, closing the door behind her.

Chapter 16

For the next two weeks Dana and Jamie e-mailed back and forth about everything from Jamie's research to Dana's family and her work on Ringlet. Dana was not afraid to reveal her innermost feelings and fears about what she should do. In return, Jamie offered understanding and support. Her advice opened Dana's eyes and let her guide herself. Jamie asked how Dana felt when she was with Shannon. How did she feel when they were apart? What were Shannon's good points and her bad? She encouraged Dana to be honest with herself. And for her efforts, Dana seemed happy, happier than she had been in months.

It was midmorning when Dana took her laptop out onto the deck, sat cross-legged in the wicker rocker and opened Jamie's e-mail.

Good morning. What's new in Budd Bay? Let me guess. You're sitting on the deck, sipping coffee and drawing cartoons? -- J.H.

Dana grinned as she opened a reply page.

Good morning, Jamie. You're close. All but the cartoon thing. I did that earlier. I'm taking a break. How about you? How's the algae? You said you were having trouble with the tests. Anything I can do? Of course, I wouldn't know an algae if I met one but I'm willing to offer assistance. It's only fair. After all, you have been there for me. -Dana.

Dana sent it, laughing at what Jamie was going to think. The reply took only a minute.

I'll be glad to introduce you to one of the algae species next time you come to the lab. Any plans to do that? P.S. Loved Ringlet yesterday. - J.H.

Dana smiled curiously as she wrote her reply.

I didn't know Ringlet was being carried in biology journals. Or is the professor actually reading real people magazines? I can't believe it. I have actually influenced the scientific community after all. Ringlet will be pleased. -Dana.

Dana hit the send key then went to make a cup of coffee, expecting Jamie's reply to be waiting when she returned but she had nothing in her inbox. After several minutes she was beginning to think she had said something wrong.

Are you there? - Dana

She sent the message and waited again. A few minutes later, an e-mail popped up.

Yes. Sorry. I was attacked by a rampant herd of algae. –J.H.

Dana burst out laughing and sent a reply.

Explain, please. Do I need to send paramedics? -Dana

Another few minutes went by before Jamie replied.

I spilled a beaker of algae suspension down my pants, converting clean tan slacks into a lovely asparagus green color. –J.H.

Dana quickly replied.

My sincerest sympathy. Might I suggest you go change? -Dana

I may have to do that. But first tell me what you drew for Ringlet. I could use a good laugh. –J.H.

I've scanned them into the computer. I'll e-mail you one. –Dana

Dana looked through the sketches she had entered, deciding which one to send. She chose the one with Ringlet curled up on the foot of her human's bed. It was the middle of the night. The woman was sound asleep with her mouth open and she was snoring loudly. Ringlet's ears were back and her forehead was furrowed disgustedly as she watched her human sleep. The bubble over Ringlet's head read: *She can make THAT noise but I can't bark at the mailman. Go figure.*

Dana attached the cartoon to her e-mail and sent it to Jamie. She sat back and waited for her reply. It didn't take long.

LOLOLOL I love it. GREAT CARTOON!!! How did you know I snore like that? –J.H.

Everybody snores, don't they? I'm sure I snore loud enough to keep the seagulls off the roof. -Dana

Dana waited but there was no reply. A few minutes later her cell phone rang. It was Jamie.

"Hello, Dr. Algae pants." Dana said with a little giggle. "What's the matter? Are you getting writer's cramp?" She loved the way she and Jamie could joke about almost anything.

"Yes. As a matter of fact, I am." She laughed. "But it wasn't from e-mailing you. I've been working on a report."

"A report on what? And remember I'm not a science brain so use small words."

"Oxygen saturation monitoring."

"When you aren't doing that what else do you do? Hobbies, I mean. Other than sailing and scuba diving, of course."

"Gosh. There's more to life than that?" Jamie chuckled.

"Yes, there is."

"Like what?"

"I don't know. There are a lot of things to do in and around Olympia. Hiking, bicycling, tennis, museums, music."

"I've seen all the museums in Seattle and Portland. As for music, I can't play a musical instrument unless you count an iPod. I like to listen to music though. Jazz, soft rock, country."

"Now there's something." Dana brightened. "There's going to be a concert in the park next to the boardwalk. A group is going to sing. They set up a little stage, and people come and sit in the grass. They had one last month. It was a great way to spend a couple hours. Would you like to go with me?"

"When?" Jamie said, showing interest.

"Tonight at seven thirty."

"Okay."

"Great. I'll meet you at the bench outside the security gate about seven fifteen. I know it will be kind of late but would you like me to make us a sack lunch? We can have dinner on a blanket."

"You don't have to do that," Jamie said.

"But I want to. What kind of sandwich would you like, or do you want something else?"

"Surprise me. Anything you make is fine with me. What can I bring?"

"Nothing."

"With your permission, may I take care of the beverage?"

"Be my guest," Dana said.

"I'll meet you there. And now, I think I should go change. I'm starting to smell like Budd Bay at low tide."

Dana smiled as she hung up the telephone. She had a date with Dr. Hughes for some reason other than to talk about Shannon. Just a plain old date and she was delighted. Dana walked to the grocery store and collected what she needed for their picnic. She spent twenty minutes trying on clothes, deciding what to wear. She dug in the back of the closet for her white jeans and white sandals. She added a teal blue blouse. She wore silver earrings with her hair down and loose. Shannon didn't like Dana to wear white jeans out in public. She said they were too revealing. Dana had argued they didn't show anything, but Shannon had been sure everyone would stare at her. Dana thought of Shannon's attitude from the other night and placed the white jeans on her bed. She would wear them anyway.

She picked up the picnic basket and headed up the dock. As she was letting herself out of the security gate, she caught her shirt on an exposed fence wire and popped off the top button. It rolled down the gangplank and dropped into the water.

"Oh, polliwogs," she muttered, looking down at her shirt.

She pulled the placket together to see if it was noticeable. It was, at least a little. She would have to go back and change, but as she reopened the gate she could hear Jamie.

"Hello, Dana," she called, striding up the boardwalk with a small tote bag over her shoulder.

"Hi," Dana said, straightening her shirt, hoping it would stay closed. "You're right on time."

Jamie was wearing a Capital State University T-shirt and well fitting jeans that showed off her long, lean legs.

"You don't look dressed for a picnic," Jamie said, looking Dana up and down. "You look nice."

"Thank you. You look good yourself." To keep her eyes off the sexy way Jamie's jeans fit through the crotch, Dana straightened the hem of Jamie's sleeve. "You should dress like this more often. And not just when you're on your boat."

"I'll take it under advisement," Jamie said, carrying the basket for Dana. "Where would you like to sit?"

"Let's find a place away from the sidewalk and away from the playground," Dana said, leading the way. They found a clear spot at the edge of the park and spread out the blanket.

"What's in here?" Jamie asked, holding up the basket. "It weighs a ton. You must have made more than just a sandwich."

"A little of this and a little of that. Have a seat and I'll show you." Dana took her place on the blanket and patted the blanket for Jamie to sit down. "What did you bring?"

"You aren't supposed to have open liquor bottles in the park so I had to improvise," she leaned in and whispered as she pulled out a thermos and two plastic cups. "Wine coolers."

"Oh, goodie," Dana giggled. "I thought something like that would taste good with dinner. It sure pays to have a smart professor supplying the beverage."

"Hey, I don't have a PhD for nothing," Jamie said then winked. "May I offer you a little thermos refreshment?" She poured them each a glass.

"Thank you very much, Doctor," Dana said and took a sip. "That's good."

"The woman at the liquor store said this was the perfect thing for a picnic. Light yet flirty." She took a sip. "I have a question. How the heck can wine be flirty? Where do they get these adjectives for wine?"

"I have no idea. I only know wine is good if I like the taste." Dana nestled her cup in the grass and went about unpacking the basket.

"What all do you have in there?" Jamie said, peeking in to see what Dana had packed.

"We are starting off with a salad," she said, taking out two small Tupperware dishes. "And then we have an assortment of cheeses and deli meats." She lined up several baggies on the blanket. Dana then pulled out a loaf of French bread. "What's a picnic without crusty bread and herb-flavored oil to dip it in? I made olive oil with a little balsamic vinegar, dill, oregano and parsley. And for dessert we are having brownies." She held up a baggie with homemade brownies.

"You made all of this just for the two of us? Wow. You can pack my picnics anytime, Dana."

Dana noticed Jamie had trouble keeping her eyes on what she was eating. Instead, her gaze kept drifting back to Dana's shirt. Dana suddenly remembered her missing button. She hadn't thought of it since they crossed the park and sat down on the blanket. She guessed the top of her bra was visible but nothing more. Dana gasped when she looked down and saw not only was her top button missing but the next two buttons were open as well, exposing her to the waist. She shrieked and pulled her shirt closed.

"Nice bra." Jamie smiled.

"Why didn't you say something?" Dana said, re-buttoning her shirt as she blushed.

"Why?" Jamie broke off a piece of bread and dipped it in the oil.

"Because I was sitting here with my shirt open, that's why."

"I may be a stuffy old science professor but I'm not stupid." Jamie leaned over and whispered. "I liked the view."

"I should have gone back and changed my shirt when I popped off the button," Dana said, doing her best to keep the placket closed.

"I'm glad you didn't. And you shouldn't be embarrassed. You look very nice with your blouse open. You've seen me in my swimsuit top."

"But that's different."

"Why? Because my swimsuit top is made to be worn outside and your bra isn't?"

"Something like that, yes."

"Would you feel better if I took off my T-shirt and sat here in my bra?" Jamie began pulling her shirt out of the waistband of her jeans.

"No! Don't do that." Dana instantly wished she hadn't stopped her. Jamie looked good in her swimsuit top. Dana was sure she would look even better in her bra.

"I won't if you promise not to get all stressed out about your missing button."

"Okay, I promise. But you have to tell me if my shirt is open and I'm making a spectacle of myself," Dana said, smoothing her shirt.

"I can't promise that." Jamie chuckled.

"Jamie!" Dana scowled.

"Well, I can't. Like I said, I like the view. Now eat your dinner. This cheese is delicious." She handed Dana a piece. "Tell me some more of your cartoon ideas. What else is Ringlet up to these days?"

"My publisher asked for me to provide panels for each of the holidays. For Halloween I've got Ringlet dressed up in a witch's costume. Black hat and all. She has a smug little look on her face, naturally."

"Naturally."

"At her feet are the chewed shredded remains of a stuffed black cat. The bubble over her head reads – *Ah, the power of a witch.*"

Jamie laughed.

"The other one is Ringlet running in circles, frantically trying to bite her rear end." Dana chomped her fingers through the air. "She has a determined, frenzied look on her face. The bubble over her head reads: *Fleas are like real estate. It's all about location, location, location.*"

Jamie laughed even louder, nearly spilling her wine.

"I love them. That's great," she said, continuing to chuckle. "Any more?"

"That's it for today. I've got some ideas but nothing concrete."

"I'm impressed. I love your work. You're very talented, Dana."

It was Dana's turn to laugh.

"It doesn't take much talent to draw a dog humping its master's leg," she said with a shy blush.

"It takes talent to find humor in everyday life and portray it through a dog's point of view."

"Thank you but I don't necessarily think that's talent."

"What do you call it?"

"Opportunistic."

"Okay, you found a market and filled it. But that takes talent, too," Jamie said, tweaking the end of Dana's nose. "Be proud of what you have accomplished."

"Oh, I am. I'm very grateful to the powers that be for providing this opportunity to me. It pays the bills. It lets me be creative. And I get to express some of my opinions, albeit surreptitiously."

"Like what?"

"Like the cartoon I did with Ringlet's human participating in a tree-hugger's sit-in, protesting clear-cutting forests. Everyone is entitled to their opinion but I bet most of those protestors live in wood-framed houses. How can you complain about harvesting trees if you consume wood in your habitat? To have any credibility, shouldn't they use alternate building materials? So I put Ringlet in the protest. She is wearing a placard that reads *Save a tree, use a hydrant.*"

Jamie smiled.

"I love it when you allow Ringlet to be a little irreverent."

"Ringlet is totally unabashed, even when I can't be," Dana said. "I know Juliana sees my cartoons so I have to be careful what I draw."

"How is Juliana?"

"Fine. They left yesterday. Steve has a conference in San Diego and he took her along. They are going to the zoo and aquarium. You should have heard her. She insisted on taking an extra camera along so she could take lots of pictures to show you all about it."

"That's great. She'll love them both. How long will they be gone?"

"Two weeks. This is their big father and daughter trip. They go someplace special every year. Last year it was Disney World in Florida. Next year he is talking about taking her to Japan."

"You'll miss them, I'm sure. It comes at a critical time for you, doesn't it?"

Dana nodded.

"How are things going with Shannon? Do you think you'll be ready to make a decision before the end of your three months?"

"I have no idea. Sometimes I think I know what I want. Other times, I'm not at all sure."

"What was the last thing you two argued about?"

"We didn't argue. We just had disagreements."

"Like what? Tell me some of the things you disagreed about."

"Well, the week before I moved out, I was planning a surprise dinner for Shannon. I didn't do all the cooking but most of it. I worked at home so it was easier for me to start things in the afternoon before she got home. I had seen a recipe in a magazine I thought she'd like. I was going to make a fabulous salad and her favorite vegetables to go with it. I worked for hours peeling shrimp and sautéing garlic cloves." Dana laughed and rolled her eyes. "I thought I was super chef or something. Anyway, Shannon came home unexpectedly in the middle of the afternoon. She asked what I was doing, and I told her it was a surprise. Shannon doesn't like surprises. She always wants to know what's going on. I told her I hated to spoil the surprise but she was insistent. She loves shrimp and Italian food with garlic, rich food. But for some unknown reason that day she hated shrimp and garlic. In fact, she didn't like anything I was making. Even the wine was wrong. The funny thing is, she had bought the wine. Said it was a good wine for seafood. She rummaged around in the freezer and found chicken breasts. She wanted fried chicken. I told her I had already started the shrimp and I hated to waste them. She said I could make shrimp cocktail if I wanted."

"Did you make fried chicken?" Jamie asked.

"Yes. But I made the shrimp dish, too."

"Did she do that often?"

"A couple times. She preferred to help plan the meals. Usually, I didn't mind." Dana giggled devilishly. "One time she called to ask what I was making for dinner. I told her spaghetti and meatballs. She said that sounded good but that's exactly what she had for lunch so I better fix something else. Then I told her that I meant I was making turkey tetrazzini. She was not happy that I tricked her. I knew she didn't have spaghetti for lunch. That was just her excuse when I planned something without asking her first."

"Do you mind if I say Shannon sounds like a control freak?" Jamie said delicately.

"I came to realize that."

"Other than meals, what else has she insisted on?"

Dana took a bite of cheese and smiled at the ground as she thought.

"Not much. Just things like the sheets we bought. She had to have beige six hundred count Egyptian cotton. And the color of the towels in the guest bathroom. The paint in my office. Every hotel and restaurant reservation. Where and when I had the oil changed in my car. What lingerie I wore. My lipstick, shampoo, conditioner and hairstyle. Things like that." Dana knew just how that sounded.

"Did you ever feel like you were sleeping with the enemy?"

"I know it sounds that way but Shannon was a very tender gentle person."

"You mean she was a tender gentle lover?"

"Yes. Very."

"Her controlling ways didn't enter the bedroom?" Jamie said.

"No, never. Well, if you mean was she forceful and domineering, no. She wasn't."

"But?"

"But lovemaking was usually her idea. Not mine."

"You mean you made love when it suited her? And if you were in the mood and suggested it, she wasn't?"

"That's right. Hey, I'm no nun," Dana laughed. "A girl has needs." She couldn't believe she confessed that to Jamie. She grimaced and clutched her hands to her head. "Now I'm completely embarrassed. First I flash my boobs for all to see, then I confess I like sex."

"What's wrong with that? You are a vibrant, attractive woman. What's wrong with admitting you enjoy sex?"

"How about you? Do you have needs?"

"As you said, I'm no nun either," Jamie said. "But we're talking about you, not me."

"Why is that? Why are we always talking about me and my fouled up relationship? How about yours? Surely you have some tales of the heart to tell."

Jamie smiled at the ground and shook her head.

"Not really."

"Ruth Ann said you were in an intimate relationship with your algae. I don't believe it. There has to be someone hidden in the shadows. Who is she? One of your students? A colleague? Who?"

"Sorry to disappoint you and Ruth Ann but there isn't anyone lurking in the shadows. I'm not dating anyone right now." Jamie adjusted her glasses, allowing her hand to hide her eyes from Dana's view.

"Why not?" Dana leaned forward to see around her hand.

"Just not," she shrugged.

Dana pulled off a piece of bread and danced it around in the oil then ate it.

"Was it Dusty?" she asked carefully.

"No," Jamie replied with a half smile.

"But I saw her kiss you. I was sure you two had a history together."

"Dusty is a close friend but not an ex-lover, if that's what you were wondering."

"Hey, I wouldn't blame you if you had. She's a good-looking woman. She has a lot of personality. And she's so kind."

"Yes, she is all that, but she's not gay." Jamie sipped her wine then refilled their glasses as if avoiding Dana's curiosity.

"I'm sorry, Jamie. Did I rake up something I shouldn't have?" Dana touched Jamie's leg.

"No. It's all right."

"Just forget it. I won't ask anything else about Dusty."

Jamie took a drink then swirled the wine in her cup, watching it intently.

"It wasn't Dusty. It was her sister." Jamie kept her eyes on her cup as she spoke. "Dr. Terry Grant. She was a marine geologist in southern California." Jamie took a deep breath at the end of her confession.

"Do you mind if I ask what happened?" Dana asked gently.

"No, I don't mind." Jamie set her cup down and began wiping her glasses on the tail of her shirt. "It was several years ago."

"You met her through your work?"

"Yes. She studied and mapped the ocean floor. Mountains, fault lines, suboceanic volcanoes. She was a very smart woman."

"Sounds like it."

"Terry and Dusty were very close. They looked a lot alike, too," Jamie added reflectively. "Dusty and I were both working at UCLA. She introduced me to Terry. Said she needed some help identifying some deepwater species. We did some diving together. There's a fault line that runs parallel to the coast of Baja. It was about two miles offshore. She mapped it for the National

Oceanographic Institute and proved their data was flawed. The slope of the fault is much steeper than formerly thought."

"Wow. That's quite a discovery."

Jamie smiled over at Dana.

"Yes, it was but it was just one of those tidbits of scientific data no one ever hears about until there's an earthquake and tsunami."

"What happened to Terry?" Dana was almost afraid to ask.

"She was diving off the coast of Louisiana doing some work for an oil company."

"Oh, God," Dana whispered, bracing herself for the worst.

"The medical examiner said Terry had a seizure. She was down pretty deep and couldn't get up in time." Jamie had a faraway look in her eyes as she stared out across the park.

"Oh, Jamie. I'm so sorry." Dana scooted over closer and rested her hand on Jamie's leg. "Was she diving alone?"

Jamie nodded.

"She wouldn't listen. I was going to fly down and dive with her the next weekend but she wouldn't wait." The muscles in Jamie's cheek rippled.

"Would it have made a difference if you had been with her?"

Jamie heaved a heavy sigh.

"At that depth, probably not," she said resolutely.

"Is Terry the last person you dated?"

Jamie drew her legs up and rested her arms on her knees then looked over at Dana.

"We didn't just date. We were partners. She was my wife. We bought a house together. It had a swimming pool. Four bedrooms. Great ocean view. We were going to have kids. She wanted a little girl. One she could name Annie Laurie, like in the song." Jamie's eyes grew misty.

"How long were you together?" Dana asked softly.

"Six years. Seven if you count the time we dated."

Dana didn't know what to say. The stoic set to Jamie's jaw and the fragility in her voice touched Dana deeply. Saying she was sorry again seemed inadequate. Instead Dana wrapped her arms around Jamie and hugged her.

"You're a good hugger," Jamie said, dabbing at her tears.

"Tell me something wonderful about Terry," Dana whispered. "Share something with me."

"Something wonderful." She sighed deeply. "There were so many things."

"Tell me one. One that will make you smile."

"She had a tattoo of a pair of dolphins." Jamie's eyes twinkled as she remembered it. "She got it when we were in Australia. It was our first trip together. It wasn't a very big tattoo. She got it put right on the cheek of her rear. She said that way only I would see it."

"Why dolphins? Just because she liked marine animals?"

"The human and the dolphin are the only two mammals that have sex for pleasure."

"I didn't know that."

"In the animal kingdom, sex is reserved for the proliferation of the species."

"Except for dolphins and humans?"

"That's right." Jamie raised her eyebrows mischievously. "She told me it was only fitting that the tattoo be of dolphins."

"Terry sounded like a very fun-loving person."

"She was."

"It must have been terrible for you."

"I sold the house and moved to Washington. Dusty already lived up here and she thought it was a great place for me to start over. To tell the truth, for the first few years I didn't know where I was or what I was doing. I went to the store but forgot what I went for. I forgot telephone numbers, even my own. I couldn't remember where I parked my car. I couldn't give a class lecture without reading it off a paper. I cried for no reason other than I couldn't stop. Everyone and everything reminded me of her. I'd go visit with Dusty just because she looked like Terry. I was a mess."

"You were hurting."

"Yeah," Jamie agreed softly. "That was six years ago. I have no idea what I did the first three of those years. It is completely a blank."

"Can I ask what Dusty said to you when we were out there for lunch? If it's too personal, I'll understand."

"She said she was glad to see me doing better."

"That's all?"

Jamie's eyes met Dana's but she didn't answer.

"I bet she said she loves you and wishes you the very best," Dana said, with a kind smile.

"Something like that."

They finished their picnic and didn't mention Shannon or Terry again. The concert had been only mildly entertaining, but they didn't mind. They walked the boardwalk, enjoying the gorgeous sunset, and picking out their favorite boats. Jamie finally walked Dana back to the security gate.

"Would you like to come down for a cup of coffee? I've got decaf."

"No thanks. I better head home. The dinner was wonderful. Thank you for making it and for inviting me," Jamie said, handing her the basket. "I had a great time."

"I'm glad you did. I'll let you know when they schedule another one. And Jamie," she said hesitantly. "Forgive me if I ask too many personal questions. It's just sometimes I feel like I should know all about you. After all, I've told you everything about me."

"That's all right. I'm learning to deal with losing Terry. I may never get past it but I'm learning to deal. Good night, Dana." Jamie leaned down and kissed Dana on the lips, her hand cradling Dana's back. This was far more than a friendly peck. There was something else in the kiss. Something warm and tingly, electrifying and sensual. Dana couldn't help but kiss her back.

"Was I supposed to tell you when your blouse was open again?" Jamie said softly, her arm still encircling Dana's waist and her lips just inches away.

"Yes. Is it?" Dana said, looking up into Jamie's big brown eyes.

Jamie stroked her hand down Dana's throat and along her exposed cleavage, sending a shiver straight to Dana's libido.

"It's open but it's beautiful. Don't close it." Jamie lowered her lips to Dana's again, this time passionately. Dana dropped the basket and threw her arms around Jamie's neck. She held on as if she never wanted to let go, pressing herself against Jamie's body. Dana could feel Jamie's hips mold to hers. There was a strong yet gentle presence to Jamie's embrace. Unlike Shannon's urgent demanding kiss, this was tender and benevolent. From the first moment she had seen Jamie on the deck of Ruth Ann's boat, Dana somehow knew she wanted this. She had tried to deny it but she had wondered what it would be like to be in Jamie's arms, feeling her lips against her own? For one moment, one fleeting microsecond of time, Dana was ready to beg Jamie to come down to the houseboat with her. And not for coffee. She wanted Jamie to make love to her, to fill her with passion and ecstasy. To come with her to the loft and spend the night in each other's arms, Shannon be damned. She wanted Jamie's long legs wrapped around her all through the night. But before she could ask, Jamie pulled away, shyly smiling and bidding her good night. Dana was left leaning against the security gate, wondering how she let her slip away.

Chapter 17

The next morning Dana was up early. She hadn't slept well and decided a walk was what she needed. The taste of Jamie's lips and the feel of her hand on her back was a pleasant memory. She knew it was silly but languishing in that fantasy put a spring in her step. *What a wonderful feeling*, she thought. She stopped at the café on the boardwalk and had breakfast, enjoying the view of the harbor and daydreaming about what might have been. She returned to the houseboat and tried to work but couldn't concentrate. She drove by Steve's house to take in the mail and feed their cat. When Dana returned to the houseboat, the telephone light was flashing. She pushed the button to hear the messages on her way to make a cup of coffee. She was sure it would be the normal litany of telemarketers.

"Dana, call me as soon as you get this message. It's important." Shannon's voice was clear and direct, telling Dana this wasn't a social call. The machine beeped and started the next message. "Dana, call me right away." Shannon's tone was now impatient and demanding. There was something else in it as well.

Dana turned off the kettle and dialed Shannon's number.

"Hi. What did you need?" she said when Shannon answered.

"Where have you been? I've been calling all morning."

"I just got home. What's up?"

"Your cell phone isn't turned on either."

"The battery won't hold a charge. I ordered a new one on eBay but it hasn't come yet."

"Damn, Dana. I've been trying to get a hold of you for hours. I've got bad news."

"What?" From her experience with Shannon's idea of bad news, it could be anything from WWIII to a flat tire.

"Maggie's mom died."

"Eva?" Dana gasped. "When? How?"

Maggie was one of Dana and Shannon's oldest friends. They had known her even before they knew each other. Maggie had introduced them. She was a sweet woman, full of energy and sincerity. At forty, she had been in countless relationships with women either far too young or far too old to understand her unique sense of humor and needs. Dana strongly suspected Shannon and Maggie had a brief history together some years ago. Shannon denied it but Maggie's coy blush at the notion was a dead giveaway. Even though Dana hadn't seen her in months, Maggie was still a good friend.

"Night before last. She was in the hospital and had bypass surgery three days ago. They think it was either a blood clot or a heart attack."

Dana sank into a chair.

"Poor Maggie. Shannon, that's awful. She has always been very close to her mother."

"She's a basket case. I called her and all she did was cry."

"I'm sure. They were more like sisters than mother and daughter. They did everything together."

"Mrs. Everett was a good old gal," Shannon said.

"Eva. She wouldn't let us call her Mrs. Everett," Dana said reflectively. "Remember the time we met them at that hamburger place by Renton on the lake? She bought everyone's lunch in honor of her great-grandmother's birthday. She said her great-grandmother loved hamburgers so she wanted to pay. Remember? She absolutely insisted."

"Yeah. And she put a match in her hamburger bun like a candle and sang happy birthday."

"I thought Maggie was going to split a seam laughing at her."

They both laughed, but their laughter soon faded to a remorseful sigh.

"Maggie will sure miss her," Dana said sorrowfully. "Have they made the arrangements yet?"

"It'll just be immediate family at graveside services but that won't be until Eva's brother and his family can get here from Virginia. There's going to be a visitation this evening at the funeral home for friends. Six o'clock to eight. I'll pick you up at five forty-five."

"I can drive myself. Which funeral home?"

"Gulleston's but they don't have a very big parking lot. It'll be better if I pick you up. I bet it'll be crowded. Everyone Eva worked with will be there."

"Where did she work? I thought she retired."

"She took a part-time job with the Port of Olympia. Some kind of clerical work. Maggie tried to talk her out of it but she insisted. Said she wanted to stay busy. She was sure she could still pull her own weight."

"She was a sweet lady. She was always very kind to me." Dana cast her eyes out the window.

"I'll be there to pick you up at a quarter to six."

"Okay," she said, her thoughts still on a pleasant woman with a quirky smile and a lusty laugh. "I'll meet you by the statue outside the security gate."

"Don't do that. I'll come down to the houseboat to get you.

213

It's supposed to be rainy," Shannon said.

Dana was about to tell her she couldn't get inside the security gate without a code when she remembered entering it after their dinner at Trinacera. Shannon undoubtedly noticed the code and it would be seared into her brain.

"I'll order some flowers," Dana said.

"I already did. Pink lilies in a glass vase. I put both our names on the card."

"Thank you. I'll pay you for my half."

"That's okay. I would have sent them anyway."

"Shannon, I want to pay my share. I didn't order them or sign the card. Could I at least pay for half?"

"Don't worry about it. I've got to go. My call waiting is lit up like a Christmas tree. I'll pick you up later. And you might want to wear that pretty pink sweater, the one with the scallops on the V-neck. It looks good on you. See you later, babe." Shannon hung up without waiting for Dana's reply.

Dana opened the telephone book and scanned the yellow pages for florists. She wanted to send her own flowers. Maggie was a dear friend, even if they didn't spend much time together anymore. And her mother had been kind. There was no reason she couldn't send a plant even if Shannon had already included her name in an arrangement. She had punched in the number of a nearby florist when she realized it was silly to send a duplicate. Maggie would question her senility if a second arrangement showed up with Dana's name on it. And Shannon would never let her hear the end of it. She hung up and went to make her coffee, a bitter taste in her mouth over Shannon's presumptive decision.

"Damn it," she said, flinging the spoon into the sink. She picked up the receiver and hit redial.

"South Sound Flowers," a woman said, picking up on the second ring.

"I'd like to order a plant. It goes to Gulleston's Funeral Home."

"And the name of the deceased?" The woman sounded as if

she did this a lot.

"Eva Everett."

"What kind of plant would you like?"

"Gosh, I don't know. I've never ordered a sympathy plant before. It's always been cut flowers. What do you recommend?"

"It can be almost anything. Amaryllis, dieffenbachia, hydrangea, miniature rose, hibiscus. You name it. I had a woman order a cactus for a funeral last week."

Dana thought a minute. This is the moment when Shannon would clear her throat, drum her fingers on the table, and volunteer to make the selection for her.

"Lilies are always nice for a funeral. Either cut or as a plant," the woman offered.

"No lilies," Dana said.

"Orchid? Gardenia? Azalea?"

It occurred to Dana that Jamie's botanical background would sure be handy right now. She also realized Jamie wouldn't tell her what to choose, but rather offer explanations and insist Dana make her own decision.

"Do you have African violets? Purple ones?" Dana asked, remembering Eva had once indicated she liked them.

"Yes. Lovely choice. What would you like on the card?"

Dana hesitated. Shannon probably spent twenty minutes on the computer looking up something clever for the card. Something profound and sappy. That was okay but not what Dana wanted.

"Just sign it—Love, Dana."

"That's all?" the woman asked curiously.

"That's all."

Dana had done it. She had sent her own flowers. Shannon wasn't going to like it but so what. Dana went to make her coffee, knowing in her heart she had done the right thing. She had just finished creaming her coffee when her telephone rang.

"Hello," she said, taking a sip.

"Hi," Jamie said with a relaxed chuckle. "I guess I'm officially an absentminded professor."

"Why? What did you do?" Dana replied, happy to hear her voice, whatever the reason.

"Your sunglasses. I had them with me to return to you that day I came by the houseboat and Juliana was there. I remembered your jacket, but I got so wrapped up in her situation I completely forgot the sunglasses. You left them in my car when I gave you a ride home from Bartolu's. Remember? It was raining."

"I wondered where I put those."

"Do you need them this evening? I could drop them off later. I've got to collect some water samples in the bay."

"What time?" Dana asked, the idea of Jamie stopping by a pleasing one.

"Late this afternoon. I'm going to take advantage of low tide around five o'clock."

"I'll be home until a quarter to six. Then I should be back by eight. Earlier if it's real crowded."

"Where are you going? A Japanese bath?" Jamie chuckled.

"A funeral."

"Oh, gosh, Dana. I'm sorry." Jamie immediately sobered.

"Actually, it's a visitation. The funeral is family only."

"I didn't mean to make fun of what you were doing." There was sincerity in Jamie's apology.

"You didn't. Making fun would be one of those gross jokes about dead people."

"Would it be terrible of me to ask whose funeral you're attending? I hope it isn't a family member."

"She was the mother of a friend but she was more like a friend herself. Lovely lady."

"I'm so sorry, Dana. What happened?"

"Complications after bypass surgery, I think."

"Was she ill a long time?"

"Not that I know of. She was mid-sixties and still very active. She walked the Pink Trail up by Seattle last year in support of breast cancer and that was twenty miles."

"I walked that event. There must have been two thousand participants. What was her name?"

"Eva Everett. Maggie Everett's mother," Dana said.

There was a gasp. Then silence.

"Jamie? Are you there?"

"Eva Everett, the lady who handles the water quality reports?"

"I don't know about that, but I know she had a part-time job with the Port of Olympia."

"Thin woman with gray hair?"

"Yes. Curly gray hair. She usually wears dangly earrings."

"That's the one. I know her. Or at least I knew her. She was very funny. And very pleasant."

"That's Eva. The family visitation is six to eight at Gulleston's Funeral Home. Would you like to go with us?"

"No, thanks."

"Shannon won't mind, I'm sure." As soon as it was out of her mouth, Dana knew that wasn't exactly true. But she didn't care. Inviting Jamie to go along seemed like the right thing to do.

"No. I'd rather not."

"Because I said Shannon was going?" Dana asked.

"That doesn't have anything to do with it."

"We've both known Maggie and her mother for years. She introduced us. It just seemed right that we go together."

"Dana, it has nothing to do with Shannon."

"Why then?"

There was another moment of silence. Dana waited.

"I just don't do funerals." Jamie's voice was soft.

"I understand."

Jamie cut the conversation short before Dana could ask if she was all right. She was tempted to call her back but she didn't have time. She had a cartoon to finish, then shower and dress before Shannon came by to pick her up.

The smaller closets on the houseboat meant Dana had to be selective about what she brought onboard. Her off-season clothes were packed away in Steve's garage. She pulled a box of sweaters from the back of the closet and rummaged through it looking for the pink sweater. Gray slacks, she thought. Or white

217

ones with white sandals. She shook out the sweater and hung it on a hanger to reshape while she took a shower.

Dana stood in front of the mirror, applying lipstick and deciding if she wanted to wear her hair down and full or back out of the way. She hadn't cut her hair since Shannon insisted cutting it would be a sin against humanity. She would always laugh when she said it, but gave Dana a suspicious glare if she even mentioned her hair getting too long and unruly.

Dana left it down, repeatedly having to pull a lock behind her ear on either side as she finished dressing. The pink sweater was still snug. In fact, a little too snug for a funeral visitation. She pulled at the hem and sides, coaxing a looser fit. She hung tiny silver loops from her ears, the earrings Shannon had given her for her birthday.

It was five thirty. Dana had fifteen minutes and she wanted to be waiting outside the security gate. She gave a last look in the mirror, reached for the door, and hesitated. She looked down at what she was wearing and groaned. This wasn't what she wanted to wear. She pulled the sweater over her head and tossed it on the chair. She put on her bright red silk blouse and the white jacket that matched her slacks. She changed her earrings for a pair of dangly gold ones that Eva had always admired. She tucked the blouse in her slacks, popped the collar outside the jacket lapels, and headed for the gangplank to wait. She scanned the marina for signs Jamie was in the bay collecting her water samples but didn't see her. Perhaps she changed her mind. Somewhere in the back of Dana's mind she hoped Jamie wouldn't return her sunglasses. If she forgot, Dana would have an excuse to drive out and pick them up herself.

"Dana," Shannon called, striding across the parking lot. "I told you I'd come down to the houseboat to get you. I didn't want you to have to wait. And I thought you were going to wear the pink sweater."

Dana could have predicted that.

"I know but I changed my mind."

"The pink sweater looks so good on you, babe."

"Yes, but it fits like a driving glove."

"So?"

"So that wasn't the look I wanted for a wake. Are you ready to go?"

Shannon looked her up and down, scrutinizing her earrings, hair and blouse.

"I suppose." She took Dana's arm and led her toward her SUV. As always, she opened the passenger door and waited for Dana to get situated before closing it.

"I feel so bad for Maggie," Dana said as Shannon pulled out of the parking lot. "She and her mom had such a special relationship."

"Uh-huh." Shannon seemed preoccupied with other things. Dana didn't pursue it.

It was a quick drive to the funeral home. Maggie and Eva may have had many friends and co-workers but the parking lot had only four cars in it.

"It's early," Shannon said, as if justifying her suggestion that Dana not drive herself.

"I wonder if Maggie is here yet. She's the only one of her family I'll know."

"Yes, she's here. I dropped her off on my way in to pick you up. She didn't want to ride in the funeral limo, and she wasn't up to driving herself so I gave her a ride."

"How is she doing?" Dana asked.

"She cried most of the way."

Shannon pulled into the first space next to the sidewalk. The funeral home was a large Victorian home converted into several offices, a chapel and a visitation room. A silver-haired man in a dark suit greeted them, invited them to sign the guest book then escorted them into the paneled room where wingback chairs and leather sofas lined the walls. A framed photograph of Eva Everett sat on a round table in the center of the room, along with a vase of lavender roses. Soft music played in the background, just loud enough to drown out the hum of the air conditioner.

Dana had been to four funerals in her life, and she didn't like

219

going to any of them. It was one of those obligatory chores she couldn't avoid. As soon as she stepped into the room and saw Maggie's tearstained face and the dark circles under her eyes she knew Jamie had the right idea. Like a knife turning in her gut, Dana wished she didn't have to do this. She always ended up crying more than the person she came to console.

"Dana," Maggie said, rushing up to her and wrapping her in a hug.

"Maggie, I'm so very sorry."

"I'm going to miss her so bad."

"I know, sweetheart. I know. She was such a wonderful woman. We'll all miss her." Dana held her and swayed, both of them sobbing. It took several minutes before Maggie had regained her composure enough to speak.

"Thank you for coming. And thank you for the flowers, Shannon. You too, Dana," she said, dabbing her nose with a tissue.

"I remember you liked pink lilies," Shannon said, giving Maggie's hand a squeeze.

"Yes. They're gorgeous. And the African violet is spectacular. Mother loved African violets. How did you know?"

"I wasn't sure, but I thought she mentioned growing them." Dana noticed a small basket containing an abundantly blooming purple plant.

"She had one in every color, I think." Maggie looked over at the plant. It brought a smile to her face. "She said they were the only houseplant she could grow. She would love it. But the lilies are very nice, too." Maggie said in Shannon's direction.

"You're welcome," Shannon said, smiling proudly at the large crystal vase holding a dozen lush pink blooms.

"I love that red blouse, Dana. Isn't that the one mom liked?"

"I think so. I thought she'd like it if I wore it." Dana wiped a tear from Maggie's cheek.

"She absolutely would." Maggie touched Dana's collar and winked. "Oh, gosh." Her eyes drifted past Dana to an elderly woman coming through the door. "There's mom's neighbor,

Mrs. Hypochondriac," she whispered. "I better go give her a hug and let her tell me how bad her gall bladder surgery was, for the tenth time." Maggie gave Dana and Shannon a hug and a kiss then moved on to greet other well-wishers. Shannon and Dana mingled for a few minutes before inching their way toward the door. The crowd had grown large enough that they could slip out and not be missed.

"You ready to go?" Shannon said.

"I think so. Maggie seems to have her hands full."

"She won't miss us." Shannon hooked her hand through Dana's arm and escorted her to the parking lot. She waited for Dana to get in then slammed the door. They rode in silence back to the marina. Dana stared out the window, remembering Eva and their times together. Shannon parked but, for once, made no effort to get out to open Dana's car door. Instead, she glared over at her.

"Did you order flowers? I told you I already took care of it," Shannon said.

"I wanted to send something from me."

"But I told you I had it covered. I put both our names on the lilies. Did you put my name on the African violets?"

"No." Dana knew Shannon had looked at the card.

"Why the hell not?"

"Because you didn't send them, that's why." Dana reached for the door handle, but Shannon stopped her.

"Is this supposed to be Make Shannon Look Stupid Day?"

"Of course not. I just wanted to send flowers myself."

"And the red blouse? I told Maggie you were going to wear your pink sweater, the one I like!"

"If you like that sweater so much, you wear it."

"It's not my size. It's way too small for me."

"It's way too small for me, too. That's why I didn't wear it." Dana touched Shannon's arm. "It had nothing to do with you, honey. Let's not argue."

"You're right." Shannon took a deep cleansing breath and turned in her seat. "We shouldn't argue about stupid little things.

I guess I'm just stressed, babe."

"Stressed about what? Work? Is the agency doing okay?"

"About us, Dana," Shannon said softly, touching a lock of Dana's hair. "This waiting for you to clear the cobwebs and come home is killing me."

Dana looked away. She didn't want to argue about that either.

"I have an idea, babe," Shannon said, lifting Dana's chin. "I've been giving it a lot of thought. I think the best way for you to come to grips with whatever is bothering you is to move back in with me." Dana opened her mouth to reply, but Shannon placed a finger on her lips. "Let me finish. I love you, Dana. You know that. We are a couple and your problems are my problems. If you are hurting, so am I. But I can't help you if you are living ten miles away on a fucking houseboat. How can I be supportive and take care of you, if we aren't together? I feel like I'm failing you, Dana. I'm not there when you need me most."

"Shannon," Dana started but before she could finish, Shannon leaned over and kissed her. It was a gentle kiss, one as tender as their first year together, when glances were soft and embraces were passionate. It was a kiss Dana craved. It was from a time she craved as well, when she felt loved and in love. The subtleness of it crept over her and made her shiver. She couldn't remember the last time Shannon had been so gentle. Dana leaned into the kiss, desperate to return to that time when their love was carefree and reassuring. Where had it gone? Where were those moments when she couldn't wait for Shannon to take her in her arms and make love to her?

"Dana, Dana, Dana," Shannon whispered, holding Dana's face in her hands, her thumbs wiping away the tears that filled Dana's eyes. "It'll be all right, babe. I promise." She reached across Dana's lap and opened her door, her hand lingering on Dana's thigh. "Let's go down to the houseboat and talk."

"Shannon, I'm not in the mood to talk." Dana didn't want to talk about the present while she was still languishing in the sweet memories of the past.

"I thought we could reminisce about Eva and the fun times we all had together."

For that, Dana would agree. She was still in shock over Eva's death and talking about it might help.

"Okay."

Shannon took Dana's hand as they crossed the parking lot and headed toward the security gate.

"Come on. Let's get drunk and laugh about all the stupid stuff we did with Maggie and her mom," she said, kissing Dana's forehead.

"Like skinny-dipping in the bay?" Dana chuckled.

"When the minister and his wife were fishing on the dock?" Shannon threw her head back and laughed, pulling Dana closer. "Maggie was so embarrassed."

"So was I. You said no one would see us," Dana said, bumping her.

"Eva wasn't embarrassed at all. She said God gave her that body and if anyone in the world should appreciate that it should be a minister."

"We all about froze our nipples off."

"It wasn't that cold," Shannon insisted.

"My lips were blue."

"Which ones?" Shannon grinned.

"Shannon!" Dana blushed and giggled.

"Seems like I remember seeing which lips for myself that night." Shannon put her hand on Dana's rear and squeezed.

"Hello, Dana." Jamie said, standing near the security gate. She was holding a bucket in one hand and a red plastic toolbox in the other. She was wearing knee-high rubber boots, a tattered gray sweatshirt, and paint-stained jeans. She was splattered with mud and slime from head to toe. The one thing the mud couldn't hide was her cold, cutting stare.

Chapter 18

"Jamie?" Dana said, still giggling from Shannon's remark. She knew Jamie was close enough to hear what they had said. Jamie's expression told her so.

"Hello, Dr. Hughes," Shannon said, keeping a firm hold on Dana. She gave Jamie's attire a disparaging glance.

"I forgot your sunglasses," Jamie said, her eyes tracing Shannon's arm around Dana's shoulder.

"That's okay. I don't need them this evening." Dana realized that sounded like she and Shannon had indoor plans together, plans that did not require sunglasses.

"How was the visitation?" Jamie asked, her eyes still on Shannon's control over Dana.

"Crowded," Shannon said before Dana could reply.

"As good as those things can be, I guess," Dana said, feeling Shannon's arm tighten around her shoulders.

"Did you know Eva?" Shannon asked.

"Yes." Jamie didn't elaborate.

"You should've gone. Everyone she worked with was there."

"I've been working." Jamie held up the bucket containing several baggies of brackish water.

"Did you get all your samples?" Dana asked.

"Half of them."

"Have fun," Shannon said, pulling Dana toward the gate.

"I'll call you about picking up my sunglasses," Dana said, unable to free herself from Shannon's firm grip.

"Anytime." Jamie headed for the parking lot.

"Can you believe that?" Shannon said, keying in the code. "Work is more important to her than a friend's funeral."

"Some people don't do funerals."

"That's no excuse." Shannon held the gate.

"Jamie has her reasons." She looked back across the parking lot.

"I'm just saying it sounds like Dr. Hughes is more involved with stinky water and slimy urchins than humans. You've got to get your priorities in line. Maggie is a friend. I can't imagine not going to show her support." She followed Dana down the gangplank. "Where's your keys?" she asked, holding out her hand as they approached the houseboat.

"I've got it." Dana said, digging in her purse. Shannon snapped her fingers, winked and took the keys from Dana's hand.

"Have you got any booze?" she asked, following Dana inside. "I could use a stiff drink."

Dana pulled out a bottle of wine from the back of the refrigerator.

"Just this." She wasn't going to offer Morgan's brandy.

Shannon examined the label, opened it, and poured them each a glass.

"It'll have to do." She held the glass up to the light as if examining its worth. "By the way, are you the one who told Jamie about Eva?"

"Yes. She called right after you did. When I mentioned who

it was, she said she knew her from where she worked."

"What's this about your sunglasses?"

"I left them in her car. And before you ask, she gave me a ride home when it was raining. She came by once before to deliver them but forgot to leave them. She was busy helping with Juliana."

"What did she do for Juliana?"

"Can you believe it? Juliana is now a woman." Dana smiled proudly.

"What the hell does that mean? Is she screwing some pimple-faced kid?"

"NO! Don't be silly." Dana scowled at her. "Juliana started her period. She didn't really know what to expect and she was upset."

"Her period? Is that all?" Shannon laughed.

"Juliana was scared. Jamie was very sweet to talk to her."

"I bet she gave her some deep scientific explanation about reproduction and genetics. The poor kid probably was more confused than before."

"She did not. Juliana said she was very kind."

Shannon finished her glass of wine and refilled her glass.

"So the kid is growing up?"

"Yes, and I don't know where all the years have gone. One minute she was a toddler eating Cheerios and the next she is picking out her first training bra."

"Drink up." Shannon held the bottle up, waiting for Dana to take another sip.

"I'm fine. I don't want anymore."

"Sure you do. Remember we're drinking to Eva." She splashed a bit more wine in Dana's glass.

"I don't need to get drunk to have fond memories about her."

"I know." Shannon downed her glass in one gulp. "By the way, babe." She gave Dana a long serious look. "You were right. You look damn good in that red shirt."

"I'm glad you like it." Dana took off her jacket and hung it

226

on the back of the stool. "And I like your pants. They look good on you. Are they new?"

"Yep. I got them a couple weeks ago in Portland when I was there for the convention." She turned to show them off. "Half price. Fifty-six bucks."

"Fifty-six dollars? And that was half price?" Dana had never paid that much for a pair of slacks in her life.

"Like you said. They look good on me. Do you want a pair? I'll get you a pair just like them. You'd look great in navy blue ones. I'll order you a pair online. Size eight, right?"

"No, Shannon. Don't. I don't need them."

"I know you don't but I want to. If they don't have navy, I'll pick something else. Don't worry. You'll love them. Your cute little ass will look great in any color."

"Shannon, please don't. I don't want fifty-six dollar slacks. But thank you for offering."

"What can I buy you then?" Shannon asked, stroking a lock of Dana's hair. "Tell me something I can get you? Earrings? I saw a pair of gold loops with tiny amethyst stones that would look so good on you, especially when you wear your hair long like this. I knew the first time I saw them they'd be perfect on you."

"Shannon, I don't need anything."

"I know you don't need anything, but surely there is something you want. How about dinner at Hartley's? Just the two of us."

"Heavens, no." Dana couldn't help but laugh. Hartley's was the most expensive restaurant in Thurston County. Coffee was six dollars. Dinner for two could easily run over two hundred dollars. "Shannon, honestly, I don't need or want anything. I'm very happy with just what I have."

"How about me? Are you happy without me?"

Dana took a sip from her wine as she decided how to answer. She didn't want to talk about it tonight but knew Shannon wasn't going to let it slide. Dana went to the window and watched a sailboat ease into its slip after a day of sailing.

"Do you remember that first summer after Maggie introduced us?" Dana said.

227

"Sure, but I don't want to talk about Maggie and Eva."

"I'm not. I'm talking about us. Do you remember our first trip together?"

"Yeah, I remember. We went down the coast and stayed at that bed-and-breakfast on Cannon Beach. I got us a great deal on that room with the ocean view."

"No. That was the second trip." Dana turned to her. "I'm talking about the very first trip we took."

Shannon scowled as if she couldn't remember.

"Oh, yeah. We went to Bremerton and rode the ferry."

"Yes. We ate hamburgers out of wax paper wrappers and watched the seagulls eat the scraps."

"Yeah." Shannon shook her head as if it was an unpleasant memory.

"And we huddled together under a blanket on the way back because it was raining. We stopped at that little café along the highway and had the best meatloaf we've ever tasted. You even said so. Then we pulled into that rest stop and kissed and talked for hours. We didn't get home until dawn."

"I'm sorry about that. I didn't know it was going to pour down rain."

"I loved it. I loved the rain and the little café and the soggy ride on the ferry. It was fun because it was spontaneous. We didn't plan it. We just did it. It was impulsive, and I loved every single minute of it."

"Damn, you're a cheap date, babe."

"Don't make fun of it, Shannon. It was very special to me."

"Why? Because it was a complete disaster?"

"Because it was us having fun. Not you making reservations and planning elaborate travel details. We just got in the car and drove. You handed me the map and said pick a spot."

"That'll teach me," Shannon said, pouring the last of the wine in her glass.

"Don't make jokes."

"Okay. I'll give you that one but that's why I made reservations at Cannon Beach. I wanted to have a real trip."

"But it was a real trip, Shannon. Don't you understand? You don't have to spend a fortune to have a good time."

"I know that, babe. But I want you to have the best my money will buy."

Dana had the perfect reply but she was stopped by a knock at the door.

"I'll get it," Shannon said, finishing her wine on the way to answer it. "Well, hello again."

"I brought Dana's sunglasses."

"Jamie?" Dana said, coming to the door.

"I decided I better do it now while it was on my mind." She held up the sunglasses. She had changed into clean jeans and shirt, her hair still wet from being washed.

"Come in," Dana said, opening the door wide in spite of Shannon's attempt to block it.

"I can't stay long. I just wanted to drop this off since I promised I would."

"Thank you." Dana took them then pulled her inside. "Can I make you some coffee or tea?"

"Sorry, doc. We already drank all the wine." Shannon held up her empty glass.

"No, nothing. Thanks."

"I hear you helped our Juliana over one of the hurdles of life," Shannon added.

"If you mean easing a little girl's fear over starting her menstrual cycles, it was my pleasure. Juliana is a very sweet girl."

"When Dana told me she was now a woman, I thought she meant the kid was humping the football team or something." Shannon laughed but was the only one who thought it was funny. Dana nudged her, hoping to stop her tactless humor.

"Why would you think that?" Jamie said curiously. "Is that what you did when you were twelve?"

The comment froze the smile on Shannon's face. Her eyes met Jamie's in a cold exchange. Dana felt the tension grow and stepped in front of Shannon.

"Come in and sit down, Jamie. Tell us about your water samples." Dana motioned toward the living room, hoping to defuse the situation.

"She said she couldn't stay," Shannon said, standing her ground.

"She's right. I can't. I've got e-mails to send this evening." Jamie, too, seemed immovable. "Did you enjoy the wine, Shannon?" She looked over at the bottle on the table. "Martin Brothers Riesling. Very nice choice, Dana. Perfect sipping wine. Interesting, firm character, never presumptuous." Jamie's description seemed to be aimed more at Shannon than the wine.

"I found it full of youth and vigor. Not one of those middle-aged wines that lack luster or firm body." Shannon's eyes narrowed as she countered.

"Ah. I can see where that would appeal to a less mature palate."

"As you might remember, age has nothing to do with a fine wine."

"Perhaps not," Jamie said, adjusting her glasses. "But maturity in wine is much more appreciated than youth."

Dana watched the two women duel. She knew they were no longer talking about wine. These barbs were personal attacks. Shannon seemed bolder in her approach, standing proudly as she faced her enemy. Jamie was more casual in battle. She wasn't intimidated, never flinching or retreating.

"Youth has its advantages in many areas outside the wine cellar." Shannon gave a cheeky grin.

"I presume you are referring to the bedroom," Jamie said, slipping her hands into the back pockets of her jeans.

"Where else?"

"Shannon," Dana interrupted. Neither woman paid any attention to her.

"I imagine you are right. Youth in the bedroom would be an asset," Jamie agreed.

Shannon smiled smugly.

"However," Jamie added. "Maturity has the vision and imagination to create a bedroom atmosphere almost anywhere."

Shannon's eyes flashed menacingly. Dana was afraid to wait for the next thrust and parry.

"Shannon. Jamie," she said, placing a hand on each woman's chest to keep them apart. "It's late. I have work to do and I'm sure you both have someplace you need to be."

The two women stood glaring at one another while Dana looked back and forth as if she was watching a tennis match. The tension was palpable. Dana wasn't sure where the casual visit had turned venomous but it was clear Jamie and Shannon were close to blows. It didn't surprise her that Shannon would lash out at someone she considered a rival, but Jamie's response did. Dana never suspected Dr. Jamie Hughes, perceptive and intellectual college professor, would lower herself to such banter. She more expected Jamie to offer some pithy remark consisting of several twelve-syllable words and then leave as quietly as she came. Instead, Shannon and Jamie stood toe to toe, acting like two cats ready to let the fur fly.

"It was nice to see you again, Shannon," Jamie said, blinking first. "Excuse my barroom behavior. I'm just tired." She extended her hand to Shannon. "Ignore the old professor with the attitude."

Shannon's frown slowly changed to an arrogant smile.

"No problem," she said, shaking her hand. "Thanks for bringing Dana's sunglasses back. You saved her a trip."

"Enjoy your evening," Jamie said, looking down at Dana. Their eyes met for a brief moment and the softness of it warmed Dana all over.

"Good night, Jamie," Dana said, following her out the door. "Thanks again." She watched as Jamie headed up the dock. Shannon came out and stood behind her, her arms folding around Dana.

"You better come inside. It's getting chilly out here."

"Shortly," Dana said, her eyes never leaving Jamie's long strides.

"Come on," Shannon said, steering her through the door.

Dana pulled away and turned to glare at her.

"What was that all about? Why were you like that to Jamie?"

"Like what? I wasn't LIKE anything. If anyone was rude, it was her. Did you hear what she said? She called me a teenage ho. Who does she think she is?" Shannon scoffed. "I know exactly who she is. She's a sexually frustrated middle-aged dyke who can't function outside her precious laboratory."

"Shannon, stop it. Jamie is not a sexually frustrated dyke. Now behave yourself or I'll ask you to leave." Dana scowled at her then went to the sink to wash the glasses.

"You'll what?" Shannon laughed.

"You heard me. I don't want to hear any more nasty remarks about Jamie or you'll have to go home. I'm not in the mood to hear it tonight."

Shannon sat down on a barstool and laughed out loud, crossing her arms judgmentally.

"Well, well. I know what's going on here. Don't think I don't. You've got the hots for her, don't you? Has good old Professor Hughes gone down on you, Dana? Is that what this is all about?"

"She has not!" Dana snapped. "Don't be stupid."

"Watch who you're calling stupid, babe. I don't take that from anyone."

"I'm sorry. But it isn't fair for you to think I've slept with Jamie either."

"You haven't?" Shannon asked it as if she wasn't going to believe her, whatever she said.

"No, I haven't."

"You're sure?"

"What is this? Twenty questions? I told you, I have not had sex with Jamie Hughes," Dana said, glaring at her. "It's late and I'm tired. I think it's time for you to go."

"I'm not going anywhere until we settle this."

"Shannon," she said, going to the door and holding it open.

"Good night."

Shannon crossed to her and closed the door, pinning Dana into the corner.

"I told you, I'm not leaving." She grabbed Dana's face and kissed her, forcing her tongue into her mouth.

"Shannon, stop it," Dana said, struggling to push her back. "Go home. You're drunk. We'll talk about this later."

"I'm not drunk," she said, forcing another kiss. Shannon's hands formed around Dana's bottom and pulled her close. "I miss you, Dana," Shannon said breathlessly as she fondled Dana's ass. "I want to make love to you right here, right now. I want you to know how much I miss you."

Dana pushed her back and leaned away from another kiss.

"Stop it. I want you to go." Dana pushed back on her chest and reached for the door.

"Like hell," Shannon said, slamming it shut again. "I said I want to fuck." She grabbed Dana by the hair and pulled her head back, forcing another kiss. Dana didn't fight her. She knew she couldn't win. Shannon was taller and stronger. If she really wanted sex, Dana couldn't stop her. Shannon ripped at the waistband of Dana's slacks, popping the button and forcing her way down inside. With one demanding thrust, her fingers curled around Dana's mound and entered her opening, probing deep and insistently. Shannon had never hurt her before, but this time it made Dana wince in pain. Dana reached down and grabbed Shannon's wrist.

"Is this the way you want it to end?" Dana glared up at her. "If you do this, it will be the last time."

Dana had never seen such anger in Shannon before. In the four years they had been together, even the most contentious argument had never brought out this kind of aggression. It was as if she didn't know her. At that moment, she was a complete stranger and it scared Dana. Like confronting a wild animal, Dana knew she shouldn't show her fear.

"It's your choice," Dana said, holding on to her emotions so Shannon couldn't see how frightened she was.

Shannon slowly withdrew her hands.

"You want it just as much as I do," she hissed. "I know you do."

"Not like this, I don't."

Shannon shot her a glare then stormed out, slamming the door. Dana quickly turned the lock and pulled the shade, her hands trembling as she leaned against the doorjamb. She closed her eyes and held her breath, trying not to cry. But it was no use. Tears began streaming down her face. She sank to the floor, beating her fist against the door and sobbing uncontrollably. How could Shannon do that to her?

Dana's first impulse was to call Jamie. At that moment, she would love to feel Jamie's strong arms around her, protecting her and keeping her safe. But this was Dana's moment of truth. She had to handle this for herself. If she wanted Shannon in her life, Dana had to make that decision. If she didn't, that too was her own choice to make. Not Jamie's.

Chapter 19

Dana hadn't slept a wink that night. She was wrapped in a blanket and sitting on the deck of the houseboat as the morning fog obscured the sunrise. It was a gray misty dawn. Dana leaned her head back against the rocker and closed her eyes. She was tired. Not from lack of sleep but from the burden that kept her awake all night. She had trusted Shannon with her heart and her love. From the first moment they moved in together, Dana had placed that trust in Shannon's care. Now to discover it was misplaced was the cruelest blow of all. Dana blamed herself. She had chosen her life with Shannon. She and she alone had allowed her to control her life. As much as Dana hated Shannon for what she had done, she hated herself for being submissive to her domination.

When she opened her eyes again, the fog had lifted. It was after eight o'clock. Shannon would be at work. Dana opened her cell phone and stared at Shannon's number in the contact list. She hated to bother her at work but the time had come for them to talk.

"Hello, babe," Shannon said as if nothing had happened last night. No apology. No remorse.

"Shannon, I need to talk with you. Could you meet me this evening?"

"This evening?" she said hesitantly. "Sure. I can rearrange my schedule. Why don't I pick you up at seven, no six thirty? I'll make us reservations at Bully's Tavern."

"No. I would like you to meet me at the bench at the end of the boardwalk. The one that overlooks the harbor. Seven o'clock." Dana said it with firm conviction.

"Why meet there? I can pick you up at the houseboat and we can go straight from there."

"We aren't going out to eat, Shannon. I just want to talk with you. No reservations. No restaurant. Just you and I having a quiet conversation."

"Okay. No reservation. Tell you what. I saw they have added some benches along the walking trail that circles Capital Lake. I'll pick you up and we can drive over there. Seven?"

"Shannon, listen to me carefully. Seven o'clock at the bench at the end of the boardwalk. Can you make it? If you can't, we can do it tomorrow evening, same time, same place." Dana tried not to be insolent but this was the way she wanted it. On her terms.

"What is so great about that damn bench? It's probably covered in seagull poop. I've given you two perfectly good options and you can't make a decision on either one of them."

"No, you have given me two alternatives to my plans. Shannon, I will be at the bench at seven. This is one time I'd advise you concede to my wishes."

Shannon laughed.

"Okay, fine, babe. I'll meet you at the bench at the end of the boardwalk at seven o'clock." She made it sound like Dana's demands were ridiculous.

"Thank you," Dana said, relieved Shannon had finally agreed.

"See you this evening. And Dana, I love you, babe."

Dana knew she was waiting for her reply. She loved Shannon but that wasn't enough. Dana knew Shannon wouldn't understand that. She pushed the button and ended the call.

Dana went inside and showered. She needed to finish some work on three of her panels but she wasn't in the mood. She couldn't sit still long enough to concentrate on anything. She paced the houseboat, from the deck to the front door, stopping at the galley to make a cup of coffee. She eyed Jamie's shirt hanging on the hook behind the bathroom door. She had washed and worn it several times, each time reminding herself she should return it to Jamie. But she liked to wear it. It was comfortable. It was a little too big and the sleeves were too long, but it fit around her like a reassuring hug. Dana sat down at her computer and opened her e-mail. She drummed her fingers on the keys, deciding how to start an e-mail. Finally, she closed the laptop and picked up her cell phone. She punched in Jamie's cell number but the call went to her voice mail. Dana tried her office number.

"Dr. Hughes's office. May I help you?" It wasn't Jamie's voice.

"Hello. Is she there?" Dana asked.

"I'm sorry but Dr. Hughes has stepped out. Can I take a message?"

"When do you expect her back?"

"I'm not sure. She had to run out to Boston Harbor Marina. Something about her boat."

"Her sailboat?"

"Yes. I think so. Do you want me to have her call you when she gets back?"

"That's all right. I'll call her later." She hung up and headed for the marina. It took her twenty minutes to wind through downtown and out Boston Harbor Road. As she pulled into the parking lot, she could see Jamie standing on the deck of her boat with her hands in her back pockets, studying the tip of the boat. She looked up and smiled at Dana as she headed down the dock.

"Hey, there," Jamie said. "This is a coincidence. What are you doing out here?" She smiled.

"Hello. I called your office. They said you were out here. Is everything all right?" Dana said from the dock.

"Somebody wasn't watching where they were going and sideswiped the bow. The marina owner thought I better take a look at it."

"Is there much damage?"

"I don't think so. A little paint got scraped off and there's a small scuff to the gunwale but it looks like only surface damage." Jamie squatted and rubbed her hand across the missing paint. "Nothing major."

"That's good news. I'm sure you were worried."

"She's a rugged old boat. I couldn't imagine someone could hit it hard enough to do much damage just backing out of a slip. But Jim wanted me to look anyway."

"Is there any damage inside?"

"It doesn't look like it." Jamie brushed off her hands. "So, what brings you out here? Everything all right with you?"

"Everything is fine." Dana said confidently. Just knowing she had come to a decision about Shannon was enough to put a smile on her face. "Can I help with something?" The wind had picked up, rocking the boat in the slip.

"I think I need to take up the slack in the lines so the stern doesn't rub on the dock. What have you got Ringlet doing this morning? Did you get any cartoons finished?" Jamie asked as she retied the lines.

"I started one, but I couldn't get into it. You know how it is. Sometimes you need a little fresh air to clear the cobwebs so I thought I'd come see what you were up to."

"How are things with Shannon?" Jamie said, looking over at Dana as she pulled another half hitch.

"Better," Dana said. "As a matter of fact, I'm meeting her this evening. We're going to have a talk."

"About what?"

"Is it okay if we don't talk about Shannon?" she asked. Dana had made her decision. She didn't need to talk about it. For now, she just wanted to visit with a friend.

"Sure. Whatever you say."

Just as Dana was about to give in and tell Jamie what had happened after she left last night, the dark clouds opened up and it began to sprinkle.

"We better get below," Jamie said, scanning the skies. "I don't like the looks of those clouds." She took Dana's hand and helped her onboard. Dana climbed down into the cabin as a clap of thunder rumbled across the heavens. Jamie followed, closing the hatch behind her.

"I think we got in just in time," Dana said, looking out the porthole at the sudden downpour.

"I think you're right," Jamie peered through Dana's porthole as she wiped the rain from her glasses. "Let's see if I've got anything to drink while we wait it out." She opened the refrigerator. "How would you like yours? Straight up or on the rocks?"

"It depends on what it is," she said, sitting down on the bench next to the tiny galley.

Jamie pulled out two bottles of spring water and read the label.

"Aquafine. Two thousand and nine. A very good year."

"How about right out of the bottle?"

"Good choice," Jamie said, releasing the cap and handing one to Dana. "I'm sorry I don't have anything to eat. I cleaned out the pantry after our trip to Hartstene. I was going to restock with fresh canned goods but I haven't gotten around to it yet."

"That's okay. I don't need anything."

"What time is it, anyway?" She looked down at her bare wrist.

"Eleven fifteen," Dana reported. "I see you forgot your watch again."

"I was running some experiments in the lab and didn't want to get it wet."

"Uh-huh," Dana snickered.

"Okay, I forgot to put it on this morning. What is it about a simple wristwatch that I don't seem to be able to remember?"

"I think that's the answer. It's too simple. It doesn't require deep analytical thought so you forget it. You're busy with other more important details." Dana took a drink, her eyes falling on Jamie's thighs, her muscles visible through her slacks.

"Is that a polite way of saying I'm absentminded?" Jamie sat down next to Dana and leaned back on the bench.

"No, not necessarily."

"Well, I am. Ask me to give the scientific name of every intertidal species in Budd Bay and I'm your girl. Ask me where I left my coffee mug, I won't have a clue." Jamie groaned disgustedly and took another drink.

"Maybe your coffee mug isn't important." Dana patted her leg reassuringly. "I think you're extremely intelligent, watch or no watch."

Jamie looked over at her and smiled.

"Thank you. I take that as a high compliment." Her eyes met Dana's. "And I think you're an extremely talented woman. I've never met anyone with so much insight and sensitivity."

"Don't tease me, Jamie," Dana said, looking away.

Jamie turned Dana's face back to hers. "I'm telling you the God's honest truth. You are very special. Never ever belittle yourself. You're smart. You're sensitive. You're funny. And most of all, you're a beautiful woman." With that, Jamie leaned over and kissed her on the cheek. "And I don't mind if you tell Shannon I said so."

Jamie opened her water bottle and poured a small puddle of water on the table. The sway of the boat threatened to spill the water onto the floor. She quickly placed her finger at the lip of the table, guiding the water to run along the edge.

"What are you doing?" Dana said, grabbing for a paper towel.

"It's a demonstration," Jamie said, sliding her finger along, keeping just ahead of the flow of water. "One of the principles of physics is that substances flow along the path of least resistance. That dribble of water would love to run off the table and onto

240

the floor. To be free to make that choice. But it can't. It can't overcome my resistance. It's forced to stay on the table and run along my finger. I'm in control." Jamie lifted her finger. The water immediately ran off the table. "It's still taking the path of least resistance, but now it has the power to go in a new direction."

"Are you saying you think I have been taking the path of least resistance?"

"I don't know. Have you?"

Like another clap of thunder, the sudden memory of what Shannon did last night sent a shudder through Dana and made her tremble.

"Are you all right?" Jamie looked concerned.

"Yes, I'm fine." Dana took a deep breath and looked out the porthole at the rain. "Just wonderful," she whispered under her breath. Slowly and without warning, tears began to stream down her face. She couldn't help it. She broke down and sobbed. Without a word, Jamie wrapped her arms around Dana and held her as she cried. Through her sobs she could feel Jamie's lips kissing her temple, soothing and reassuring her. It was the most secure she had felt in months.

"Oh, Jamie. How did I lose control of my life?" she said through her tears.

"You haven't, Dana. All you have to do is realize it."

Dana couldn't speak as she cried even harder, her body shaking within Jamie's embrace.

"Shh," Jamie cooed, stroking her hair. "I'm here. Dr. Hughes is right here."

Dana wanted to scream *Where were you last night when Shannon forced her hand inside of me?* But that wasn't Jamie's responsibility. It was Dana's and Dana's alone. She continued to cry.

"I should never have put you in the middle of this," she finally managed. "I'm sorry."

"Dana, no." Jamie hugged her tighter.

"This is my problem. Not yours."

"It's mine, too," she whispered, turning Dana's face up to hers. "Believe me, it's mine, too." With that, Jamie kissed her more

241

tenderly and more passionately than Dana ever expected.

Dana closed her eyes and accepted the kiss. It was exactly what she needed at that moment. Someone who cared and cared deeply. It was more than a kiss. It was an emotional security blanket so real and so soft it blocked out the pain and the anger that had driven her to tears. She threw her arms around Jamie's neck and pressed herself against her, desperate for more. The feel of Jamie's tongue in her mouth sent a tingle through Dana all the way to that spot Shannon had so callously invaded. Dana eagerly devoured Jamie's mouth. Jamie leaned her back on the bench as the kiss became more urgent, both of them moaning and moving against each other. Jamie pressed her knee between Dana's thighs, holding it against her crotch. Her hand brushed over Dana's breast. The wonderfulness of it ignited a flame in both of them. Dana wanted more and Jamie seemed to sense it. She unbuttoned Dana's shirt and cupped her hand over her breast, massaging her nipple between her thumb and finger. Dana could feel a fire smoldering from within, a fire she hadn't felt in months.

Dana pulled Jamie's shirt over her head then released her bra. Touching her erect nipples brought on a guttural moan as Jamie nuzzled against Dana.

"Make love to me," Dana whispered.

Somewhere between kisses, Dana felt her slacks slide down over her hips, followed by her panties. Jamie released Dana's bra and dropped it on the floor.

"You are gorgeous," Jamie said, running her hand over her body. Dana could feel herself melting like butter beneath Jamie's touch. Dana closed her eyes as Jamie took one of her nipples in her mouth.

"Oh, Jamie. That feels so good," she gasped, holding Jamie's head to her chest.

Dana had never felt anything like the electric thrill when Jamie's fingers entered her wetness.

"Yes," she sighed, clamping her hand over Jamie's as she plunged deeper.

The rhythmic swaying of the boat acted to heighten Dana's ecstasy as Jamie's fingers moved in and out of her. Jamie began to methodically kiss down Dana's body, her tongue moving tantalizingly closer to Dana's valley. Jamie knelt on the floor and cradled Dana's hips in her arms, painting kisses up the inside of her thighs. Dana gasped and writhed in her arms, impatiently waiting for Jamie's mouth to take her in.

"Take me, Jamie. Let me feel your hot mouth on me," Dana said, grimacing with anticipation.

Jamie's tongue parted Dana's folds and entered her just as a crack of thunder and a flash of lightning split the air. Dana grabbed the back of the bench, digging her nails into the cushion. Dana had never been a screamer during sex, but she couldn't hold back. She felt an orgasm growing in her so profound and so intense that she couldn't imagine surviving it. She pressed her hips down against Jamie's mouth and held her breath, waiting for it to consume her. Sweat rolled down her face and she began to pant. She finally screamed out as her orgasm exploded through her. Jamie held on, delivering shock after shock. Every muscle in Dana's body clenched. Just when she thought she could endure no more, Jamie plunged her fingers deep inside and held them there, pressing an aftershock up through Dana's body.

"Oh, yes," she gasped, breathlessly stiffening as the last waves washed through her. Jamie lay down next to her, stroking her face as she regained her breath. "Oh, Jamie. You were right. Age definitely has its benefits," she said, smiling contentedly. Dana was exhausted, but she had never felt so satisfied.

Jamie pulled a blanket over them, holding Dana against her as they listened to the raindrops on the cabin.

"I love the sound of the rain," Jamie said, folding her arm over Dana.

"And I love sailboats." Dana kissed Jamie's arm. "Can we stay here all day?"

"I'd love to, sweetheart, but I have to be back at the lab soon." Jamie said, kissing the back of Dana's neck. "I already miss you though."

"Do you really have to go?"

"Regrettably, yes, I do. Can I call you this evening?"

"You better. Oh, wait. I almost forgot. I'm meeting Shannon at seven. I'm not sure how long that will take."

"How about tomorrow morning? Say ten o'clock. I should have my lab techs occupied by then."

"I'll look forward to it," Dana said then began to laugh wickedly.

"What?"

"Boy, am I going to have fun with Ringlet. No telling what I'll have her doing. She is definitely in for a treat."

"You wouldn't?"

"Oh, yes, I would." Dana wiggled against Jamie. "It's about time I let Ringlet have a little sex. She deserves it."

"She most certainly does." She kissed Dana softly then slid off the bench and began to dress. Dana rolled onto her side and watched, grinning seductively.

"You look good in your wet suit but you look even better out of it."

Jamie blushed as she hooked her bra.

"Are you flirting with me?"

"Uh-huh." Dana let her eyes drift down and up Jamie's body.

"I wish I didn't have to go," she said, kissing her softly, her hand lingering on Dana's cheek. "I wish I could take you with me but I'd never get anything done."

It was still raining as Dana headed back to town. She busied herself with the rest of her day as she waited anxiously for her meeting with Shannon. Dana arrived at the bench at precisely seven o'clock. To her amazement, Shannon was late. Fifteen minutes late. Something she almost never was. Dana wondered if it was intentional to show her displeasure and to remain in control.

"Hello, babe," Shannon said. She leaned down to kiss her but Dana turned her face, accepting the kiss on the cheek. "What's the deal? Why are we meeting here?"

"Sit down, honey," Dana said, patting the bench next to her. "We need to talk."

"I don't need to sit down," Shannon grumbled and went to the railing. When she finally turned around she had a stern look on her face. "What do you need to talk about?"

Dana came to the railing, trying to ease into it gently. She didn't want to hurt Shannon's feelings but she knew this wasn't going to be a happy conversation.

"Shannon, I made a phone call today. I called Morgan, my landlord."

"I know who she is."

"I told her I'd like to extend my lease on the houseboat for another three months, maybe more." Dana let that soak in for a moment before continuing. "I told her I may want a long-term lease. I like living on the houseboat."

"That's crazy. Why do you need a long-term lease? You're wasting your money. If you want a vacation home, we'll find something."

"I plan on living here year round, Shannon. I'm not talking about a vacation home. The houseboat is perfect for one."

"What do you mean, perfect for one? You've got another week and your three months are up. I can't wait for you to move back home and put this craziness behind you. I missed you, baby," she said, wrapping her arms around her but Dana pushed her back and moved away.

"I've decided to live on my own."

"You've decided what?" Shannon demanded. "How can you say that? That isn't what the deal was at all. It was three months. That's it. Then you were coming home. I didn't like it, but I agreed to it. Dana, this is nuts. I'm supposed to rearrange my life all over again just because you can't make up your mind?"

"Shannon, I *have* made up my mind. When I moved out, I told you we had some problems. I wasn't happy and I couldn't move back until I had a chance to think things through. I'm sorry it has taken me so long but I now know what's best for me. I'm not moving back to Lacey with you."

"*What?*" Shannon said loudly, loud enough a couple well down the boardwalk turned to look. "What do you mean you aren't moving back to Lacey?"

"Shannon, I'm not what you need. You deserve someone special, someone who can appreciate what you have to offer. And that just isn't me."

"Does this have anything to do with last night? Are you breaking up with me because of that?" She leaned back against the railing and crossed her arms.

"No, not entirely. But, yes. It had a factor in it. I'd be lying if I said it didn't." Dana took a deep breath and continued. "I loved you, Shannon. And I thought you loved me. But what you did last night hurt me, both physically and emotionally. The girl of my dreams would never force herself on me like that."

"So you asked me here to dump me?" she said angrily, as if it came out of the blue. "One minute I've got a girlfriend. The next I don't."

"What you and I want in a girlfriend are two completely different things. I'm only sorry it took me so long to realize it."

Shannon suddenly narrowed her eyes and glared at Dana. "It's that professor, isn't it? She's responsible for this. Isn't she?"

"No, she isn't. Jamie has nothing to do with this. I moved out three months ago, Shannon. Surely you must have considered this might happen. We haven't been happy for a long time."

"Are you telling me you never talked to her about us, about you and me?"

"I won't lie to you. Yes, I have talked to her. But this is my decision. Mine and mine alone. Jamie never told me what to do. I merely talked with her as a friend. I told her I was confused about what I wanted in my life. She listened and gave me support to make decisions for myself."

"Yeah, right. I told you she was a sexually frustrated, middle-aged dyke. You can't tell me she doesn't have an interest in what you do. She can't wait for you to dump me so she can move in on my girl. I can't believe you didn't see her ulterior motives."

"Jamie never ever tried to influence me on what I should do.

246

I know I have to make a change. It's time for me to make my own decisions. Good or bad, right or wrong. For my own sanity and my own happiness, I need to start over. And you deserve that, too. Can't we do this amicably?"

"I don't know, Dana. How should I react when my girl tells me it's over? Should I laugh and said, hey, that's great. Or should I just nod and walk away with my tail between my legs? You tell me. I knew I should have insisted on meeting somewhere else. I hate this damn marina crap." She groaned and turned away. "I love you, Dana," she said quietly. "Have you forgotten that?"

"No, I haven't forgotten." Dana went to stand next to her. "I haven't forgotten, honestly, I haven't. And I love you, too. I'm just not in love with you. I deserve to be in love. So do you, honey. So do you."

Shannon stood staring out at a passing boat. Her face had lost all expression. Dana couldn't help but feel sorry for her.

"I wish you happiness, Shannon. I really truly do. It just can't be with me." Dana squeezed Shannon's arm, turned, and headed up the boardwalk.

"Dana?" Shannon called. "Would your decision have been different if you hadn't met Jamie Hughes?"

Dana thought a moment and then turned around.

"Yes, it might have been. But you wouldn't have wanted that girl. She wasn't being honest with herself." Dana pulled her jacket closed and continued up the boardwalk.

Chapter 20

Jamie unlocked her office and flipped on the light. She planned to call Dana as soon as she checked her messages. She had fought the urge to call her as soon as she got up but decided six fifteen was too early for a social call. She had fumbled with her cell phone all the way across the parking lot and up the stairs of the science building, anxious for a quiet moment she could spend visiting with Dana. She had so much to tell her. How special yesterday was. How much she looked forward to seeing her again, perhaps for dinner. And how much she hoped Dana's meeting with Shannon had gone well. Jamie was also wrestling with her own guilt. Guilt for making love to a woman who wasn't free. As far as Jamie was concerned, Shannon didn't deserve Dana but that wasn't her place to say. If they could work out their differences, who was Jamie to say otherwise? From that first time they met on Ruth Ann's boat, she knew Dana had the intelligence and determination to sift through her feelings and find an answer to her uncertainty. All Jamie had to do was offer encouragement and support. She had to admit making love to Dana may have been wrong, but at that moment it felt so right. If she had the chance to do it over again, Jamie wasn't sure she would do it differently. And that thought angered her.

Jamie reached for the telephone. Before she finished dialing Dana's number, there was a knock at her office door.

"Come in," she said, hesitating before entering the last number. The door opened and Shannon stood in the doorway.

"Hello, Dr. Hughes."

Jamie could tell she had something on her mind.

"Hello, Shannon." Jamie replaced the receiver in the cradle and stood up, offering Shannon a handshake. "Is there something I can help you with? Please, have a seat."

"No, thanks. This won't take long. I've come to tell you I don't think you have Dana's best interest at heart, professor."

"I beg your pardon."

"Dana tells me she has been talking to you about us. I don't think it's fair for you to offer opinions when you don't know what's going on."

"I have no idea what you are talking about. But I assure you I haven't told Dana to do anything. And what's more, don't you think what she and I talk about is our business? Not yours." Jamie sat on the corner of her desk, nonchalantly folding her hands across her lap.

"No, I don't. When you're talking about my relationship with my girlfriend, that *is* my business. I love her, professor, and I would do anything to protect her. Ever since you knocked her key ring overboard, you have been forcing your way into our lives. I'm getting a little tired of hearing Jamie this and Jamie that. You know what I think? I think you knocked her key ring off the railing on purpose."

"Ah, yes. The infamous key ring. Your gift to Dana."

"Damn right. I designed it especially for her. I wanted her to have the best."

"Silver, right?"

"No, not cheap silver. Gold. White gold. It looks like silver but it's pure gold. Dana likes that."

"What girl wouldn't like gold? I'm glad I could retrieve it for her." Jamie sat down in her desk chair and opened the drawer. "As a matter of fact, I thought about getting one for myself. I was going to call you and ask where I could order one. But as luck would have it, I found one at an open-air craft market a couple weeks ago. It isn't exactly like Dana's but it's pretty close." Jamie continued to sort through the papers and junk at the back of the drawer. "Here it is." She took out a small brown sack with the receipt stapled across the flap. She opened the sack and pulled out a key ring, suspending it from her index finger. Shannon's expression instantly changed to a scowl. The key ring looked identical to Dana's, right down to the engraved interlocking hearts. "It's not exactly like Dana's," Jamie said, wiggling her finger. "I didn't have the lady put initials on it. It only cost an extra two bucks, but I like it plain. What do you think, Shannon?"

"Where did you get that?" Shannon snapped.

"Of course, adding initials does give it a personalized touch. I could have had block letters or script letters, like Dana's. I'm more of a block letter kind of person myself," Jamie said as Shannon stared at it in horror. "It was even on sale. Regularly fourteen ninety-five, on sale for nine bucks. It's only silver plate, but what the heck. Right?"

"That may look like Dana's but hers is gold. White gold."

"The lady said they looked like white gold," Jamie said, examining it. "Sometimes it's hard to tell. I guess it could pass as white gold if you didn't know the difference."

"Well, Dana's is gold," Shannon insisted. "Not cheap silver plate."

"Right. That's what she said."

"I know the difference between silver and gold."

"The big difference being cost, right?" Jamie dropped the key ring back in the drawer and closed it. "Of course, there's a simple way to make sure you get what you pay for when it comes to gold."

"What's that?" Shannon asked skeptically.

"I'm glad you asked. I've been conducting a little experiment." Jamie pointed to the two beakers of brackish water on the file cabinet next to her desk. "Silver has a bad habit of tarnishing. You know how silverware turns black in the drawer." She used a pair of tongs to lift out a blackened ring. "Anything containing sulfur will cause silver to tarnish. Eggs, fossil fuels, onions and even oily hands will cause silver to tarnish. Humidity only accelerates it. Ocean water, for example." She placed the ring back in the beaker. "It's a chemical reaction between the sulfur and the surface of the silver." She used the tongs to fish a ring out of the second beaker. It was silver in color without a speck of tarnish on it. "Gold, on the other hand, even white gold, doesn't tarnish. That's why it's used to make the connections on silicon chips in integrated circuit boards. Unlike silver, it isn't affected by atmospheric conditions." Jamie looked over at Shannon. She could see her mind scrambling to make sense of what she was saying. "You could drop a gold ingot in Budd Bay, bring it up a month later and it would look just as good as new. It might have a little sediment and algae overgrowth but not tarnish." Jamie dropped the gold ring back in the beaker then turned to Shannon.

"So what?" Shannon frowned.

"When I was looking for Dana's key ring on the bottom of the bay, I almost didn't see it. It was so black and tarnished it was nearly invisible."

"What are you driving at?"

"I'm just saying, it's hard to argue with science. If Dana's key ring had been white gold, like you said, it wouldn't have tarnished. Don't you think that's a fair assumption?" Jamie watched Shannon begin to squirm. "I'm not sure what your motives are, but who are you trying to fool? That key ring was silver, Shannon. Not gold. What did you pay for it? Ten bucks? Why did you tell Dana it was gold?"

"You don't know what you're talking about. It's gold, I tell you. Gold," she shouted. "That one you have is just a cheap imitation."

"Do you think so little of Dana that you have to impress her with expensive gifts?"

"You're crazy. You're just trying to make me look bad in her eyes. You told her this crap, didn't you?"

"Dana doesn't know. She still thinks hers is gold and for all she knows, gold tarnishes. She'll never hear a word about it from me. It isn't my place to tell her."

"I don't believe you."

Jamie shrugged.

"That's your prerogative. But I'm telling you I haven't said a word. Why would I? Why would I want to deliberately hurt her?"

Shannon's eyes narrowed.

"I don't want to hurt her, either," she said. "I love her. I only want to protect her."

"Protect her or control her?" Jamie asked.

"Protect her," she scowled. "She needs someone to take care of her."

"Dana needs someone to share her life, not run it for her."

"What the hell do you know?" Shannon opened the office door, ready to leave. "I love her and she'd still be mine if you hadn't interfered."

"What are you talking about?" Jamie frowned.

"She broke up with me last night. She said you told her to. You and your advice. She even admitted you were the reason." Shannon gave a last bitter look and stormed out.

Jamie opened the door and stepped out into the hall but Shannon had gone, her footsteps echoing down the hall.

"SHE WHAT?!!!" Jamie shouted, but there was no reply. "I didn't tell her to do that."

She went back in her office and grabbed the telephone, ready to call Dana and find out what had happened. But she hung up just as it began to ring. Jamie sank back in her chair, trying to make sense of it. She hoped Shannon was wrong. The last thing

Jamie wanted to do was break up anyone's relationship. She would never forgive herself if Dana's decision to end her relationship with Shannon came out of a moment of vulnerability. What if Shannon was right? What if Dana's decision was made from the heat of passion?

"Shit," Jamie said, locking her hands behind her head. "What have I done?"

"Are you talking to me?" Hanna said from the doorway to the lab. She was carrying a stack of textbooks.

"No," Jamie said, absentmindedly. She continued to stare out in space, wrinkling her forehead as she thought.

"The bookstore called. They can't get enough copies of Dr. Osborn's book before classes start. What are you going to do? Should we use last year's text?"

"She should never have listened to me. What did I think I was doing?" She stood up and stormed out of the office without answering Hanna.

"Dr. Hughes?" Hanna said, following her out into the hall, trying to balance the heavy stack of books. "Dr. Hughes, what do I tell them?"

"Don't tell anybody anything," Jamie shouted without looking back. "It'll only cause heartache."

"Where are you going?"

"To hell, probably." Jamie hurried down the stairs and across the parking lot. She had just one thing in mind. She had to tell Dana she was wrong. Her advice was tainted by her own emotions. She raced toward downtown Olympia. The closer she got to the marina, the more she realized that might not be the best plan. Jamie wasn't sure she could tell Dana she was wrong. She had an undeniable attraction for Dana, one she felt the first moment their eyes met. She had tried to tell herself there wasn't a physical attraction but there was. It was stronger than anything she had ever felt. Every fiber of Jamie's being longed for one more precious touch and kiss.

Jamie pulled into the parking lot. She sat staring at the security gate. She knew the code and could easily descend the dock to the houseboat. Dana would be there, working on her cartoons or sitting on the deck with her laptop, sending out e-mail. Jamie could almost see her, curled up in the rocker, her long hair stirred by the breeze off the bay. Jamie didn't trust herself. How could she tell Dana she was wrong when deep down inside she couldn't wait to hold Dana in her arms again? Jamie restarted the car and returned to her office to busy herself in work. Dana called several times but Jamie didn't answer. As she was locking her office to leave for the day, the telephone on her desk rang again. It was Dana's number on the ID. Jamie hesitated then finally answered it.

"Hello. Dr. Hughes, here," she said, standing at her desk.

"Hello, yourself," Dana said with a chuckle. "I was beginning to think you fell in one of your beakers of slime. I've tried to get you all day. I thought you were going to call this morning."

"I'm sorry. We got busy. Problems with the textbooks. And I had to finish up my syllabi. The week before classes start is always hectic."

"I can guess. I bet you are exhausted."

"A little."

"How would you like to come to the houseboat for dinner? You can sit on the deck and watch the sailboats while I cook for you. I make a mean chicken salad." She gave one of her soft laughs that turned Jamie on like nothing she had ever experienced. "After dinner we can watch the sunset from the loft."

"I'm sorry, Dana. I can't. I've got a faculty meeting tonight." Jamie wasn't lying. Three of the professors were meeting for pizza and a pitcher of beer. She could easily get out of it but she couldn't, in good faith, do that. She didn't want to encourage a situation she knew would end up in bed. She didn't want to take advantage of Dana like that again.

"How about afterward? The sunset is going to be really spectacular tonight. I guarantee it."

"I'm sure it is but I'm sorry. We've got a lot to go over."

"Okay. Not tonight. Tomorrow night. I'll make something special for dinner."

"We've got faculty meetings all this week."

"All week?" Dana said, obviously disappointed. "But Jamie, I need to talk to you. When can I schedule an appointment, Dr. Hughes?"

"It may be a while, Dana. Once the semester starts I'll be pretty busy. I've got field trips scheduled for almost every weekend. I'll have reports to grade and labs to setup. I don't have much free time." Jamie sat down in her chair and removed her glasses.

"Are you trying to say you're too busy for me?"

"No. I'm just saying for a while I'll be busy with my classes." She propped her hand against her forehead and closed her eyes. "I'm sorry, Dana, but summer is over and I don't have time to do much of anything. Maybe we can work something out during the holidays."

"What holidays?" she asked warily.

"Thanksgiving. Maybe Christmas." Jamie moved the receiver away from her mouth, worried Dana would hear the anguish in her sigh.

"Jamie, this is September. Are you saying I won't see you until November or December?" There was a tremble of disbelief in Dana's voice.

"Being department chair has its drawbacks."

"Could I at least come out and meet you for lunch sometime?"

"It's hard to say. The middle of the day is when I make myself available to my students for conferences and assistance in the lab."

The silence before Dana's reply was heart wrenching for Jamie. She wiped a tear from her eye and cleared her throat.

"But Jamie, I need to talk with you. I have something important to tell you. It can't wait until November. One evening. A few hours. That's all I'm asking. It's about Shannon."

"I'm concerned my hectic schedule will interfere with my ability to be objective. I really think you need to find someone else to talk with, someone who doesn't have a conflict of interest. I have to go, Dana. I'll be late. I'll call you when I have some free time. Okay?" She waited for Dana's reply. It was a long time in coming.

"Okay." Dana hung up.

Jamie locked her office and walked the darkened hallway to the stairs. She sat down on the top step, unable to see through her tears. If she stepped out of the picture, perhaps Dana would reconsider and return to Shannon. Jamie told herself it was for Dana's own good. She ripped the glasses from her face and threw them down the stairs, mashing them into a million pieces. In her mind, she knew it was the right thing to do but in her heart, she would never forgive herself for throwing away the best thing she had ever known.

Chapter 21

Dana couldn't believe what she had heard. Jamie had gone from passionate one day to distant the next. And nothing had happened in the interim. Nothing except Dana had finally come to her senses and ended Shannon's four-year domination of her life. But that shouldn't have had anything to do with it. In fact, Jamie hadn't even allowed her to tell her that news. It was as if Jamie no longer cared what Dana did or thought. The months of her friendship and encouragement had ended as suddenly as they began. And Dana didn't know why. What had she done to push Jamie away? If there was blame to place, she thought it must have something to do with the afternoon they spent together on the sailboat. Perhaps Dana had lured Jamie into something she wasn't ready for. Maybe she wasn't completely over Terry and making love to Dana only reminded her of that. Whatever it was, Dana had to know.

It didn't take much detective work to find a telephone number for Dusty Hooten on Hartstene Island. If there was anyone who might know what was going on with Jamie, it had to be Dusty, Terry's sister.

"Robbins, D," Dusty said, answering the call cheerfully. "That has to be our Dana girl." She laughed robustly. "Hello, you sweet thing. How's my favorite cartoonist?"

"Hi, Dusty," Dana replied, not really expecting such a warm welcome. "I'm fine. How are you and Bo?"

"Bo has grown another foot, I think. We're dandy. She and a group of friends are spending the day in Seattle, eating and shopping all over Pikes Place Market. Moi was NOT invited. Thank goodness." Dusty chuckled. "When are you and Jamie coming up for the weekend? I've got extra beds."

"Good question."

"What do you mean?"

"Dusty, that's why I called. Have you talked to Jamie recently? In the past few days?"

"No, I haven't heard from her since you two were up here for lunch. What's this about Jamie? What's going on with the two of you?"

"Oh, it isn't us. I'm just asking about her."

"If it has anything to do with Jamie and you are asking, it has to do with the two of you," Dusty said in a perceptive tone. "Now, what's up?"

"It's sort of difficult to explain."

"That sounds ominous."

"Jamie has all of a sudden closed the door to our friendship. She has conveniently become so busy at school she doesn't have time to have lunch with me. Or even a conversation. I don't know what I did or didn't do but I thought maybe she had said something to you about it."

"Did you two have an argument?"

"No. That's the strange part of it." Dana couldn't decide if she should admit she and Jamie made love on her boat or not. Jamie might considerate that private. "We went from fine one day, laughing and having fun on her boat, to her having a dozen reasons she didn't have time for me the next."

"What were you doing on her boat? Arguing about something? Although I can't imagine Jamie arguing about anything. She isn't that kind of person. She's pretty passive most of the time. She relies on rationale to solve problems. I don't think I ever heard her and Terry raise their voice to each other. I assume she told you about Terry."

"Yes. My sincerest sympathy, Dusty."

"Thanks, honey. She was a great gal. But let's talk about this problem you are having with Jamie. How long has this been going on?"

"The last time I talked with her for more than two minutes was a week ago. I've tried to call her but she's either too busy to talk for more than a few minutes or won't return my calls at all. When I mention having her over, she cuts the conversation short. I know she's busy, but surely she has some time to at least talk to me. I don't know what I've done, Dusty. If it's something I said, I wish she'd tell me."

"Can I ask a personal question?"

"Sure." Dana had a good idea what she was going to ask.

"Have you and Jamie been intimate? And believe me when I say, I hope so."

"Yes. It was on her sailboat the afternoon before she became too busy for us anymore," Dana said, surprised at how easy it was to confide in Dusty, almost as easy as it was to confide her feelings to Jamie. "It was our first time."

"I'm afraid all I can say is keep trying to get a hold of her. Eventually she'll give in and talk to you. I'm sure of it. She is very practical about stuff like that."

"Do you mind if I ask you a personal question?"

"Go ahead, but if you want to know if Jamie and I have slept together, the answer is no," she said with a little chuckle. "Although, if I decided to swap sides, it would be with someone exactly like her. She's a wonderful caring person. And I know something else. She loves you, Dana."

"That wasn't what I was going to ask but first things first. How do you know she loves me? Did she tell you that?"

"No. But I could tell. I've never seen her so at ease with someone before, not even with Terry. Oh, she loves you all right. She may not know it yet herself but she does. If there is one thing I know about Jamie, it's that she wouldn't have had sex with you unless she was in love with you. You can take that to the bank. But I think you already knew that about her character. Now, what did you want to ask me?"

"This may sound nosy but I was wondering what you whispered to Jamie that day when we were getting ready to leave the island?"

Dusty laughed. "Is that all?"

"Whatever it was, I saw her look a little misty-eyed. Then she looked angry. I was just curious. I was wondering if Jamie still has issues over losing Terry I should know about."

"Jamie Hughes has lived in the painful past long enough. Ever since Terry died, she has buried herself in work so she won't have to commit to anyone. For years she's been talking herself out of love. God only knows why but she doesn't think she has anything to offer a woman anymore. I just told her it was time to take a new tack, for her heart's sake. I told her she needed to be in love again. Terry would want her to. I may be overstepping my bounds here, but I told her I thought she had already found love if she would just open her eyes and look around. If you love her, Dana, you need to let her know. And you need to be patient with her. Falling in love again scares the hell out of her. But I guarantee she's worth the wait, honey." Dana could hear a doorbell ringing in the background. "Dana, sweetheart, I have to go. I've got a client at the door. Call me later, okay? Just remember. She may be a stuffy old science professor but she's a keeper. You'll see. Bye-bye."

Dana stood on the deck of the houseboat, staring down at the murky water. Jamie loved her. Knowing that, even if it was only Dusty's hunch, brought a smile to her face. She hadn't realized it until that very moment, but yes, she loved Jamie, too. She didn't know how she could have missed it. She hadn't ended her relationship with Shannon to attract Jamie. That much she did know. If it hadn't been for Jamie's support she might not have found the courage to free herself from Shannon's domination. And for that she would be forever grateful. But that wasn't why she did it. How was she going to tell her how much she really cared if Jamie wouldn't talk to her? For a week Dana worked on her cartoons, enjoyed the solitude of the houseboat and made twice-daily calls to Jamie's voice mail. She was being patient, just as Dusty suggested.

"Hello, Jamie," she said, as her voice mail picked up. "This is Dana with your afternoon call. Ringlet has a girlfriend. They meet in the backyard and rub noses through the fence. I think I'll put a Band-Aid on her nose and call it a love wound. What do you think? I hope classes are going well. I'm sure you're busy, but I hope you have time to call soon. I feel so good about my decision to end things with Shannon. I guess I had to wait until I had had enough. It's amazing how that works. One minute you can't do something. The next you can. It helps to have someone special in your corner cheering you on. Thank you, Jamie. And believe it or not, Shannon has moved on, too. I understand she has a new girlfriend. Actually, it's an old one. Maggie, Eva's daughter. According to reliable sources, she was spending the night at Shannon's apartment right after I moved into the houseboat. I wonder what Shannon would have done if I gave in and offered to move back to Lacey with her. Start a harem? Anyway, I hope they find happiness. I guess that's all for this message." Dana hesitated before hanging up. "And Jamie, in case it matters, I love you. With all my heart and soul, I love you. I love you so much it hurts that I can't be with you. Please call me."

Dana hung up and went for a walk along the boardwalk. Autumn colors speckled the trees and the air had lost its summer warmth. September in Washington was a beautiful month with sailboats still filling the harbor. Dana wrapped her jacket around her and leaned against the railing as she watched a small cabin cruiser drift with the tide. The skipper was taking in the fenders, not paying any attention that his boat was drifting precariously close to another. He finally started the engine and steered into open water before the tide could push the boats together. Dana had often wondered what would happen if the houseboat got loose and floated out into the harbor. Without a motor she wouldn't be able to steer it back to the slip. Morgan had assured her it wouldn't happen since marina residents looked out for one another, but it crossed Dana's mind, nonetheless. The last place she wanted to be was floating helplessly across Puget Sound in the middle of the night.

Or did she?

Dana arched an eyebrow curiously. What would happen if she was adrift at sea? Could that possibly be reason enough to get Jamie to come help? She had a motorboat to tow the houseboat back to the marina, and she lived close enough to be only a few minutes away.

"Could I get her to do that?" Dana muttered, smiling mischievously. "If Dr. Hughes hasn't got time to return my calls could I get her to rescue the houseboat?"

Dana hurried back up the boardwalk to the bulletin board where the marina owners posted the tidal chart. She hadn't paid much attention to the comings and goings of the tides other than she knew it was easier to carry heavy things up the gangplank during high tide when it wasn't as steep. According to the chart, high tide tonight would be just after midnight. That was perfect. The tide would start to go out by one and by two a.m. anything floating on the surface of Budd Bay would be on its way out to sea, or at least out to Puget Sound. And if her scheme worked, Morgan Faylor's turquoise houseboat would be one of those things adrift with the current.

"Sorry, Morgan," Dana said to herself, keying in the security code. "Forgive me but this is one of those things you do for love."

Dana did a little housework then waited impatiently for the sun to go down. Just after eleven o'clock she began preparing the houseboat for its journey. She unhooked the hose to the dock water supply and pulled the plug from the electric meter. With a flashlight in hand, she watched as the tide climbed up the dock post, covering the nests of mussels and barnacles. High tide in Budd Bay came at twelve ten. She waited nervously, worried someone would notice what she was doing. Or worse, call Morgan or the harbor patrol that a crazy woman was setting a houseboat adrift in the middle of the night. Slowly, the water mark on the post at the end of the finger pier began to recede. The tide was going out. Dana untied the ropes that secured the boat in place then hurried inside, ready to be carried away from the dock. But nothing happened. The boat just sat in the slip, seemingly unaware it was free to move with the tide. Dana opened the door and peeked out. The lights along the dock cast enough light for her to see all the way to the gangplank. When she saw the coast was clear, she stepped out and gave the dock a shove with her foot, hoping to get the cumbersome boat moving. It was like pushing a barn. She tried again, leaning heavily against the end of the boat.

"Come on," she grunted as she pushed. "It's time to move. We're going to take a nice little trip out in the harbor." She braced her feet on the dock cleats and leaned all her weight against the boat. A wave rolled ashore and lapped at the dock. As the wave rolled out again the boat moved with it, inching away from the dock. Dana stepped onboard and watched as the rolling action of the waves slowly floated the houseboat out of the slip. She took a deep breath as the boat cleared the end of the finger pier. She had passed the point of no return. She couldn't get the houseboat back into its secure moorage now if she wanted to. She was committed to this foolishness. And the further out into the harbor she floated, the more she realized it was just that. She ran through the living room and out onto the deck, squinting out into the darkness. It was a starless sky and she couldn't see ten feet in front of the boat.

"Oh, my God. What have I done?" she gasped in horror. She hurried back to the dock side door and rummaged in the storage bin, looking for something she could use to pull the boat back to the dock but by now she could barely see the slip through the darkness, let alone reach it.

"No, no, no. I've changed my mind." She shined the flashlight at the dock, hoping to see someone she could hail to help pull her back to safety. There was no one. Not one light from a single boat. She tried rocking the boat, jumping up and down on the deck to change the boat's direction but it was no use. She was on her way out of Budd Bay. And she felt stupid. Too stupid to call Jamie and tell her what had happened. Who else could she call at two o'clock in the morning and ask for help getting her boat back to the marina? Not anyone she knew. Steve didn't have a boat and he would never let her live it down. Ruth Ann and Connie had a boat but she couldn't call them in the middle of the night. Besides, she thought she had heard Ruth Ann say their motor was on the fritz. Shannon would be the last person on the earth she would call, not since she found out the sheets weren't even cold before she had Maggie on them. She'd swim ashore first. There was only one person she could call. Only one person with a boat and who had the nautical knowledge to help. Dana pulled out her cell phone and punched in Jamie's number. It went to her voice mail. She had no choice but leave a message.

"I'm sorry to bother you, Jamie. It's two a.m. and I'm on my houseboat, floating out to sea. Don't ask why. The tide is going out and I'm going with it. I'm sorry but I didn't know who else to call. I don't know what to do. I don't even have an anchor. Help!" Dana hung up and clutched the phone to her chest, trying to decide what she should do. As the tide continued out, the houseboat drifted toward the lighted buoy in the middle of the harbor. Dana wished she had electricity so she could at least show a light from the window. She pointed her flashlight out the front like a headlight but the batteries were fading and she didn't have anymore. She wished she had planned better.

"Where's the harbor patrol issuing citations when you need them?" she said, using the last of her flashlight to scan the harbor for help. Her light finally went out, leaving her in darkness. She opened her cell phone, using the dim light of the screen for comfort. Jamie hadn't called back and Dana knew she wasn't going to. If the houseboat didn't hit something on its way out into Puget Sound, Dana wondered how far she would drift before someone noticed and came to help. Miles, probably. After all, it wouldn't be light for hours. Dana wasn't sure if she should remain on the deck, expecting to hit something or if she should go inside, away from the railing and the inevitable collision. Before she could decide, she heard two blasts from a ship's horn. Judging by the sound of the horn, it wasn't a large boat. Probably a sailboat she was about to hit.

"Ahoy, the houseboat," a voice called over the sound of the approaching motor.

"Yes, ahoy," Dana shouted, waving her arms. She squinted into the boat's bright searchlight, trying to see who it was. "I need a tow. Can you help me, please?"

The motor on the approaching boat revved as it eased up to the deck of the houseboat.

"I'm coming alongside," the skipper said, the light still blindingly bright in Dana's eyes. As the boat gently nudged the stern Dana could make out the outline of the pilothouse and an inflatable dinghy tied to the top. She could also see a metal cage suspended from a winch on the back of the boat. Jamie had a cage like that. In fact Jamie had a boat like that as well. Just like that, right down to the air tank rack.

"Jamie?" she said, holding her breath at the possibility it could actually be her.

"Who else did you expect?" she said from somewhere behind the light. "You called, didn't you?"

"Yes." Dana was never so relieved in her life. Embarrassed but relieved.

"Well, here I am. Are you okay?"

"I'm okay. I feel really stupid but I'm okay."

Jamie lowered the light and wrapped a line around the railing of the houseboat.

"Stand back in case the line breaks." She went back to the pilothouse and urged the throttle forward.

"Are you going to push me back to my slip?" she asked hopefully.

"No. I'm just pushing you into deeper water so you won't run aground. By dawn this part of the bay will be an exposed mud flat."

Dana hung over the side, staring down into the black water. Jamie pointed the searchlight at the spot where she was looking. Sure enough, even through the murky waters, she could see the rocky bottom. How would she ever explain to Morgan why her lovely turquoise houseboat was perched on a mud flat in the middle of the bay? It would be hard to conceal since the harbor was visible from almost any vantage point in downtown Olympia. Jamie finally dropped anchor and turned off the motor. She secured another line to the houseboat, keeping it snug against the side of the research boat.

"Can I ask how you ended up floating toward West Side Marina?" Jamie said, dropping rubber fenders between the two boats to keep them from rubbing. She was dressed in jeans, sandals and a bright yellow rain jacket with the hood crowded up around the back of her neck. She had an understandably disgusted look on her face.

"West Side Marina? I thought I was headed out into Puget Sound."

"The wind was pushing you northwest. Another twenty minutes and you would have entered the marina channel. My guess is you would have bounced around in there like a pinball."

"Do you think I would have hit another boat?" Dana asked fearfully. Jamie only chuckled. "I didn't mean to hit anyone. Really I didn't. It was just an accident."

"Just an accident that all six dock lines came loose at the same time?"

"Could you just push me back to my marina?" Dana asked, realizing her plan was totally irresponsible.

"Not in the dark, I can't. It's hard enough to maneuver a big tub like this in the daylight. Fitting it into that narrow slip at night is next to impossible. And I don't think you want to put a hole in the hull." Jamie grinned at her own pun. "Besides, I can't push it. I'll have to rig a tow sling through the metal eyelets. I don't want to do any damage moving it. It's just an epoxy covered wood frame."

"Is this your technical way of telling me I have to spend the rest of the night out here in the middle of the bay?"

"This is my way of telling you this was a bad idea. I'm not sure what you had in mind but ask next time."

"I would have loved to but I couldn't. You won't return my calls. When you do, it's ten seconds of hi, how are you then you have to go."

"You were going to ask if you should set the houseboat adrift in Budd Bay?" Jamie said, raising her eyebrows.

"If you really want to know, I set the houseboat adrift in Budd Bay so I could ask you something."

"Ask me what?" she said, shoving her hands in her jacket pockets as the wind picked up, stirring her hair.

"Why don't you come onboard so we don't have to shout?" Dana said, waving her over.

"Ask me what?" Jamie didn't move.

"Ask you why you won't talk to me. Don't you think it's time you tell me why?" Dana stood at the railing, waiting for Jamie's reply.

"I told you, Dana, I've been busy at school. The first few weeks of the semester are always busy."

"I don't believe you. I think there is something else. And I think it has something to do with that afternoon we spent on your sailboat. Something happened between that afternoon and the next. I don't know what but it must be important. Now I want to know what it is."

"Nothing happened."

"Are you going to come onboard or not?" Dana said, scowling over at her. "Because if you aren't, I'm coming over there." She grabbed the post and climbed onto the railing.

"Dana, wait. You're going to fall overboard," Jamie said, reaching across and grabbing her legs. "Get down."

"No. I'm going to stay right here." She wrapped both arms around the post and looked down triumphantly. "At least I've got your attention. That's more than I've had in a week."

"Please, get down and we'll talk."

"But I like it up here," Dana said, looking across the bay at the lights from the marina. "I've got a great view."

Jamie started to laugh. Soft at first. But it grew louder.

"I guess I shouldn't tell you what to do, should I? You're a free woman, free to make your own decisions."

"Yes, I am. For the first time in four years, I can stand on the railing on this boat and no one can tell me not to."

"You've always been able to do that. You just didn't realize it."

Dana took one more look around and smiled down at Jamie.

"Would you help me down?"

Jamie took her hand and helped her back onto the deck.

"Jamie, if I said or did something to upset you, I wish you'd tell me."

"It isn't you, Dana. It's me. I'm worried I may have said something to influence your decision to break up with Shannon. It wasn't my place to do that. I had become personally involved and that meant I could no longer be objective. That wasn't fair to you or to Shannon. What we did on my boat was wrong if it in any way changed your decision. I feel very guilty about that."

"Jamie, I had already made up my mind what I was going to do before I came out to Boston Harbor to see you that day. I knew I had to end it with Shannon. I think I knew it a long time before that. Maybe from the moment I moved out of her apartment. I just had to get it through my thick head. Like you said, I think I was taking the path of least resistance. It was easier to give in than to stand up for myself. And yes, you helped me come to that decision but in a good way. You let me see I could be on my own. You showed me how to start over," Dana said, shaking her head. "Let's just say, thank my lucky stars I did. I hate to think where I would be if I hadn't. You didn't make the decision for me. You let me make it. And I love you for it," she said fondly. Dana leaned over and kissed Jamie, the two of them leaning across the gap between the boats. Just then the houseboat moved, throwing Dana into the railing.

"Are you okay?" Jamie grabbed for her.

"Yes," she said, holding onto the post. "What was that? Did we hit something?"

Jamie checked the other side.

"No. But I need to drop another anchor to keep us from spinning on the anchor chain. Be right back."

"I have to go in for a minute." Dana disappeared inside while Jamie set the anchor and checked the lines. When Dana didn't return after a few minutes, Jamie tilted the searchlight into the living room of the houseboat.

"Are you in there?" she called, scanning the light across the windows. "Are you all right?"

"Yes," Dana said, stepping back out onto the deck. She had on Jamie's blue chambray shirt and nothing else. Only the bottom button kept it from falling open. The top was open, exposing her bare cleavage down to her navel. The cuffs of the shirt were turned back and the collar was up, standing seductively close to her chin. "I'm right here," she said coyly.

Jamie's jaw dropped. She looked Dana up and down, slowly pulling a smile.

"I'm officially a liberated woman," Dana said, placing her hands on her hips. "I just thought you'd like to see what one looks like. What do you think, Dr. Hughes?"

"That shirt never looked that good on me," Jamie said, unable to take her eyes off of Dana's youthful figure.

"I forgot to give it back. Would you like to come get it?" Dana said as she ran her hand down the opening, pulling the shirt open slightly.

"I was going to let you keep it," Jamie said, flipping the searchlight to dim and hopping over the railing. "But maybe I should reclaim it," she grinned.

"By all means. Anything you see that you like, you should claim it," Dana said seductively.

"Are you sure it's mine?" Jamie said, unbuttoning the bottom button and slipping her hands inside the shirt.

"Maybe you should try it on," Dana said, stepping closer. "If you like it, it's all yours."

"Oh, I like it," Jamie whispered, taking Dana in her arms. "But do I deserve it? That's what worries me. I'm just an old professor. You're a gorgeous sexy woman."

"You really shouldn't worry," Dana said, hooking her arms around Jamie's waist and looking deep into her eyes. "From my point of view, you are one sexy professor, Dr. Hughes. And I can't wait to show you how much." She grinned up at her. "Kiss me, professor."

Jamie kissed her, lifting her off the ground.

"Wait," Dana said, suddenly pushing her away. "I need to do something first." She ran inside, leaving Jamie on the deck with a confused look on her face. A minute later she returned with the key ring. "We have some unfinished business."

"Are we still discussing who was at fault for knocking that thing overboard? Okay. I take the blame completely."

"No. We are discussing how deep the water is here. If I dropped it here, would you be able to find it and get it back for me?"

"No." Jamie laughed. "It's forty feet deep. With ships coming and going through the channel I'd never find it. So be careful with it."

"Oh, I will." Dana wrapped her fingers around it, securing it in her hand. "I want to put it where I'll always know where it is." She walked to the railing and threw the key ring as far as she could into the darkness. All they heard was a plunk. She brushed off her hands. Then, she threw herself back into Jamie's arms. "There. I took real good care of it."

"Is that the beginning of your new life as a liberated woman?"

"Yes."

"What's the first thing you're going to do?"

"I don't know yet," Dana said, twirling a lock of Jamie's hair around her finger. "Any suggestions?"

"I do have something to tell you, in case it matters."

"What's that?" Dana said, draping her arms around Jamie's neck.

"I love you madly?" Jamie said, kissing the end of Dana's nose. "I never thought I'd find love again but I absolutely have. And it's completely your fault."

"I'm so glad. I love you, too, Jamie. Could I interest you in a tour of my houseboat?" Dana whispered. "I'd like to start with the loft."

"I thought you'd never ask." Jamie took Dana's hand and followed her inside.

SIDE ORDER OF LOVE by Tracey Richardson. Television foodie star Grace Wellwood is not going to be golf phenom Torrie Cannon's side order of romance for the summer tour. No, she's not. Absolutely not. $14.95

WORTH EVERY STEP by KG MacGregor. Climbing Africa's highest peak isn't nearly so hard as coming back down to earth. Join two women who risk their futures and hearts on the journey of their lives. $14.95

WHACKED by Josie Gordon. Death by family values. Lonnie Squires knows that if they'd warned her about this possibility in seminary, she'd remember. $14.95

BECKA'S SONG by Frankie J. Jones. Mysterious, beautiful women with secrets are to be avoided. Leanne Dresher knows it with her head, but her heart has other plans. Becka James is simply unavoidable. 14.95

PARTNERS by Gerri Hill. Detective Casey O'Connor has had difficult cases, but what she needs most from fellow detective Tori Hunter is help understanding her new partner, Leslie Tucker. 14.95

AS FAR AS FAR ENOUGH by Claire Rooney. Two very different women from two very different worlds meet by accident—literally. Collier and Meri find their love threatened on all sides. There's only one way to survive: together. $14.95